Broken Identity

A NOVEL

Broken Identity

ASHLEY WILLIAMS

DESTINY IMAGE® PUBLISHERS, INC.

P.O. Box 310, Shippensburg, PA 17257-0310

"Speaking to the Purposes of God for This Generation and for the Generations to Come."

This book and all other Destiny Image, Revival Press, MercyPlace, Fresh Bread, Destiny Image Fiction, and Treasure House books are available at Christian bookstores and distributors worldwide.

For a U.S. bookstore nearest you, call 1-800-722-6774.

For more information on foreign distributors, call 717-532-3040.

Reach us on the Internet: www.destinyimage.com.

Trade Paper ISBN: 978-0-7684-3921-2

Ebook ISBN: 978-0-7684-8950-7

For Worldwide Distribution, Printed in the U.S.A.

1 2 3 4 5 6 / 14 13 12 11

Dedication

To my family...

All I can say is, I have a great team. You can't even begin to know how much your encouragement has made a difference in my life and in my writing. You always said that God, then family, are the two most important things. Thanks for being the best example of that.

And to my Lord and Savior Jesus Christ...

I want You to know that I have enjoyed every step of the way. Keep calling me higher; because the day I stop climbing marks the day I stop dreaming. What You have waiting for me at the top sure must be special, and I look forward to it with all my heart.

Contents

$\mathcal{P}\,r\,o\,l\,o\,g\,u\,e$

Name's Drake. Drake Spyridon Pearson, if you wanna get that specific. Yeah, thought about changing my middle name a long time ago after I realized I couldn't even spell it by the first grade, but I won't go into that. Guess Mom thought an unusual name would make me sound important or sump'n, but I'm still the same old me doing the same old stuff the same old way. My life's pretty much routine...if what I'm doing is routine for most teens my age. Kinda embarrassing when you go to fill out scholarships online and they ask you to list any achievements you've made, and then you realize you don't have any. But college isn't that great anyway. If it's filled with the kind of people I'm used to here at my school, you couldn't pay me to go.

So far, my life story hasn't been that great. Life's stressful, to say the least. The only thing that really matters to me anymore is an old, slightly torn picture I carry around in the sleeve of my wallet. But that's another story.

Here's mine.

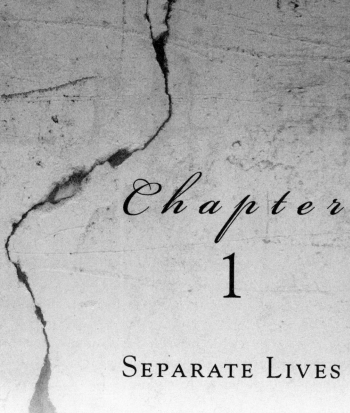

Chapter 1

SEPARATE LIVES

Drake Pearson eased his 1981 Ford truck into the driveway of his shabby trailer home, careful to keep it from rocking wildly across the yard every time his tires hit holes. Stupid dogs. A shotgun would take care of that. New tires were a killer to afford, so better the mutts disappear than his sanity.

Linhurst Peak, Missouri, was all heat by the time May rolled around. Dirt concreted to a hard crust, wild roses and dogwoods bloomed prematurely, parents drowned their kids in Gatorade and sunscreen, and even the local scrooges were desperately singing "Let it Snow" by the time Christmas rolled around. Of course, it wasn't all that bad if you could afford air conditioning, which Drake's old man couldn't.

Along with the heat, everything else in life pretty much went along routinely. Drake went to school, avoided home when at all possible, slept long hours just to find peace in blackness, and endured the ugliness of life in cruise control. No, he wasn't calling it quits altogether. He just hadn't found an alternative to living yet.

Drake steered to the right and braked in a patch of dead, twisted weeds, half-noticing that the clunker his dad owned was gone. Again. He pulled his keys from the ignition and sat there, thinking only for the pure sake of the silence it brought. He pressed his head back against the sweat-stained headrest and closed his eyes. *Welcome home, man. Last on the list of places I want to be right now.*

The smell of cut grass filled Drake's nostrils as he stepped out of his truck and walked up to the front door. Another downpour last night had left the rickety porch saturated with water. He was certain that one day he'd come home and find it disintegrated from rotting. Then again, if the porch ever did collapse, there wouldn't be much of a fall. All the empty cigarette cartons and beer cans piled high underneath would surely bolster the four-foot drop. Drake really didn't care what happened either way. He even made a point to hit the steps harder and listen to them crack with every step he took, if only to give his dad something else to cuss about once he got home.

Drake kicked the neighbor's stray cat away from the screen door and grabbed the doorknob, finding it unlocked as usual. A thousand thoughts flashed through his mind. After tomorrow, he would be forever done with twelfth grade. That meant the real sting was on the way— get a job and do something useful with your life, punk. Yeah, if only he knew what that meant. While his dad was gone and with his head cleared from exams, Drake determined he would spend the rest of the afternoon sorting out what he might dare call his future.

He bit his lip and shrugged. Ah, save it for another day.

Another blast of scorching heat blanketed him as he walked inside. Drake took off his shirt and flung it over the side of the couch. Might as well get a full tan in this furnace of a house. He went to the freezer and scattered the last handful of crinkle-cut fries on a rusted cooking sheet. Maybe the oven would work long enough to at least thaw them out.

Drake stared down at the food, starving for more to eat. He had to get a job soon. This wasn't life. It was poverty. Something had to give soon. Everything was lacking in his life. He wanted more, needed more. Something to drive him on and give his life purpose.

He combed through his shaggy black hair with his fingers and sighed. Maybe someday things would be different. But not now. Now was just too far away and confusing.

Andrew Tavner moved the dial on the iron to low and slowly pressed his best slacks. Stress made his right hand tremble and his heart beat furiously within him. Only two more hours of this edginess, and then he would hear the judge's verdict on the case he had so long been fighting. Almost a year had passed...had it really been that long?

Andrew quickly lifted the iron and made sure he hadn't burned his pants. Yes, it had been almost a year since he had decided to take his own brother to court. What he hadn't known was that the battle would continue to this day. So many sleepless nights, so many court hearings, so much pain. Somehow, in light of it all, he had not allowed himself to grow weary. At least he was doing something about it, even if some family relationships had to die in the process. This was all about the kid now. Only when the courts handed the child over to his care could he finally set his mind at ease.

After knotting his tie a little tight, Andrew adjusted his collar with shaky hands and briskly combed through his graying hair once more. *God, help me*, he prayed, unable to maintain eye contact with the sad, red-veined eyes looking back at him in the mirror. *You know how much Ronnie means to me. You know I'll always take care of him and do everything I can to get him into church.*

He wasn't trying to bribe God by telling Him he would take the kid to church; but it was a reputable argument, and he meant every word of it. Besides, just getting the child out of foster care was a good enough reason to win this case. His attorney wasn't the greatest in the world, but then again, he didn't have to be. Anyone with eyes could see that the kid desperately needed a better home.

Drake was tense as he walked to his last class the next morning. Something about the words "test results" made his mind go into overload and fear the worst—another year of high school. He had a lot on the line and wasn't sure yet if he could handle seeing anything lower than a D on his paper.

Drake found his seat near the back and sat down, hands jittery and ankles crossed so no one would see them shake. It felt as if this room were ten degrees hotter than any of the others as the teacher reached for the papers on his desk and began passing them out, starting with the front and ending in the back. Drake tapped his fingers nervously against his desk as the teacher approached him and laid down his exam.

Drake slowly lowered his stiff neck until his eyes fell on the page below him. His mouth nearly fell open.

A beautiful, scrawled C-. The breath rushed from his lungs as his entire body trembled with relief. *I passed. I can't believe it. I really passed.*

"Is that you, Drake?" a voice hollered from the bathroom.

"No, it's a robber!" Drake shouted back, letting the screen door bang shut behind him. *Idiot.* "Who do ya think it is?"

His dad, Ben, staggered into the room with his typical attire of worn, blue-jean shorts and a seafood restaurant tee. The smell of alcohol lingered in his breath.

Drake parked himself on the tattered, blue couch in the living room and glared with repulsion at his father. "You never came home last night."

Ben sat down hard on the other end of the couch and rubbed his head.

"You gonna answer me? I just spoke to you."

"Go away," Ben slurred. He moaned at the sudden throbbing that rushed to his head.

Glad to see you too, Drake thought. "You spent your entire check on booze and joints again, didn't you?"

Ben rolled his eyes. Why so much talking? He didn't ask for a conversation. "Whadda you care how I spend my money?"

Drake slapped himself on the knee. "Gah, I knew it! Dad, we need groceries! There's no more food in the house, and..."

"I don't need no food," Ben said tersely, scratching the line of poison ivy embedded on his bulging arm. "I need a high, that's all I need. Sump'n to take the edge off every now and then." His eyes were red and vacant as they stared straight ahead at no particular thing.

"Well, it's gonna kill ya someday, and frankly, I don't care. If you wanna die, sure, fine, that's your business. Wonderful. But there's another member of this house who actually likes to eat. So how much money you got left?"

Ben fanned his shirt and shook his head. "As if you don't enjoy a little alcohol every now and then. Gimme a break."

"Oh, oh, OK, I see. Takin' shots at me now, cause you're so...so... well, why do ya think I drink? To be like you?"

"I really don't care."

"Well, I'll tell ya why. So I can forget what kind of a life I'm living here, that's why! That makes perfect sense. Least I have a reason."

"Always an excuse, isn't there?"

"'Sides, I can control it," Drake flared back, ignoring his question. "You don't see beer running my life. Or *ruining* it, for that matter."

15

Ben belted out a long, grating laugh. The salmon on his shirt rippled with every mocking chuckle. "I've heard that one before! Yeah, you control it all right. Enough to keep you up half the night over the toilet barfing your guts up!"

Drake pursed his lips tightly. "Whatever," he mumbled. "Just answer my question. How much cash did you save for food?"

Ben pulled out his wallet and revealed a five and two one-dollar bills.

"You disgust me," Drake said coldly, shaking his head. "Guess you didn't think to pick up the medicine for my allergies either, did ya?"

"At those prices? Even the off-brands are through the roof."

"Then sacrifice a pack of cigarettes this week and there you go. Man, your priorities are so outta whack."

Ben glared at him. "Watch your mouth. We may not see eye to eye—"

"You got that part right," Drake said, just as bold.

"—but I'm still your father, and you have to respect me."

Now Drake was laughing. "Respect *you*? I wouldn't even know where to start! How do you respect someone who wastes his life away on drugs and walks around like a zombie all the time? I'm sorry and maybe that's just me, but I don't respect that. I'm ashamed of it."

Ben stood brusquely. "Now you listen here—"

"No, *you* listen, Dad! I'm tired of coming back from school every day wonderin' if you're either passed out on the couch, over at your stupid, *married* girlfriend's house, or dead."

Ben exhaled slowly. "Dead?"

"You're puttin' way too much stuff in your body—more drugs than I care to count—and I can't help but wonder if today'll be the day you just keel over and die. Or tomorrow. Or the day after that. The worrying never stops, and I don't think it ever will stop until you stop your addictions first!"

"Oh, listen to the pot calling the kettle black! You smoke too, but you never hear me houndin' you 'bout that!"

"You're the one who got me addicted! But least I got sense enough to know eating's more important! You still haven't figured that out yet." Drake stood and paced to the other end of the room to keep from looking at his father.

Ben followed him. "Oh, so smoking's different for you? It's called being weak, Drake. Face it."

Drake whirled. "Yeah, and I guess I inherited it from you."

"I can do whatever I want to with my life, so stay out of it!"

"You sound like a child. Fine. You say stay outta mine, I'll stay outta yours. Drink yourself to death. See if I care. But before you do every weekend, remind yourself to at least leave more than seven dollars for your son so he can buy himself some food. Unlike yours, my body can't survive on just drugs."

"Sell your truck. It's what I've told you all along."

"I need it."

"Learn to hitchhike! You want money, there it is."

"I'm not sellin' it."

"Then quit whining! You're just as able as I am to get your lazy self out of bed in the morning and work."

"Oh, and I look forward to it," Drake seethed. "I'm gonna find me a job somewhere so I can make my own money and leave this dump for good. It's time I leave your Stone Age and start livin' like everybody else."

"Like everybody else?" his dad repeated, letting out another throaty laugh. "You really think that a no-account like you can ever climb up the ladder and be like everybody else? Have you looked in the mirror, Drake? You ain't goin' nowhere—not because I ain't lettin' ya, but because you can't raise enough money to leave. You're trash, just like me. Everyone knows it. You're branded with my name and you're stuck with it for life. Nothing good's ever happened to the Pearsons and it sure ain't gonna start with you."

Drake stared into the distance. "I'll show you. Tomorrow, I'm coming back with a job, and then you'll wish you hadn't said anything after seeing my first paycheck."

His dad cackled louder, "We'll see."

Chapter
2

UNANSWERED QUESTIONS

Andrew Tavner felt a soothing sense of peace as he stepped into the courtroom and took his seat. His chest felt warm inside. Fear was still knocking with questions, but overall it just felt right this time. No more angry letters or court dates or lingering phone calls after this. It would all end today.

Andrew's brother hadn't arrived yet, which was annoyingly typical of him, but perhaps that was a blessing in disguise. Just the sight of his brother sent enraged thoughts swarming through his mind, and he regularly found himself asking God for forgiveness for it later. *Not today. Today will be different. It has to be. I have enough gray hairs as it is.*

Andrew straightened his silk garnet tie and peeked up at the clock on the wall to check the time once more. He was a little early if the clock was right, so he spent most of his time praying or studying the military ring on his finger as he waited. There wasn't much to look at—just the same, mind-numbing courtroom he had seen one too many times before—and the combined smells of old papers and lemon furniture polish attacked his senses, quickly giving him a headache.

A hand lightly patted his back. "How you feelin' today?" Joe Calbert, his attorney, said as he took a seat beside him. He dropped his heavy briefcase on the polished, hickory table in front of him and glanced at the clock.

"Surprisingly, a little more calm than last time," Andrew said, managing a weak smile. "You did a good job. I really believe we've finally won this thing."

Joe nodded his head and exhaled slowly. "Let's hope so. The judge'll be out in a moment to decide that, but personally..." He smiled back at Andrew and said, "I think you're right. You'll make a good father to that boy."

Father. No, he could never replace that figure in Ronnie's life. That definition wouldn't work. It represented abuse, not love, so he would just keep it at "uncle" unless Ronnie ever wanted to change it.

Kevin Tavner, Andrew's brother, finally arrived at ten minutes before eleven o'clock. What a sight. No tie, half-ironed slacks that barely matched his button-up, and speed-combed hair. Andrew shook his head. Was this nothing more than a game to him? He glanced at Joe, who said with his eyes that he was thinking the same thing.

Kevin purposefully snubbed his brother's presence. He jerked his seat back, ignoring the grating shrill it brought as it scraped the floor. Along with his sweat-matted, black hair and livid eyes, his face was a splotchy, blood red. Andrew knew what that meant and didn't care to think about it. He was just relieved that Ronnie was now safely out of Kevin's reach, especially on a day like today. If Kevin ever dared to touch that kid again, Andrew would handle him himself—this time without the help of a judge.

Kevin's wife entered next, smearing away her thick, caked-on makeup as she wiped her eyes with a tissue. Her mascara spread in streaks under her eyes like the windswept grass that forced itself through the cracks of Andrew's front porch. But Andrew felt no compassion for her. She was just as much part of this as her husband was; and since neither of them had taken proper care of their own son, he found it his duty—and his privilege—to assume responsibility of the boy.

Andrew barely shifted his eyes to look over at his brother discussing something with his attorney. He closed his eyes, praying, hoping that today would be the last time he ever had to come back to this nightmare of a place.

Saturday morning brought on a rush of emotions. Scared, sure. Nervous, maybe. Excited...yes, definitely excited. More excited than he had ever remembered feeling.

Drake Pearson found the best clothes he owned and smoothed them out over his bed. Still wrinkled, but good grief, it wasn't like he was applying for manager at a restaurant or something. A simple job of flipping burgers or bagging groceries was as far as he expected to get.

He had already figured out on his calculator last night how much cash he would need to save each week before he would finally have enough to ditch this house and start his own life. The figures were disappointing, but the gamble of living on the street for a while didn't seem so bad. People did it all the time and came out OK, depending on how hard they tried. At least, that was his analysis. No matter what the cost, he would find a way. Whatever it took to get away from his old man would be worth it in the long run.

His dad was still snoring deeply in the next room, giving off sounds like he was hacking up a log. That's all the fool ever did. Sleep his life away as if his days would last forever. Well, the world was still spinning and the hourglass still sifting sand; and now, Drake wasn't going to watch life pass him by. He was going to pursue it.

He hastily threw on his clothes and splashed his face with water. Most of his acne had cleared up in the last few months—definitely a plus considering appearance had a lot to do with being hired. After patting down a stray hair above his ear, Drake snatched up his wallet and keys and stole quietly out the door.

A local pizza place situated between a nail salon and insurance company was Drake's first stop. He had had his eye on that place ever since he first considered getting a job, which in reality hadn't been longer than a month. It didn't seem like much on the outside, especially with the cracks in the bricks being crammed full of gum and the windows still advertising last year's Christmas parade. But outside appearances didn't matter much, Drake guessed. As long as he received a paycheck every week that he could call his own, he would be thrilled.

A tiny bell jingled as Drake pushed open the door. Instantly, the aroma of hamburger and pepperoni pizza rushed to fill his nostrils.

"What can I do for you?" The 42-year-old owner's New York accent was still as sharp and defined as it had been twelve years ago when he moved to Missouri. He wiped his greasy fingers clean on his apron, which had the company's giant logo printed on it, and grabbed a pen from his pocket. "Our specials today are—"

"Uh, actually I saw your now-hiring sign out front and wondered if you still had positions available," Drake interrupted, doing his best to keep the quiver in his voice unnoticeable. "I'm a hard worker, and—"

"Sorry, kid," the man said, cutting his sentence short. "Interviewed a guy and girl yesterday. Gave 'em the job on the spot."

Drake melted inside. "You don't have anything? I mean, I could wash the floors or clean the pans or something. Anything. Please, I need this job."

"Already filled. Besides, we don't hire students."

"In two days I'll be eighteen," Drake protested.

The man sighed and returned his pen to his shirt pocket, obviously realizing he wasn't going to make a sale. "Look, we aren't hiring anymore," he said flatly. "*Period.* Meant to take the sign down yesterday and forgot, OK? Sorry."

Drake caught the emphasis. This man clearly wasn't interested in him and probably would never be. He doubted the man had even interviewed anyone. It was just as his dad had told him yesterday: People didn't hire trash, especially the son of a man this town knew too well for all the wrong reasons. Besides, this pathetic excuse for a county was too small anyway, cutting his chances for work to an even scarier fraction. So it wasn't like the blame was all on him; opposition was plainly stacked against him on all sides. *It's just one place, Drake. Don't beat yourself up over it. There's plenty more places willing to hire.*

The next four places gave him the same message—not hiring. Tired and feeling as if his confidence had fallen lower than a zero, Drake followed their advice and went home.

Andrew's heart thumped rapidly against his rib cage as the judge commanded the defendant to rise.

Say it. Say it.

The air seemed to rush from the room. Andrew tried to read the judge's face, but all he saw were Ronnie's eyes and the cluster of freckles underneath them instead. His pulse quickened, his heart pleaded for an answer. *God, let it be good. Let Ronnie come home with me today. Please, please let today be the last day I ever have to come back to this courtroom.*

The courtroom was dead silent as the judge cleared his throat and pushed his thin-rimmed glasses higher up his nose.

I'll never ask You for another thing again. Just let him say the words I've been waiting to hear.

Kevin watched like a stone-faced gargoyle, beyond caring any longer. This was all a boring formality that needed to end today.

The judge made eye contact with both Andrew and Kevin before finally uttering his verdict. "I rule this case in favor of Mr. Andrew Tavner. This court grants full custody of Ronnie Tavner to his uncle, Andrew Tavner, effective immediately."

Andrew almost collapsed into the chair behind him. A sudden coolness swept over his entire body, as if life and peace were welcoming themselves in again. So long...too long. Tears burned his eyes as he thanked God. *Oh, God, thank You. You've answered my prayers. Now all I ask is that You help me raise this child right.*

"All visitation rights for Mr. and Mrs. Kevin Tavner are terminated at this time," the judge continued, his deep voice booming as it reverberated off the walls.

Andrew rubbed his eyes, finding it hard to listen to the rest of what the judge had to say when all he could think about was Ronnie.

Drake burst through the front door too quickly and collided smack into his father. He ducked his head and walked toward his bedroom.

"Don't go runnin' off now, Drake!" Ben said with a curling sneer. "I wanna hear all about your little experience of finding a job!"

"Go take a bath. You reek of old beer and body odor." Drake rounded the corner to his room.

Ben followed close behind him. "So will you be taking fast-food orders, or..."

"Leave me alone!"

"Didn't get one, did ya?" He cackled with laughter. "How does it feel to stoop to the level of admitting your old man was right and you were wrong?"

Drake swore. "Don't start with me today!"

"I asked you a question, you disrespectful brat!"

Drake braked in his tracks and whirled around. "No, Dad, I didn't. Does it make you feel better knowing your son's a failure just like you?"

Ben held up his hands innocently, though a cynical smile still covered his face. "Don't blame me for it," he said cheerily, slurping down the rest of his stale beer. "I tried to tell ya, but nooooo, you wanted to do it your own way. Didn't want my help, when I plainly told ya—"

"Yeah, always trying to watch my back aren't ya? I'd probably fall over dead if you actually encouraged me just once instead of spotlighting every one of my flaws. But I guess that's askin' too much, isn't it? Especially from a waste like you."

Ben slammed his fist lividly against the already dented wall and cursed. "Encourage you how? By feeding you lies? I try to be honest with my own son, and I get hated for it!" The veins in his neck grew taut.

"I'm still leaving!" Drake shouted angrily, not willing to accept defeat this soon. "I hate this house, I hate my going-nowhere life, and I—" He clenched his keys in his hand and held them in a fist in front of his face. "I'll drive a thousand miles away and steal, kill, do whatever it takes to get my break in life. I'm ready to explode on the inside, and you're about to set me off!"

"You're all talk and no guts. Going away takes money. Lots of it. And stealin' ain't as easy as you think, else I would have had my hands on plenty of it years ago."

Those words cut deep. Not have the money to leave? He'd do anything before he let that happen. He could pull it off and make it work.

"I don't know, but I'll find a way!" he yelled, sick and tired of the constant nagging. "With or without the money, I'm leaving. Just get off my case!"

"You remind me of your mother," Ben said, slowly crushing the beer can in his hand.

Drake stared at him, wondering why those words sounded so much more threatening when coming from his mouth. "Oh, so now that's a bad thing?"

"Will I never see Daddy or Mommy again?" Ronnie said during the long drive back to Andrew's home in Springfield, Illinois.

Andrew pressed his lips closed and watched the 7-year-old cuddle his overstuffed panda as he gazed curiously out the window. He swallowed and said hesitantly, "Do you want to, Ronnie?"

Ronnie shrugged and hugged his bear tighter. "No," he said, so quietly Andrew almost didn't hear him. "They were mean to me. I dunno why."

Andrew felt terrible for the kid. He remembered a little over a year ago when Ronnie had come to visit him one Christmas—that was when he had first noticed the cigarette burns on the young child's skin and the small bruises that Ronnie's parents had always justified by saying, "He's always running into things." Andrew had known it was a lie. Pain always had a way of surfacing itself, whether through a kid's sad eyes or his tense body when his father came too close.

Andrew wilted like a dead leaf on the inside just thinking about it. He wanted it to be different for Ronnie this time, for relationship to mean something. He just prayed he was strong enough to reach out and pull Ronnie back to love again.

Ronnie hardly blinked. His eyebrows were tilted in confusion as rows of shadows swept across his expressionless face. Slowly, he pulled the bear closer to his heart and buried his frown in the fur of its head.

Andrew shifted a little in his seat, dreading that the thin ice he was tiptoeing on would crack under his feet at any moment. Ronnie was happy, wasn't he? Surely he hadn't made a mistake. "Were your foster parents good to you, Ronnie?"

Ronnie shrugged.

"I mean, I know we talked on the phone about it a lot, but..."

Silence.

"Did they treat you all right? Feed you and give you a bed?"

"Sure."

Andrew glanced in the mirror and hesitated. "You don't make it sound that way now."

"They were OK, I guess. The man worked a lot, and the lady liked to talk on the phone."

Straightforward, Ronnie. Please answer my questions and don't walk around them. "Did they have any kids?"

Now Ronnie met his gaze. "Two boys, both older than me," he answered. "I don't think they liked me very much, though. Called me names sometimes when their parents weren't around. One of them told me I was there just so their parents could make more money."

The ice shattered, along with what was left of Andrew's bruised heart. "I'm sorry, Ronnie. People are just mean like that sometimes. You know why?"

Ronnie shook his head.

"Because they're jealous."

Ronnie blew air out of his nostrils. "Jealous? I don't think so."

"Sure. Why else would they say mean things about you? I'll bet it's because they know they can never be you, and that makes them mad. You're special. There will never be another Ronnie, you know that?"

Ronnie stared at him doubtfully. "A lot of people are named Ronnie."

"But they're not my Ronnie," Andrew said, smiling.

Ronnie shyly smiled back. "You're silly."

"Forget about your foster home. You're going to be living with me from now on, and those stairs are practically begging for someone to run up and down them every day."

"Can I still keep all my toys?"

Andrew smiled. *Just like a kid to be worried about his toys at a time like this.* "Of course you can."

"And my other stuffed animals too?"

"And all your stuffed animals too. You're going to stay with your grandma this evening while I go get your stuff, and when I get back, we can—"

"But I want to go with you, Uncle Andy," Ronnie said softly, struggling to peer over the headrest.

Andrew frowned. "I don't think that's a good idea, Ronnie."

Ronnie had a puzzled look on his face, but Andrew decided it best not to explain further. "Hey, I promise as soon as I get back, I'll make you the biggest fruit smoothie you've ever seen. That's something worth waiting for, huh?"

Ronnie considered that for a moment. "Can you make mine banana? That's my favorite."

"Why not? Then after that, maybe we could play a board game or something."

Ronnie yawned and used his panda bear as a pillow against the window. "OK...Uncle Andy?"

"Yeah?"

"Why are Mommy and Daddy mad at me? Did I do something wrong?"

So they were back on that subject again. Andrew's heart ached to know that Ronnie was taking the blame for what was happening to him. "No, Ronnie," he said, surprised at how weak his voice suddenly sounded. "You've never done anything wrong."

"Then why don't they like me?"

"Ronnie, your mom and dad...well, they just..."

"Don't love me?"

"No, I wouldn't say that," Andrew said, his tired eyes looking everywhere but in the rearview mirror.

"Then what?"

Seven-year-olds can ask the hardest questions. How do I tell him the truth about his parents without crushing his heart? "Do you know why I'm taking you home with me, Ronnie?"

"Because they were mean to me?"

"Because I love you and want the very best for you. You know that, don't you?"

Ronnie nodded his head, listening intently to every word.

"We just need to pray for Mommy and Daddy and ask God to help them. Do you know how to pray?"

Ronnie knocked his knees together and said timidly, "I don't know. Maybe...I guess."

"Well, then, tonight I'll show you. It's not hard, Ronnie. You know how to talk, right?"

That got a smile out of him. "You know I can talk."

Andrew returned the smile. "Praying is that easy."

The salmon-colored clouds arranged in the sky like the dotted scales on a sunfish. They gradually faded into a long stretch of gray, giving the darkening landscape the appearance of an ancient sketch drawing. The moon was suspended high in the sky like a ghost emerging from the fog, and the flutelike songs of meadowlarks and wood thrushes faded away with the sunset as the sound of crickets and throaty toads welcomed the night. An osprey left its perch from a barbed wire fence and soared toward the pond in the distance where bending, ragged marsh grass dipped into the water.

This was supposed to be one of the happiest days of Drake's life, yet here he was, more interested in the wildlife outdoors than what was going on in his own life. Not surprisingly, his dad was out late doing who knew what while he watched the clock tick by. He shouldn't have to live like this, a parent to his own dad—don't blow all your money, don't stay past curfew, don't do drugs, don't be a louse all your life. And on, and on, and on.

Three more hours dragged by. Soon even the crickets and frogs got tired of their own singing and called it a night. This was ridiculous, and Drake was tired of waiting. His dad had probably drunk himself into a high again and was under a tree somewhere talking to his own shadow. Who knew anymore? Toss a coin.

Drake ambled back into the living room and reclined on the couch with his feet elevated on the armrest. He didn't know why, but at the strangest times, thoughts of his mom flooded his mind. He had only one picture of her holding him as a baby that he kept tucked away in his wallet. Though he realized he should be outraged with her for leaving him years ago, he couldn't make himself resent her for what she had done.

His heart stung. Why did he torture himself this way? Why did he have to dream about her again last night when those days of dreaming should be over? It was too far away now, too many years behind him. As hard as he tried to reflect into the past, the only thing he seemed to remember about her were the tiny dimples that formed in her smooth cheeks when she smiled.

And that she was beautiful—the most beautiful person in the world. He was 5 years old when he first told her he wanted to marry her. She had pulled his small frame against her warm body and hugged him, kissed him, and reminded him repeatedly how much her love for him grew every day.

Drake brushed a tear away and wished he could envision her clearly in his mind. His dad had thrown away almost every reminder, but it wasn't another picture of her Drake wanted to see. He wanted to remember her as she really was—in motion, talking, breathing, and all the other things pictures fell short of. That part of her was so hard to see anymore.

The way her long, dark hair flowed down her shoulders was still surprisingly clear to Drake, but the rest of her face was one huge blur. The picture he had of her was almost impossible to see any longer because of all the ugly creases in it. His dad had never said anything to him about his mom; but for years, Drake had blamed himself for her sudden leaving. Maybe he wasn't the perfect child she had always dreamed of having. Perhaps he had asked for a specific toy one Christmas, even though he knew his parents were broke and in enough debt already. It had to be something, Drake told himself. She wouldn't have simply packed her bags and left for no reason.

But the part that killed him the most was that there was never any discussion of her. It was almost as if he and his dad had a silent understanding between themselves. Drake never asked questions—for the most part, anyway—and his dad never offered to answer any. At times, it felt as if she had never even been a part of their lives. But Drake knew otherwise; and tonight, he was determined to find answers.

Drake sat up suddenly as the doorknob twisted. He watched the door swing open as the large silhouette of his father stumbled inside.

Ben jumped and put a hand to his chest. "What're you tryin' to do, scare me half to death? What're you up past midnight for anyway? Don't you have school tomorrow or somethin'?"

Drake rolled his eyes at the empty beer bottle his dad still clung to, as if it were some sort of trophy of the night's events. Disgusting. "I graduated, remember?" He sighed and said, "No, I shouldn't expect you to remember anything when you're drunk like this. After you go to the bathroom and throw your guts up for an hour straight, your son would like to talk to you."

Ben glowered at him and stumbled toward his chair so he could relieve his unsteady legs. "I'm not drunk. I can talk."

Drake brusquely stood up and strode over to the other end of the room. He turned only slightly to see his father. "Do you remember what today is?"

"Monday, I think," Ben mumbled, massaging his aching head. "Yeah, that's right. Monday, cause Paul and Albert—"

"I swear, I'll strangle the life outta those friends of yours if they keep makin' you come home like this!" Drake said, landing a solid kick in the side of his dad's recliner. The fabric ripped at the seams.

"Oh, go to bed. They bought my beer tonight. I had to join 'em."

"Bought your beer," Drake repeated sarcastically. "Bought you another sleepless night, you mean."

"You're just jealous you didn't go. I know what it is."

"No, I have a life. May not be much, but it's a lot more'n you got." He shook his head and shoved his hands in his pockets. "Point is, I knew you'd forget."

"Forget what?"

"Your own son's eighteenth birthday." Drake paced back over to the couch and rested his forehead in his hands. "What an accomplishment," he mumbled. "Another year's come and gone, and my life still stinks just as bad as it did a year ago."

"Oh, brother, just spit it out!" Ben said finally, slapping the armrest beside him. "What do you want? Money? Too late for that. Don't have any left."

"No, something else."

"What?"

"Mom's journal," Drake said slowly, watching his dad's reaction out of the corner of his eye.

Ben stuttered, attaching curses to most of his words. "What? Why? What could you possibly want with that old thing?"

"Do you still have it?"

"Yeah, uh...in that old video box, I think. But what does that have to do with you?"

Drake forced a laugh, despite his rage. "Because she's my mom, and I'd finally like to have some of my questions answered. I want to know why she left and where she was going."

His dad snorted. "You want it, you can have it. I ain't got no use for it."

Drake clasped his hands together and leaned forward in his seat, more serious now. Maybe in his drunken state of mind, his dad would finally open up. "Why did Mom leave?"

Ben heaved a sigh and straightened out of his chair. "Don't use that voice on me. It stopped working years ago."

"Dad, I need to know. I can't keep wondering like this forever."

"I don't want to talk about it."

"What do you mean you don't want to talk about it? She was *your* wife and *my* mother. You can't just push her away and act like she never existed. What's wrong with you anyway? Why do you keep avoiding my questions?"

"I'm going to bed."

Drake seized his dad by the arm and yanked him back. "No! I've waited for hours for you to come home because this is important to me. I deserve an answer!"

"You don't want to know her."

"What are you talking about? Of course, I want to know her! I can't help but want to know. She's my mom. I've studied the pictures, Dad. I'm not blind. I look just like her. At least you can tell me something about—"

"That's enough!" Ben said fiercely, jerking away from Drake's hold. "I refuse to discuss this any longer. Good night!" He stomped off to his bedroom and slammed the door shut.

"You don't have to tell me," Drake said under his breath, infuriated with his father's stubbornness. "I'll just find out for myself."

He went outside to the shed and flicked on the single bulb. Old car parts and insulation pieces littered the floor. He pushed aside empty paint cans and plastic bags and winter boxes until his hands touched a wrinkled cardboard box marked *Videos*.

A chill ran through his body. Here was the only thing left that would ever link him to his mother.

Chapter 3

EMPTY PAGES

Ronnie seemed out of place, hesitant. He approached every object, even the staircase, as if it belonged in a "Do Not Touch" museum. Finally, he turned to Andrew with a questioning look.

"Hey, you act like you've never seen this place before, even though you've been here several times." Andrew sat on the second stair to get on eye-level with Ronnie. "You're not second-thinking any of this, are you?"

Ronnie kept his mouth tight.

Andrew began to grow worried. "Ronnie, I..."

"I wanna stay."

"You do?"

"Don't let them take me back."

"Oh, no. No, Ronnie. Let who take you back?"

"Mommy and Daddy."

Andrew blinked several times to keep his eyes dry. "Ronnie, you're not leaving here. This isn't a visit anymore. You're really staying. We... we talked about all this."

"I know. I just didn't know if it was really real or not."

Andrew smiled gently. "It's really real. We're gonna have a lot of fun together, you and me. Baseball games, sledding, you name it."

Ronnie surveyed the room again. "It's weird to think about."

Even these things take time, Andrew assured himself. He asked God privately in his heart if he had acted too quickly. Or maybe, if anything, he had just been too late.

He rose to his feet and slid a hand in his pocket. "Tell you what. Why don't we go to Grandma's house, and you can spend some time with her while I go get your toys?"

Ronnie showed a smile. "OK."

Andrew reached his mom's house in nineteen minutes. The picturesque, farm-looking house framed in by a simple nut-brown fence was a place he never got tired of seeing. He had phoned his mom already to let her know they would be coming. He only hoped that when he came back to pick Ronnie up, he would be just as cheerful as he was now.

Andrew's mom ran to embrace Ronnie before he even reached the porch. After a moment of brief greetings, Andrew checked his watch. He gave his mom an anxious look before he bent down to give Ronnie a hug. "I won't be gone long, buddy."

"Promise?" Ronnie said, clinging to his uncle's sleeves.

"I promise." Andrew lifted Ronnie's chin with his finger and stared into those mysterious, dark eyes of his that harbored something so vastly profound and yet somehow simple all at the same time. "I'll bring back all your toys, and then I'll help you set up everything just the way you want it in your new bedroom."

"And the banana smoothie?" Ronnie reminded him. "You won't forget?"

"How could I?" Andrew ruffled Ronnie's light brown hair, then looked up at his mom. "I appreciate your watching him till I get back. I uh..."

Kara, Andrew's mother, sensed that Andrew needed to talk to her in private. "Why don't you go inside and find your uncle's old container of cars?"

"Can I?" Ronnie scurried into the house as if in search of buried treasure, making Andrew laugh. "It's good to see him so happy and full of life," he said, holding the door open for his mother.

"It's good to see *you* happy and full of life," Kara said, taking his hands in hers. "Your life will be full again, but don't expect to keep him over there all the time. I want to see him often too, you know."

"You got it, Sergeant," Andrew said, saluting her.

"Oh, stop it," Kara said, waving him on. "Now, really, tell me about your trip. What did he say?"

"Ronnie's a great kid, considering all he's been through." Andrew jingled his keys around in his pocket, trying to think of what to say next. "Just pray for me as I go up to Kevin's, will you? I don't want this to turn into a fight."

"Do you think they'll give you Ronnie's things?" Kara said. "Willingly, I mean?"

"I'd think so, but maybe that's just my wishful thinking breaking through again. After all, they don't have any use for them anymore, and Kevin sure isn't the sentimental type who'd keep things just for memory's sake." He looked at the ceiling and sighed forcefully. "I dread even going up there, but I have to keep reminding myself that this is for Ronnie's good, not mine."

"When do you expect to be back?"

"I'm guessing seven o'clock. Will you be OK for that long?"

Kara rolled her eyes at him. "Andrew, your eyes deceive you. With every day that goes by, I grow younger inside. Don't worry about us." She paused and listened to the sounds of wheels rattling against furniture and Ronnie making rumbling engine noises. "See? He already sounds like he's having a good time."

Andrew decided to leave the conversation at that and took hold of the doorknob. "I noticed your mailbox when I turned into the driveway. The mystery mailbox-smashers are still at it, I see."

Kara just shook her head. "It happened again last night."

"Why didn't you call me?"

"It was past midnight, and by that time, even I was too tired to care. Nicole's husband heard them when they smashed my mailbox, though, and ran outside just in time with a flashlight to get a glimpse of their license plate. He gave it to the police this morning."

"Man, I'd give anything to have that guy's eyesight when I turn his age," Andrew said, amazed that a 70-year-old man still had such incredible vision. "What are you going to do about your mailbox until the police catch the culprits?"

"Oh, I haven't even started worrying about that. Maybe you could get me a new one for my birthday next month," Kara said, smiling.

"A mailbox isn't exactly a birthday gift, Mom. I'll pick up one on my way back." He winked at her and added, "I'll see if I can find a thick, metal one. Make 'em think twice before they come back to this house again." Then he turned serious and cracked the door open, sending a burst of cool air inside. He rubbed his arms and stared in the distance at the red clouds hovering over the sunset. Something inside him clawed at his heart, something much colder than the evening air. Fear? Possibly. But more than anything else, it was that wrenching feeling of stepping out into the unknown. "I guess I'll be on my way then," he said, barely moving his lips. "Don't hesitate to call if you need anything."

"Be careful, Andrew."

Drake Pearson became so engrossed in his mother's journal that he frequently had to remind himself to breathe. As if through a hazy dream, he felt he was seeing her again for the first time in years—her feelings, her joys...her love for him. So she really did love him before she left. That brought peace to his heart. He wanted to believe that she had always loved him and that it had pained her to leave him, for whatever reason that might have been.

Drake took in every word she had written down, sometimes reading a sentence two or three times because this was the only opening he had left to her past. She had begun the journal a few months after she and Ben had gotten married, and had continued writing throughout her pregnancy and through Drake's early years as a toddler, which was where Drake was reading now.

I took Drake with me to the grocery store the other day, which he seemed to enjoy very much. Other than wanting to put everything on the shelf into our buggy, he was very helpful and often stretched his little arms up to push the buggy around for me. He's so sweet at this age. Sometimes I wish he would stay like this forever, but I'm looking forward to the years ahead I'll spend with him.

Drake wiped his eyes and ran his tongue over his bottom lip, wishing he were hearing his mom tell him this in person rather than reading on paper what took place so long ago. He turned the page and continued reading.

At the checkout, there was a stack of free booklets, so I picked one up and stuck it in my purse to read later. I love to read, but because Ben and I don't make much money, I've never been able to actually buy books. As soon as I got home, I opened the booklet and began reading. It was about a man named Jesus and how He came to love people, even enough to allow Himself to be crucified for them. It said something about God sending His Son to die so that we could live forever with Him one day. I don't know when it happened, but I soon realized that I was crying because there were tearstains covering the small pages I was reading. The next thing I knew, I was on my knees saying something about how sorry I was for my sins. Drake must have heard me, because he walked in and asked why I was crying. I knew I should have felt embarrassed at this strange, sudden emotion welling up inside me, but all I could think about was that someone out there loved me enough to die for me. I read more until I reached the end of the booklet. It said that if I wanted to know more about Jesus, I could find it all and more in the Bible. I went straight to the trunk at the end of my bed and found a Bible a friend had given me at a Bible camp I had attended as a little girl. It was a children's version, but the message inside was for children and adults alike. I found the verse I had read–John 3:16–and continued reading until my eyes were so blurred with tears that I couldn't read anymore.

Drake tore his eyes away from the pages to stare out the foggy window in front of him. *Mom read the Bible? I never knew that about her. Then again, I guess I never knew much about anything in her life until now.*

He glanced back down and turned the page, noticing from the date that the next entry in her diary had been written three days later.

For the last three days, Ben has been irate. I told him I had asked Jesus into my heart and explained to him everything the book had explained to me; but his response was very, very different from mine. He doesn't want anything to do with Christianity or the Bible, and his attitude toward me has been nothing but anger and resentment. I keep trying to tell him about Jesus and His sacrifice for us on the cross because we're sinners, but he refuses to listen. I've tried praying for him, but sometimes words are hard to find when you're praying for someone you love who you know despises everything you believe in. I don't know if I'll ever be able to get through to him or not, but I do know one thing–I will continue to try to help him understand, and when Drake is old enough, I will do the same for him because I love him.

Drake slid his mom's neon green bookmark between the pages and placed the journal under his mattress. He had anticipated ahead of time that he would get a few shockers by reading his mom's journal, but nothing could have prepared him for this. His mom, a Christian? They weren't church people. No one in his family had ever fallen for the redemption bait. His mom was already a good person and had never lied or stolen, so why did she of all people need God? Maybe that was where she went, going off to join a church somewhere and enlighten the rest of the world about this Jesus guy. But what about him, her own son? Why would she have left him behind?

I'm not gonna hold it against her. I can't. Whatever she did, she would have only done it to help us. His mom may have become a Christian, but she was no lunatic. She wouldn't have abandoned him without a reason. Drake only wished he knew what that reason was.

Andrew finished what was left of the lukewarm cappuccino froth clinging to the bottom of his cup as he pulled into his brother's driveway. After resisting the urge to toss the cup into Kevin's front yard, he closed his eyes and silently prayed to God once more for peace. He didn't want to do this, wasn't looking forward to it, and frankly, didn't mind if he and Kevin *did* get into a fighting match because, in a way, he wanted to give Kevin a couple of bruises himself and have a good excuse for doing it.

Andrew relaxed in his seat. So much anger inside. *God, I'm sorry for feeling this way, but it's hard not to remember what he did to that kid. When I think of that monster shoving Ronnie against a wall or gripping his arms so he can...* He cut his words short as a tremble coursed through his body. Who was he trying to kid? He wanted nothing to do with his brother, let alone talk to him. Then again, he couldn't simply go barging into Kevin's house without saying a word and start loading his car with Ronnie's toys either. *Just help me handle this like You would, Jesus. I don't want to cause more trouble than what's already been started.*

Aware that he was being watched through one of the bay windows, Andrew maintained his firm posture and stepped out of the car. He walked promptly up the front porch and knocked forcefully on the solid oak door—his way of announcing that Kevin's shallow attempts to scare him weren't working.

After making Andrew wait several minutes, Kevin finally came and unbolted the door.

Andrew nodded to his brother without blinking. "Suppose you know why I'm here."

Kevin said something under his breath and seemed to breathe down Andrew's neck as he walked inside. "Get what you came for and get out," he warned.

Your thoughts are the same as mine. I don't want to stay here any longer than I have to, believe me. Andrew turned around halfway in the living room and said, "Where's Ronnie's bedroom?" It had been so long since he had been allowed in this house that he honestly couldn't remember.

"You mean where *was* it?" Kevin said gruffly. "End of the hall."

"Thank you." Andrew stepped around Kevin and found Ronnie's old bedroom. An undersized toy box in the corner of the room, a simple nightstand and dresser, a few strewn items on the floor, and a couple of glued puzzles hidden underneath his slim twin bed were all Ronnie had to call his own. Andrew searched the room for the toys he had bought Ronnie for his birthday and Christmas, but they were nowhere in sight. *Kevin probably sold them and pocketed the money. What a jerk.*

Andrew had estimated a few hours work to get everything cleared out, but now he questioned if it would even take him half that long. He started first with the toy box, dumping most of its contents into a sleeping bag he found stuffed high in the closet. It took two trips to get all the toys out using the sleeping bag method, and he started next with the clothes. Every time he walked out to his car carrying an armload of

Ronnie's things, Kevin was standing at the end of the hall with hateful eyes, watching him.

Drake stopped reading only to sneak into the kitchen and grab a quick snack. Still so many questions and not enough answers. At least, not any satisfying ones. With every assumption he had made about how his mom might have left, a loophole always left him craving more answers. Then again, maybe he was searching for something that didn't even exist. Could it be that he was trying to make logical excuses for his mom's disappearance when the fact was none remained but the obvious? *So she just left, is that it? Just packed up her things and walked away from me forever?*

Drake threw a lumpy pillow behind his back and flipped to the page he had left marked with the green bookmark. *No goodbye, no letters, no phone calls, and yet I'm supposed to somehow leave it at that and go on with my life?* Trying to keep his mind objective, Drake decided to at least finish the journal before coming to any real conclusion.

Out of the blue today, Ben surprised me by telling me he was going to take me on a trip. I'm so excited! He didn't say where, and I have to be honest, it came as a shock at first. Dad agreed to watch Drake while we were gone, so we dropped him off this afternoon. He started to cry when I told him goodbye, but I assured him that he would have a wonderful time with his grandpa and that I would come back for him soon. Almost immediately, he was laughing and playing off in another room, so I closed the door and we left.

Ben and I are driving now and will probably have to spend the night in a hotel. I told him we could sleep in the car so it would be cheaper, but he insisted we stay at the hotel. You should see how many bags I brought. Ben said I was overdoing it, but, hey, that's what vacations are all about, right? I'm looking forward to tomorrow already. Ben still hasn't told me anything yet, so I guess it'll all be a big surprise. But that's OK. I'm sure whatever it is, I'll love it.

I'm not being very good company to Ben writing like this, so I'll stop now. (But I'm sure I'll be filling lots of pages tomorrow telling about all the fun we've had!)

Despite his mental turmoil, Drake smiled at the excitement his mom must have felt. Going on a big trip to who knows where sounded like a dream, even if it meant just going a few miles out of town to see new places. All the scenery Drake had to bore his eyes with every day was corroded barbed wire fences and cracked roads. He honestly believed that the wildlife had better living conditions than most people here did.

Anxious to see what his mom wrote next, Drake pressed his back deeper into his pillow and turned the page.

Blank. No words. No date.

Nothing.

What? Drake furrowed his brow and turned over another page.

Nothing but more empty pages.

Frustrated and even more bewildered, Drake took the diary in his hands and flipped the pages until he reached the end.

Every page was blank.

Drake's stomach felt as if it were coiling into knots as an even bigger wave of confusion ruptured in his heart. From everything he had read, his mom certainly didn't seem like the type of person who had a reason to leave. She was happy, full of life, energetic, excited...

So what happened?

Drake checked his watch and found it to be a little past three in the morning. *I wonder if I could find her,* he thought. *I can't keep wondering like this for the rest of my life, and Dad's sure not gonna spill any time soon. I know the chances are slim, but it's worth a shot.*

Not completely sure what he was doing but determined to do it anyway, Drake snatched a duffel bag from his closet and began packing his clothes, his mom's journal, and what little money he owned. This was crazy, but oh well. Too much time had already passed. Now it was time to take it a step further and do something about it.

Ben stumbled into the room, awakened by the sudden noise. He wiped his eyes and tried to avoid looking into the light. "What are you doing, Drake?" he groaned.

Drake hardly acknowledged his dad's presence. "Going to find Mom," he said simply, stuffing his jacket in the side pocket.

Ben braced himself against the doorframe. "You're *what?!*"

Drake rolled his eyes. "You heard me. She's out there somewhere, and I'm gonna find her."

"And how exactly do you expect to do that?"

Drake ignored him and kept packing. "Don't worry about me," he said sarcastically. "You never have before."

"You won't last a day on your own. And what about the money you'll need?"

Drake stopped what he was doing and faced his dad. "All I know is that you and her were going on a trip and stopped at some hotel on the way. After that, the journal stops. No explanation. No *nothing*."

"Your mom left," Ben said bluntly. "You're wasting your time."

Drake zipped up his bag and tossed it on his bed. "What really happened that night? She sounded so happy, and then—"

"Oh, your mom was happy, all right. Ever since she got hold of a stupid book she found, she turned into a religious nut!"

"I know she was a Christian. I read it. But that still doesn't explain why she would just suddenly pack up and hit the road. There's a big gap missing, and the least you can do is tell me what happened—"

"I already told—"

"—so that maybe I can understand this a little more. You're forgetting that I'm eighteen years old, Dad. If Mom was involved in some kind of an affair or left you for someone else, please tell me now so I don't go searching for something that isn't even there."

"You don't wanna know the truth," Ben said gravely, turning away.

"I can only read so much in her journal, but now I need more than that. I'm a grown man now. You can tell me."

Ben stared at him a long time until Drake finally got tired of waiting. "Fine," Drake said. "I guess I'll just have to find out for myself, won't I?" He slung his duffel bag over one shoulder and pushed past his dad. "You're about as much help as—"

Ben grabbed Drake's wrist and yanked him back. "Tell me!" he demanded. "Tell me to my face what you really think of me!"

"You'd be worth more to me if you were dead," Drake said, jerking away.

"Just like your mama, aren't ya?"

"At least she had sense enough to leave. I think I'm finally beginning to understand why she left."

"Which is?"

"The same reason I wanna leave. *You.* If you treated her like you treat me, no wonder she went away. Now I'm leaving too and it's for good."

"I've heard that line before. Same story all the time with you, only you're too coward to back up your own words."

"It'll be the last time. Don't expect me to come back to this dump of a trailer, because I'd sooner kill myself before crawling back to you and your trash hole. Whether Mom was smart to leave or she was just plain crazy, I dunno, but I'll make my own judgment of that."

Ben grated his teeth. "What do you expect to find, Drake? That your mom left us for a good reason? She didn't leave because of me, no matter what she put in that journal of hers. She left because of you. There, I said it. It's not hard to put two and two together. You come into the picture, she leaves. Get it?"

"You're lying," Drake said evenly, trying to clear his mind of what his dad had just told him. "I don't believe you."

"She got tired of it, and my guess is that during the trip we took, she liked the idea of freedom and what life was like without a six-year-old following her around asking her questions all the time. Next day, she was gone."

Drake picked up his bag and stormed from the room.

"Good! Leave!" Ben shouted as he heard the front door yank open and slam shut. "That's all you're good at!"

Andrew struggled to wrap his arms around the last of Ronnie's clothes, thanking God in his heart that he was finally about to leave this stress-cloaked environment. He closed the bedroom door behind him with his foot and walked down the hall for the last time.

Kevin was still standing there, glaring at him. Andrew thought he looked like a time bomb ready to explode at the slightest amount of pressure. *And I'll bet he's just waiting for me to set it off too. It's your call, Kevin. I'm not one to start a fight, but I'll sure finish one.*

This time, Andrew made a point not to even look at his brother as he walked by. It was his last attempt at peace, but Kevin saw it as a challenge. Andrew sensed the pressure in the room begin to build as he headed for the door.

Kevin bolted from the kitchen and deliberately stepped in front of Andrew's path, forcing him to come to a sudden halt. "No one ignores me in my house," he snarled.

"Didn't know you wanted to talk," Andrew said, advancing a step.

Kevin didn't budge. "I plan to see Ronnie at least once a month, is that clear?"

Andrew felt his heart pick up speed. He caught a glimpse of Kevin's wife, Louise, watching them intently from the kitchen in her slippers and tattered, navy blue robe. "You heard the judge this afternoon," Andrew answered, keeping his voice steady. "You're not allowed visitation rights."

"He's my son!"

"Living in my house now."

"You don't have the right—"

"Who started this, Kevin? Me or you? You beat Ronnie up like he was—"

"You're a liar! I never touched—"

"Oh, don't try to play that card with me!" Andrew threatened, finding it necessary to raise his voice if he could ever hope to make a point in this house. "Every time you got angry, you treated him like he was your personal punching bag."

"How dare you accuse me of harming him! He caused those bruises on himself by acting clumsy all the time like seven-year-olds do."

"And the cigarette burns? I suppose he smokes too? Nothing's your fault, is it, Kevin? Always passing the blame on someone else, even if that someone else is an innocent child!"

"He's still mine," Kevin fumed.

"You lost that right."

Kevin's face grew redder.

"If you had gotten your way in court today, you would have done nothing but beat Ronnie all night long, accusing him by saying that *your* mess is *his* fault. Well, I couldn't take it anymore, seeing Ronnie just 'happen' to have a black eye the day you lost your job or finding purple bruises all over his body every time you got drunk and lost your self-control. He's safe now, and I don't want you anywhere near him. No visitation rights, no phone calls, *nothing*. Is that clear enough for you, or do I need to slam you against a wall to get your attention like you did to Ronnie?"

Kevin inhaled as if preparing to raise his voice, but Andrew stopped him by saying, "You're lucky you didn't go to jail. Next time you go near Ronnie—if you even dare cross that line with me—I'll be the judge, and I promise, I *will* stop you."

He forced his way past Kevin and only barely restrained himself from slamming the front door on his way out.

Chapter 4

STARTLING TRUTH

Drake Pearson snatched the keys from his duffel bag and heatedly started his truck. He jolted the gear into reverse and sped out of the driveway, taking part of the curb on his way out. He was fuming, and wanted more than anything to pummel someone. It didn't matter who it was as long as it made him feel better. Still, he had to face the fact that this whole mess could partly be his fault. Had he been so bratty of a kid to his mom that she wanted to leave him? Maybe he had been too hard on his dad all this time. After all, she had left his dad the burden of raising a child and keeping a job. *I have to find answers*, Drake thought. *Dad may be right, but he could also be lying. I have to know for sure.*

Drake withdrew his hand from the steering wheel and rested it over his heart. He was too young to have heart problems, so it must have been stress causing these pains. He was carrying too much, he knew. The irony that his dad was the negligent one and he was the one trying to hold it all together was completely undeserved. While other teens his age were facing their futures with clear minds only flecked with the fear of getting a job or succeeding in college, his future remained clouded by a past that had never been resolved—or even discovered, for that matter.

Drake drove toward the library, knowing that if he could get to a computer, he might be able to find some real information. People reunited all the time these days over the Internet, so why should it be any different for him? He only knew a little about his mom, but he was sure that what he had was enough. If he could only find out where she lived now—even if she had remarried and had a new family—he would find her. Despite the fact that she had walked out of his life so many years ago, she was still his mother, and that fact alone kept him from resenting her.

Drake slowly pulled into the library's small parking lot, suddenly feeling stupid. *Closed. Duh, Drake. They aren't open at four o'clock in the morning!* He ripped the keys from the ignition and decided to stay parked. No point in going home unless he wanted to give his vocal cords some more unneeded exercise. The library opened at eight—that gave him a whopping four hours of sleep. Right now, even eternity didn't seem like a long enough rest for the fatigue he was feeling.

Drake tilted his head back, determined to at least try to catch some rest. He wedged his hands snugly underneath his arms and pulled his legs close to his body, suddenly feeling chilled. *Wonder what Dad's doing right now,* he thought, sensing the muscles in his back and neck slacken as his body gradually conformed to the uncomfortable shape of his seat. *Probably cussin' me out for leaving like that. Oh, well, let him rant. He brought it on himself by not tellin' me 'bout Mom. It wouldn't have killed him to at least tell me what color her eyes were or if she was left-handed or right-handed. But Dad wouldn't even remember stuff like that. All he cares about now is hanging out and drinking with his stupid friends, whatever kind of a life that is.*

He looked up at the black, starless sky and wondered if that's what the inside of his soul looked like right now. Empty. He was really no better than his dad when it came down to it, was he? *Stop doing this to yourself, Drake. You know you're tired. Get some sleep.* He had a lot to do when he woke up, and sleep would not be an option once he was typing away at the keyboard.

He closed his eyes and listened to himself breathe. *Three more hours. Maybe then, I'll know the truth.*

Andrew Tavner arrived at his mother's house at precisely a quarter till seven with a mailbox tucked under his arm, just as he had promised.

"I didn't know you'd go buy one tonight," Kara said, taking the box from his arms. "Thank you."

"Ah, no problem."

"Such an expensive-looking one. I could have gotten along with a cheaper one just as fine."

"Quit worrying about how I spend my money, Mom. At least your mail won't be on the ground tomorrow." Andrew meant for it to come across as a lighthearted comment, but it ended up sounding more irritable than intended. Was he still that angry over what had happened at his brother's house? He found a chair and collapsed in it, guessing that he wouldn't be leaving any time soon without first explaining to his mom why he was acting this way.

"Don't slump, Andrew," Kara said, seating herself across from him. "You know what that does to your posture."

I'm sitting here stressing my mind to no end about keeping my brother away from Ronnie, and all you're worried about is whether I'll turn into a hunchback. Andrew reluctantly scooted himself up higher just to be left alone. "I've been doing it for years, so I guess my vertebrae are still strong enough to take it," he said flatly. *If only I could say the same thing about my nerves.*

"You look tired, Andrew," Kara said with concern. "Is everything all right?"

Andrew glanced around the room and asked where Ronnie was.

Kara paused to listen to the soft sounds of the television coming from the bedroom. "In the other room watching cartoons. We can talk."

Andrew clasped his hands together and looked at his mother through weary eyes. "It's about Kevin." He snorted and said, "Course, who else would it be about? He asked to—well, no, it was more of a demand—to see Ronnie once a month. Can you believe the gall of him to ask such a thing?"

"But he can't—"

"I know he can't, and I told him. And boy, did I tell him. Made him mad, of course, but I wasn't going to let his hateful stares and balled fists push me around...not like he did to Ronnie. Mom, I swear—"

"Don't say that. I know you love Ronnie, just like I know you'll take good care of him. Ronnie knows that too. I can see it on his face that he feels safe around you."

Andrew could feel his blood pressure rising. "It isn't just about that. Mom, you don't understand. I wanted to *hit* Kevin. I'm talking about a full one-two punch in the face. I wanted revenge. A scar he could remember for life every time he looked in the mirror. I know he's your son too, Mom, and he's my brother, but do you ever just find yourself... I don't know, almost hating someone?"

Kara looked away and fingered the delicate indentions of flower petals around the handle of her empty coffee cup. "I still have to love him, Andrew," she said quietly. "I can't hate him. I may disagree with him—"

"Oh, definitely that."

"—and it may turn to anger, but never to hate. A mother can never hate her son."

Andrew rubbed the palms of his hands together and said almost hesitantly, "I know in the Bible Jesus commands me to love my enemies

54

and pray for those who persecute me, but what about the people who persecute my family? A child? Is He saying to forgive them and pray for them too? I try my hardest, but I can't make that fit."

His mother was silent, so he took it to be a yes.

Andrew studied the beige carpet between his shoes, unwilling to accept a response like that this soon. "I guess I know what the answer is, but it's still hard. I can't look into Ronnie's eyes without seeing years of hurt and abuse there. Sometimes, I honestly don't know if I can ever forgive Kevin for what he did."

Kara thought for a moment. "Do you mind if I read you something I read in the Bible yesterday?"

Andrew winced. "Is it gonna make me feel like a jerk?"

Kara smiled. "Probably, but that's OK. Good stuff to build on." She picked up her worn, leather-bound Bible and turned to Romans chapter 12. "Repay no one evil for evil. Have regard for good things in the sight of all men. If it is possible, as much as depends on you, live peaceably with all men."

"Notice Paul says, 'If it is possible,'" Andrew pointed out.

"True, but you have to at least put forth an effort first and try. After that, if Kevin still refuses to be peaceable, at least you know you've done what's right and that's all God requires. The verse goes on to say, 'Beloved, do not avenge yourselves, but rather give place to wrath; for it is written, "Vengeance is Mine, I will repay," says the Lord. Therefore, "If your enemy is hungry, feed him; if he is thirsty, give him a drink; for in so doing you will heap coals of fire on his head." Do not be overcome by evil, but overcome evil with good.'"

She closed her Bible and stared at Andrew, his face partially darkened by the shadowy lines of her staircase. "Andrew, no matter what you feel in your heart, no matter what situation you're put through, you can't make exceptions for God's Word. If Jesus tells us to forgive, we forgive. He never tells us to trust that person again or make ourselves vulnerable to their attacks. He only tells us to forgive. Release Kevin from what he's done. I'm not saying you have to trust him or open yourself up to more hurt, but release him. That way you've done your part, and by doing so, have untied God's hands so He can begin to bring healing."

Andrew nodded and massaged the back of his sore neck. "You're right," he admitted. "I'm sorry."

"God's right. He always is. I've had your same struggle too, Andrew. You're not alone. But when I turn to God and not to my anger, somehow the peace God instructs me to give comes naturally when I'm willing to listen and obey Him."

Andrew turned his head as a shadow crept along the wall and saw Ronnie.

"You're back!" Ronnie exclaimed, his eyes lighting up at the sight of his uncle. "You got my toys?"

Andrew smiled. "Everything. I also stopped by the grocery store on my way home and picked up some vanilla ice cream and lots of bananas. You know what that means, right?"

"Banana smoothie!" Ronnie shouted. He reached for his uncle's hand and pulled him to his feet. "Come on before the ice cream melts!"

Andrew waved to his mom as Ronnie tugged him toward the door. "I'm being taken prisoner, but I'll see if I can sneak a phone call to you tomorrow!"

"Don't wear yourself out!" Kara called after him.

"I won't!" Ronnie said.

"I was talking to your uncle!" Kara said, now laughing.

Andrew barely pulled the door shut behind him before being dragged down the porch steps. He felt so incredibly blessed to have

Ronnie and his mother filling his life with joy at times he needed it the most.

Drake sat up suddenly, fully awakened by the jarring sound of a jackhammer breaking up concrete some fifty yards away from his truck. He blinked several times until his eyes adjusted to the light, his heart still racing to keep time with the jackhammer. Why was he surprised he had a headache? If it wasn't caused by his dad, it would be from that idiot across the street. He lazily raised his arm to check the time on his watch.

The library had been open for nearly two hours now! Drake hurriedly pressed down his uncombed hair, shoved his keys in his pocket, and flung the truck door open. He had expected some emotion, but he was completely taken off guard by the tightness in his chest. He hadn't found a single thing out yet, and already he felt sick.

Drake found an unoccupied computer next to the wall and jiggled the mouse to wake up the screen. He breathed slowly through his nose and ran his thoughts one last time through his mind. *Here we go, pal.*

He moved the pointer to one of the search engines at the top of the Web page. He decided to use the hunt-and-peck method for typing *Stephanie Pearson, Missouri* for fear that the memory of anything beyond home-row keys would fail him. He hit the enter button and waited as the computer loaded the search results.

Fifty-two thousand, three hundred results. *What?* He quickly scanned down the list of web links. *Stephanie Pearson's new ocean drilling program... find Stephanie Pearson, age 15, on MySpace...breakthrough made in new stem-cell research...Stephanie's recipe book...* He let out a sigh and leaned back in his chair. Not even two minutes in front of the computer screen, and already he had run smack into a brick wall. *I can't go through all these. I gotta be more specific.*

He sat drumming his fingers lightly against the keys, wondering what he should type that would help narrow his search to a number preferably in the hundreds. *Looking for mom who left me twelve years ago? Man, what am I supposed to type? I don't even know where she lives or if her last name's changed by now.* Drake didn't know his mom's exact age and definitely had no clue as to what her maiden name was. He was literally left with nothing to go on and no one to turn to. He sure couldn't rely on his dad for any help—that would be a joke. His situation suddenly seemed doomed to failure, and made him realize how foolish he had been for believing he could actually find information on someone he hardly knew anything about. *But if I don't try—even if I have to go through every one of these fifty-two thousand links—I'll never forgive myself.*

Drake cleared the search and retyped *Stephanie and Ben Pearson Linhurst Peak Missouri.* Even though she no longer lived here and his dad was out of her life, it was all he had to work with. He had nothing else.

The page popped up almost instantly. Drake could feel the air escaping from his lungs. The first link captivated him, and for the longest time, he could do nothing but stare at the title. *The Stephanie Pearson trial.* With trembling hands still on the mouse, Drake leaned closer to the computer screen and read the small type beneath the headline. *Court rules death by drowning on November 14, 1997, an accident due to a sleeping disorder. Though there was substantial convicting evidence presented in the autopsy report, Ben Pearson was found innocent after presenting...*

Drake felt as if his mind was shutting down. The room, the lights, the voices...everything began fading into a silent, distorted haze.

The headline drew his eyes in again. This must be talking about his mom, because there was his dad's name directly beneath it. *Then that means she's...*

Leaving the Web page up, Drake darted outside to his truck and tore through his bag for his mom's journal. He knew what he would find, yet he opened it anyway and frantically turned to the last written page.

Drake clamped a hand over his mouth as a surge of acidic vomit inflamed his throat. *No, it's a lie. It has to be wrong.* He let the journal slip from his grasp and fall to the floor as he covered his face in his hands and sobbed.

In the top left corner, slightly smeared by blue ink, was the date November 14, 1997.

Ronnie slurped the last of his melted smoothie through his straw and dramatically patted his stomach. "I'm so full, I feel like I could bust!"

Andrew poked at a banana clump with his straw and decided he wouldn't try to finish his. "Oh, you are, are you?" he said casually. "Then you're probably too tired to help me get your toys out of the car and—"

"No, wait! I can do that! I'm not so full I can't walk."

Andrew stood and took their glasses to the sink. "All right, then. Follow me."

Ronnie was overjoyed to discover that his uncle hadn't forgotten a single item. He busied himself by lining up his stuffed animals against the wall as Andrew lugged in the heavier things.

"No, I want my toy box over there, next to the giraffe," Ronnie said as he stood on his bed, ordering his uncle all over his room every time he changed his mind about something. He gave him a thumbs-up when the last item was set in place. "Perfect."

Andrew wiped his forehead and sat beside Ronnie on the edge of the bed, bowing the mattress with his weight. "And we're done."

"You're sweaty," Ronnie said, as if that weren't already a well-known reality to Andrew.

Andrew looked down at his wet shirt and sucked in another deep breath of air. "Thanks to you. Do you mind?"

"As long as you don't smell," Ronnie said, flashing him a cautioning look.

Andrew laughed out loud. "Thank you for your bluntness."

"I don't know what *bluntness* means, but you're welcome anyway."

Andrew gazed around the room and guessed it to be almost twice the size of Ronnie's old bedroom. "Wait...one thing's missing."

Ronnie looked around him, confused. "What?"

Andrew pulled out a container of colorful thumbtacks from his pocket. "Your puzzles. Don't tell me you're going to keep them under your bed where no one can see them. You ought to cover the walls with them."

Ronnie looked stunned. "You mean you'll let me do that? Poke holes in the wall?"

Andrew pulled out a puzzle of an underwater scene and held it out in front of him. "I think these masterpieces deserve to be seen."

Ronnie smiled sheepishly and threw his arms around his uncle. "Thanks, Uncle Andy. Here, let me help."

Andrew hung all six puzzles, letting Ronnie once again decide for himself where each one would go. "Now the room's complete. Like it?"

Ronnie nodded. "A lot. It's really big too. Bigger than my other room was."

Andrew sat down beside Ronnie again and said, "Do you know what tomorrow is, Ronnie?"

Ronnie stared up at the ceiling as he thought. "Wednesday? Because today's Tuesday, right?"

"Yes. Wednesday is a church day. Have you ever been to church?"

"A little. Sometimes Daddy and Mommy would take me at Christmas to watch a play." Ronnie's voice cracked slightly at the mention of his parents. He wasn't sure if that scar would ever leave his life. He looked up at Andrew and said, "Are they having a play tomorrow at your church?"

Andrew chuckled and shook his head. "No."

"Then why are you going? I thought that's why people go. That's why Daddy and Mommy went."

"Well, you see, Ronnie, church is where we go to learn about Jesus and sing songs to Him. It's a place where we go so we can get close to God and hear about the Bible. It's important that we go to church."

Ronnie nodded his head, even though he still didn't quite understand. "How come?"

"Because Jesus loves us. Do you know that?"

Ronnie shrugged. The only love he had ever felt in his life came from the one sitting beside him now. As far as he knew, no other form of love existed. "Why do you love Jesus, Uncle Andy? Did He do something for you?"

Andrew tried not to appear disappointed. *Oh, Ronnie. If you only knew.*

Drake still tasted vomit. Still felt the anesthetic of shock. He had his hands on the steering wheel like he was going to strangle it. Someone was not going to be happy to know he had found out. Everything.

Drake hit the brakes midway into his driveway and let the screeching sound be the only warning. As he jumped out of his truck and banged the door shut behind him, he realized he was still shaking.

You're dead. Nothin' but a dirty liar. Drake felt sick again and gripped his stomach. A mass of emotions was about to send him over the edge. Every step forward felt like electricity. *You're dead, old man. Your secret's finally come out.*

Rain pelted against Drake's light jacket as he took the stairs with heavy, crushing steps. He tried the screen door and found it locked. He slapped the palms of his hands against the cheap glass and yelled, "Let me in! We need to talk!"

The lights were all off, but Drake could vaguely make out a large figure moving toward the door at a snail's pace. "Hurry up!" he shouted, striking the door harder. He heard several screen doors creaking open across the street and knew he had attracted an audience. Well, if they wanted a show, then they might as well pull out the lawn chairs now and start the popcorn, because Drake was about to give the whole neighborhood the shock of its life.

"I'm comin', I'm comin'!" Ben yelled back. He was wearing a ratty pair of blue-jean shorts and had a shirt draped over his shoulder. "What's wrong with you, Drake? You high or somethin'?"

"Why did you lie to me?" Drake said strictly, forcing his way inside.

"Leave me alone. I'm going out."

Drake blocked the door. "Don't think you're going to run off to get drunk somewhere before explaining to me why you lied about Mom!"

"I don't know what you took last night or where you got it from, but it'll probably wear off in a few hours, so I suggest you go to bed before the migraine starts," Ben said indifferently, still thinking his son to be drunk from too much beer.

Drake refused to budge. "Why did you kill her?"

Ben spun around. He said nothing, but his stunned face said all Drake needed to know. "Your theatrics are getting old, Drake. Like I said, go to bed."

"You know exactly what I'm talking about!" Drake pressed, his voice still raised. "I read it online. Her drowning, her trial, and how you tried to cover it up!"

Ben felt the breath drain out of him. He swallowed and looked away.

"Oh, but I wasn't supposed to know, was I?" Drake said coldly, his hands trembling to hit something. "It was my fault. She left because of me. Wasn't that the story?" He swatted the lamp to the left of him onto the ground just to hear it shatter.

"Breaking everything in this house isn't gonna change things!"

"Then what's it gonna take?! What's it gonna take to penetrate through those stone layers of your skull?"

"Out!" Ben yelled, pointing his finger to the door. "If this is what I can expect of you being out of school now, you can go. I'm not gonna waste time and money supporting you anymore."

"I'm not done talking."

"Well, I'm done listening."

"No, you're gonna listen. You drowned the only person who cared anything about—"

"All right! So you found out she died! But before you go accusin' me of somethin', it might interest you to know that she—"

"I know she had a sleeping disorder!" Drake interrupted. "Narcolepsy. I read it in her journal."

"Well, there you go. That's how she drowned. Every time it hit her, she just conked out and stayed asleep for up to half an hour sometimes.

I found her like that in the bathtub at the hotel, but I never told you because I wanted to protect you."

Drake made himself laugh despite his rage. "Protect me? Protect *me?* You mean protect yourself. When the matter went to court, all you had to do was show the judge Mom's doctor reports, and you were a free man. I read all that online too. Probably even had to buy a bottle of eye drops to put in your eyes so your tears would look believable to the jury."

"That's a lie!"

"This is the same old story you told the jury twelve years ago, isn't it? Isn't it?! Just say it! I want to hear you admit—"

"Enough! Get out of my house!"

"I'm not listening to you anymore," Drake said through clenched teeth. "You've kept me blind for too long, and I'm not gonna take it anymore."

"I said *get out!*"

"The autopsy report showed bruising under her skin. She didn't fall asleep; you held her down under the water and watched her die."

Ben began to show fear.

"You're a fool. You should've known I'd find out."

"I didn't—"

"You should've known I wouldn't stay little forever. I grew up, got stronger...you really didn't think about that, did you?"

"About what?"

The muscles in Drake's face contracted as he said, "I'm going to kill you for what you did."

Ben took a step back and defensively held out a hand in front of him. "You don't know what you're doing, Drake."

"You knew what you were doing when you killed Mom," Drake snarled, moving closer.

"I had no other choice! She was fine one day, and then the next she just...just changed. That wasn't my fault though! I couldn't stand hearing her talk about God and Jesus all the time. *He* wasn't her husband; I was. But she wouldn't listen. She never listened to me."

"You were jealous over a *Book* she was reading? Is that it? Is that what you're trying to tell me? I don't know whether to believe this or call it insanity."

"She wasn't the woman I married. She stopped wanting to have fun after she got God."

"No, it went deeper with you."

"I had nothing to do with—"

"Then why not divorce her? Gah, you held her *underwater*? You sick—"

"It wasn't supposed to go that far."

"That's why you sent me away to Grandpa's that day. So you could perform your sick little murder while I was away without any problems. For twelve years, you thought you got away with it, but now you're going to pay. And you're going to feel every drop of pain like you made her feel."

"Don't try me, Drake!" Ben cautioned, stepping back toward the fireplace. "I'm warning you!"

Drake saw his dad craftily move his arm around his body. He immediately jumped back as soon as his dad brought down an iron poker on the spot where he was standing only a second before. Before his dad had a chance to raise the poker again and swing it at him, Drake made his move.

He swung his right fist around and let it sink deep into his dad's cheekbone.

Ben stumbled and tried to maintain his balance. He swatted at the air as he fell.

Too late. Drake watched the back of his head land directly on the cold, hard stone of the fireplace hearth.

Thud.

Drake stood there guardedly, waiting for his dad to get up. "Stand up and fight! I'm not finished with you yet!"

Ben never moved. Drake wasn't even sure if he saw him breathing.

Drake took a few steps back as soon as he saw the pool of blood begin to flow from the back of his dad's head.

What have I done?

Chapter

5

FUGITIVE

Drake Pearson didn't know what he was doing or where he was going, only that he had to get as far away as he could from his home. A *murderer*, he kept repeating to himself. *I'm a murderer. That means prison, life, or worse...death row.*

OK, back up, back up. It had started off all talk. Arguing. There were threats...he said he was going to kill him, but that was just an offshoot of his anger. From the beginning, he had never actually intended on killing his father.

A lot of good that does now. He had planned on a fight, though. A long, bloody fight, even if it meant just as many bruises on him as he gave his father. Anything to make his dad feel a percentage of the pain his mom must have endured as she gasped for air during the last moments of her life. He had had no idea what kind of shape his old man was in, but he certainly hadn't planned on the fight being over in one blow.

Now there was a dead body. He had sentenced himself to this fate. The guilt had been shifted, and with the authorities after him, who knew if he would be able to get away? *Stupid, Drake. Real stupid. You've really outdone yourself this time. Can't you ever do anything right?*

Drake slowed to a stop in front of the railroad tracks bordering the outskirts of town as soon as he saw whirling lights in the distance, warning him of an oncoming train. He struck his hand against the steering wheel but held his tongue from saying anything only because he knew it wouldn't do any good.

Where are you going? He braced his forehead in his hand and realized he had no plan. *Leave the state. Go anywhere. Isn't much else you can do now.*

His duffel bag was still in the passenger seat like a quiet companion. Hard to believe all this started from a few empty pages in a journal. One argument. One blow. It was never meant to lead to this.

Drake's eyes followed the train as it rumbled past. He listened to the tracks shudder and groan beneath the weight as he let his mind drift. He hadn't been here in so long that he had almost forgotten its name. Though not official, this railroad was known by all the townsfolk as Penny Tracks, due to a legend almost as old as the scrub brush that had fossilized itself against the tarnished metal plates of the tracks.

For generations, a legend had floated around that over ten thousand wheat pennies had been mixed in with the concrete used for the crossties. Though no one ever knew for sure whether the myth was fact or fiction, the old-timers wouldn't give it up just because it gave them something to talk about every Sunday afternoon at the gas station. Sometimes the story changed from wheat pennies to buffalo head nickels to occasionally even arrowheads, but every time it was told, it was like a new story engraving itself into the very history of Linhurst Peak.

But Drake was tired of legends. Tired of secrets. The only thing they were good for was bringing pain. And now look at him, the biggest secret of them all. Running away from a murder sure wouldn't help things, but neither would going to jail. Either way, his life was fated to crash at some point, so the least he could do was prolong what little freedom he had left.

Freight cars rattled by as the train continued to make its lengthy journey across a stretch of tracks concealed by dense thickets of goldenrod, wild grapes, and honeysuckle. Drake hated living so close to the tracks. Every night, it was the same thing. The screeching whistle would blow—*long, long, short, long*—and shake him from his dreams at three-something every morning. Plus, the sight of the dingy rail cars slowly rumbling by was a constant reminder that he was still here as the rest of the world passed him by, trapped inside his miserable life. Now he was finally crossing over these tracks, but he had always planned to leave in hopes of starting a new life, not flee from a murder scene.

Drake glanced down to check his gas level and was relieved to find that he had slightly over half a tank. He killed the engine as he waited for the train to pass and dug through his bag for his wallet. He cracked it open and counted again what he knew was already there.

Fifty-two dollars. He shoved the wallet in his back pocket. Wouldn't last long. He would have to use it strictly for food. Nothing else.

He sighed and pressed his head against the steering wheel. *So I guess that means I'll have to kick cigarettes...Man, that'll be torture. But I'm doing it only to save the money. No cigarettes, no gas. Just food. When I run out of gas, I'll just have to walk.*

What a plan. When the money ran out—and boy, would fifty-two dollars run out fast—he would be stuck. Then, he would either need to find a job, hit the streets, or turn himself in. He knew he would never give himself up, regardless of what kind of life he would have to learn to adjust to. That was for the weak who were afraid to sleep in the rain or go a few days without a meal. He wasn't like that.

Dad deserved it. I didn't mean to do it, but it happened. Why should I be sorry for that? He rubbed his head and closed his tired eyes. *What a day.*

"Proverbs 21:13 says, 'Whoever shuts his ears to the cry of the poor will also cry himself and not be heard,'" Pastor Don Bauer said earnestly from behind his glass pulpit. A congregation pushing sixty people sat drinking in his every word while fatigued children leaned against their parents with bobbing heads, wishing this man would say what he needed to say and close in prayer. Usually there was more of an attendance on Wednesday nights, but perhaps the heavy rainfall had deterred those living farther away from coming—as was apparently the case with the children's teacher tonight.

"How can we ever hope to reach the lost if we aren't even willing to reach out of our comfort zones first and show them Christ's love?" Pastor Don said, straying away from his notes again as he walked the length of the platform. "Do you want to know why eighty to ninety percent of people who become saved fall away from the faith? It's most likely because they got caught up in emotion during praise and worship or an altar call, but have never actually had a relationship with Jesus, because the Church as a whole is too afraid to tell them the truth."

Andrew liked it when his pastor got this way. Once he began talking about witnessing and reaching the lost, it was hard for him to talk about anything else. His forehead would gleam with sweat as he paced back and forth, reaching out to the audience with excitement and passion in his voice. Of course, Andrew understood why his pastor was this way. It was because a friend of Don's had been bold enough to share his faith with him that the gospel finally became clear to him, and he had immediately accepted Jesus into his heart. Ever since that day, Don had been a changed man and witnessing became his number one obsession.

Andrew sneaked a peek at Ronnie as Pastor Don Bauer retreated behind his pulpit. "What do you think, Ronnie?" he whispered.

Ronnie sat like a still statue with his legs dangling over the edge of the pew, gathering his own thoughts about the church in stride. "I don't know yet. I kinda like him. He's funny when he starts talking fast."

Andrew rested his hand on Ronnie's knee and flipped through pages in his Bible as the pastor told everyone to turn to Matthew 25:34-40.

70

"Read with me," Pastor Don said loudly, picking up his Bible. "Then the King will say to those on His right hand, 'Come, you blessed of My Father, inherit the kingdom prepared for you from the foundation of the world: for I was hungry and you gave Me food; I was thirsty and you gave Me drink; I was a stranger and you took Me in; I was naked and you clothed Me; I was sick and you visited Me; I was in prison and you came to Me.'

"Then the righteous will answer Him, saying, 'Lord, when did we see You hungry and feed You, or thirsty and give You drink? When did we see You a stranger and take You in, or naked and clothe You? Or when did we see You sick, or in prison, and come to You?' And the King will answer and say to them, 'Assuredly, I say to you, inasmuch as you did it to one of the least of these My brethren, you did it to Me.'"

Pastor Don closed his Bible and stared out into the congregation with teary eyes. "These duties mentioned here—feeding the hungry and giving drink to the thirsty—are duties that *anyone* can perform. We have to remind ourselves that Jesus once did the same for us. I'm not saying that you give money to every person you see on the side of the road asking for it; God instructs us to use wisdom. Ask God to give you discernment and let Him use you. All the deeds mentioned here in these verses are deeds of love; not one of them consists of words, but involves action and even sacrifice."

Andrew nodded his head softly in agreement.

"I'll say that again, 'cause I don't think you all heard me. *Sacrifice.* It means giving up something to God that hurts, something of personal importance to you. God has to see that He's got your heart and your obedience before His anointing can ever enter your life."

Pastor Don stepped down from the stage again and got personal with the congregation. "Believers, *we're* going to Heaven. We have life and a wonderful future to look forward to. But it's not enough to come to church week after week so we can feel like we've fulfilled some sort of a religious duty. What was it Jesus commanded us to do right before He left the world to go back to Heaven?"

"Go unto all the world and preach the gospel," Andrew muttered under his breath.

"He told us to go unto all the world and preach the gospel," Pastor Don said. "Yes, we're going to Heaven. Yes, Jesus saved us. But let's make sure we take as many people with us as we can. It hurts me to know that even one soul is in hell today. It can be avoided, but it's up to us."

He smiled in spite of his tears and said, "In conclusion, I'd like to remind you all of the verse in Hebrews 13:2 that says, 'Do not forget to entertain strangers, for by doing so, some have unwittingly entertained angels.' Live your lives as sacrifices to God and He will direct your paths. He'll use you if you're willing to be used by Him."

Once Drake's headache progressed into a migraine, he decided it was time to turn off the '80s station he had been listening to for the past three hours of driving and give his head a rest. He rolled up his window and tried to relax in the silence, but his throbbing head made every effort impossible. His unyielding craving for nicotine was probably also a major contributor to his headache—especially because he usually took a smoke when he felt stressed.

He popped open his glove box and scanned the inside just one more time, in case he might have overlooked it. Surely he had just one cigarette left in there somewhere. He slammed it shut and shoved a piece of gum in his mouth. Cinnamon wasn't the flavor he was looking for.

Several times, he had been tempted to turn into a gas station and buy a pack of cigarettes, but he had to keep reminding himself that he'd be thankful he saved his money later. *Boloney*, he thought. *The only thing I care about right now is a cigarette and a lighter.* He pressed his left foot hard against the floor and chewed faster.

He spotted a gas station in the distance and felt his stomach churn. *One couldn't hurt, could it? What's a few bucks outta fifty, anyway?* In time, those few bucks would hold a greater value when he was searching the trash cans for food. *But I need this.*

Drake put his trembling hand on his seat and gripped a fistful of the padding, fighting the gut-wrenching urge to give in to his addiction. With only a second more to decide, he passed up the exit leading to the gas station and stared blankly ahead at the long strip of highway that lay before him. *I can do this. I can do this. It feels like I'm dying, but I can do this.* Withdrawal. Wonderful way to top off his day.

Drake felt stupid wasting gas like this. Driving in no definite direction was probably a mistake that would later come back to haunt him. He just wanted to get away. He had to get safe somehow; prison wasn't an option as far as he was concerned. His past was covered in dirt like everyone else's, and he sure hadn't been a saint, but he had always hoped he would never cross paths with the law. Some thugs he knew blew off prison as if it were nothing more than a visit to the doctor. For some reason, it had always been a bigger deal to him. If for no one else, he had to live for himself. Speeding tickets were one thing. Electric chairs were quite another.

But maybe I'm doing myself more harm by running away. If I go back and confess, they might go easy on me and cut my sentence short. Drake squinted in the glare of the setting sun and bit the inside of his cheek. *Nah. I'm not gonna go back and beg for their mercy. I stand on my own two feet. I don't crawl. 'Sides, who knows if they'll even be able to pin the murder on me? How do they know that someone didn't break in, get in a fight with Dad, and leave? No, they won't be able to find me here. I can escape. Maybe this is just the kinda break I've been looking for.*

An alarm beeped and a red exclamation point lit up beside the gas tank level. "Oh, no," Drake moaned. "Outta gas already?" He looked up just in time to see a large sign with the words "Welcome to Springfield, Illinois" printed boldly in white. "Springfield, eh?" he muttered to himself. He turned his attention back to the flashing red light and let out a long breath. "Might as well get used to it. Looks like Springfield's gonna be my new home."

Drake knew he had a little more gas left in his tank but decided not to chance it. He made a quick U-turn and pulled into the small, used car lot he had seen a couple miles back. *This old set of wheels probably isn't worth a dime, but maybe I'll be able to squeeze a few bucks out of it to give me some more food money. Won't be no good to me anymore without gas.*

He parked his truck and wiped the sweat off his face. Presentable and not guilty—that was the key. Just a guy who wanted to sell his truck. A face everyone would see, then hopefully forget. Easy.

Just as he was about to get out, he caught a glimpse of himself in the rearview mirror and leaned back slowly in his seat. *That's...me?* His whole complexion was masked in anger, as if his resentment had manifested itself into some sort of visible disease that had stained his entire face. And his eyes. They looked so strange, so different from ever before. Hollow. Cold. Like he would almost be willing to do anything to get what he wanted now.

What is it I want? The question took him by surprise. He put his hand on the door, ready to go talk to the salesman about this truck so he could hit the road, not be lectured by his conscience. *I want to be free, that's what I want. To be left alone finally. I want to live without being screamed at and hated. I want to prove to the world that Drake Pearson doesn't have to live at the bottom anymore. That's what I want, and I finally got the chance to get it.*

He stepped out of his truck and jogged up the short flight of steps that led to the office building, but he stopped when he saw a sign posted on the door. *"Some trust in chariots, and some in horses; but we will remember the name of the Lord our God"* (Psalm 20:7). He read over the words again and wrinkled his brow. *Whatever that's supposed to mean.* He tapped lightly on the door and hesitantly took a step inside. "Hello?"

A tall, black man in his late forties stood and greeted him with a glowing smile. "Hello! Guess I didn't even hear you drive up."

I ain't here to buy any of your cars, pal. Drake forced a smile back and tried to remember to keep his words polite. Selling his truck might take about every trick in the book, so he extended his hand and kept smiling. "Good morning, sir," he said, trying to sound as educated and respectful as possible.

The man returned the greeting and identified himself as Bruno Gorman. "See anything you're interested in, Mr...."

"Drake," he answered politely. "Drake Pearson." He wanted to slap himself as soon as he gave the man his last name. *You idiot! What are you thinking throwing your last name out there when you're a wanted man? How could you be so stupid?* He tried to conceal his fear with another smile, but felt as if the look on his face was giving him away. *Just another guy with nothing to hide, remember? Easy.*

Of course, Bruno didn't seem to notice as he shuffled past Drake and held open the door for him. "Shall we take a look around outside then, Drake, or do you already have your eye on one?"

"Sir..." Drake started, debating whether he should be direct with the man or leave now before getting laughed at. He could still leave. The man would think he was crazy, of course, but he could handle that much easier than being told by this upper-class gentleman that his dilapidated vehicle would be better off in a junkyard than on the road. "I might as well tell you now. I don't even have a fraction of the money I need to buy a car, used or not. I brought my truck down here today to see if you might be...well, if you might be interested in buying it."

Bruno maintained his smile, which Drake found particularly odd. Why hadn't this guy already run him out of his office? Drake almost left, but Bruno stopped him by saying, "I can't make any promises, but I'll be happy to look at your truck."

Drake knew he should feel ecstatic at those words, but he couldn't ignore the looming dread of being turned down as he led the man outside. *Don't hold your breath, Drake. Once he sees your truck, you're gone.*

"I can't find my toothbrush *anywhere*," Ronnie complained as he searched again through his unpacked bags.

"Did you check the zippers?" Andrew called from downstairs.

"All empty."

"Hang on, I'm coming." Andrew hustled up the stairs, wishing his body would stop reminding him of his age. "Wait..." he stopped. "Then you didn't brush your teeth last night?"

"Uh...no."

"Then I must have forgotten it," Andrew said, mounting the last stair. "I didn't even think to get your things out of the bathroom before I left." He thought for a moment and snapped his fingers. "Ronnie, hold on. I think I have an extra toothbrush in the bottom left drawer in the bathroom cabinet. You're welcome to it until I buy you a new one."

Ronnie made a face. "You mean a *used* one?" he said, dragging out the word "used" as if it were the most nauseating thing on earth.

Andrew stifled a laugh. "No, I don't mean a *used* one." He walked to the bathroom with Ronnie following close behind him. He found the toothbrush and held it up. "See? Still in the package. Here you go."

Ronnie took the toothbrush in his hands and examined it, nearly making Andrew laugh again.

"Still not completely convinced, eh?" he joked.

"It's really big," Ronnie said. "You must have a big mouth."

Andrew knew Ronnie hadn't meant for that to be an insult, so he didn't take it as one. "Well, I can't argue with that," he answered truthfully, rubbing his jaw. "I'll find you your own toothbrush tomorrow. But for now..." He observed the toothbrush and couldn't help but smile. Ronnie was right; it was rather big. "I guess you'll just have to somehow fit that monstrous thing in your mouth and get it over with."

Ronnie sighed and trudged over to the sink, but Andrew detected a smile on his face before he disappeared from view. Andrew wondered what it must be like for Ronnie to at last live in a peaceful environment where it was normal to joke around and have fun. Ronnie seemed relaxed here, not tense like Andrew had seen him when he was around Kevin. He was 7 years old, and for the first time in his life, he was allowed to be a kid.

"Uncle Andy?" Ronnie said in a garbled voice from the bathroom, his mouth overflowing with foamy toothpaste.

"Yes, Ronnie?"

Ronnie trudged into Andrew's bedroom and found him already pulling the covers back on his bed. "Mind if I make a pallet in your room again tonight?"

Andrew let go of the covers and met Ronnie's eyes. "You mean you don't want to try out your soft, new bed yet?"

Ronnie halfheartedly turned his head to the side in a yes-and-no answer.

Andrew noticed the disappointment on Ronnie's face as soon as those words left his mouth, so he said quickly, "Of course you can, Ronnie. I just didn't want you to think you couldn't stay in your room because I enjoy your company so much. You know, I sometimes get lonely too in this big old house by myself."

"Really?"

"Sure. C'mon, I'll pull out the inflatable mattress while you go get the blanket and sheet off your bed."

Chapter

6

STRANGE REACTIONS

Bruno Gorman did appear somewhat stunned when he caught sight of Drake's 1981 Ford truck. However, if he was completely uninterested, he did an excellent job of hiding it. "I'll be honest with you, Drake. You got a nice vehicle, but it's in pretty rough condition. Sides are beaten in; some of the scrapes are pretty deep. That's coming from a guy who's spent most of his life around used cars."

Drake rubbed the back of his neck and unwillingly nodded his head in agreement. "Yeah, I kinda figured you'd say that."

"Has the vehicle ever been involved in any accidents? I mean, other than the obvious bumps and scratches. Any internal damage?"

Drake paused for a moment, questioning if he would kill his chances for selling this man on his car if he told the truth. "Well..." This guy looked, acted, and talked professional, and Drake was sure he knew his stuff like the back of his hand. He may have been able to get away with some things, but to say that his truck had never been in an accident would be an obvious lie. "Yeah," he admitted, much to his dislike. "Twice, actually."

"Minor or major?"

"The first one was...well, I wouldn't call it major, but it was pretty close. Second one just involved the fender getting smashed, and I already replaced the side mirror that got tore off." As if that was a big plus.

Bruno found the indention and examined it for himself.

"Might as well go ahead and save you the time by telling you that the airbags don't work either. Found that out the hard way in my first accident."

Bruno cringed. "Ouch. Were you hurt badly?"

"My head and shoulder hit the steering wheel." Drake lifted up his hair and pointed to a small line across the left side of his forehead. "Took six stitches to patch it up."

Bruno popped the hood and took his time inspecting every part, taking a few mental notes on loose parts and anything that appeared to need immediate fixing.

Jump him. The thought came out of nowhere as Drake watched how occupied Bruno was under the hood of his truck. Drake debated the temptation in his mind and glanced back at the office.

Vacant. *Imagine how much cash he has stashed inside that huge desk.* Drake considered his own weight and strength and looked again at Bruno, whose head was now almost entirely out of sight as he examined the truck more meticulously. *Are you crazy, Drake? Don't you realize you've already committed a murder? Do you want theft added to your sentence too?* His stomach churned restlessly as he realized the stupidity of his idea. *Besides, even if you got one-up on this guy, he's likely to overpower you in two seconds instead of vice versa. It'd be suicide.*

Bruno lowered the hood and moved to the back of the truck. He casually glanced at the license plate. "From Missouri, eh? Long way from home."

Drake snapped out of his thoughts and faced Bruno. "What'd you say?"

"I noticed your Missouri plates. Haven't been there in years."

"Yeah, well, I pronounce it as *Misery* instead of *Missouri*. Not a lot of good memories."

Bruno forced a grim smile. "Sorry to hear that."

How little you know, buddy. And I plan to keep it that way.

Bruno opened the driver's door and sat down in the seat. "Mind if I have the keys?" he said, stretching out his hand.

"You wanna drive it?"

"If that's all right with you."

"'Course," Drake said. He handed him his keys and climbed in the passenger seat beside him.

"Oh, almost out of gas," Bruno remarked once he saw the warning near the gas tank level. "I'll make it a quick ride, then." Bruno took the truck a mile down the road, turned around, and finally pulled back into the car lot. "A little bumpy, but overall it rides fairly well. Brakes are a bit worn down and I heard some air gushing through from somewhere—"

"The floorboard," Drake interrupted, lifting up a soiled green towel he used as a mat to reveal a tiny puncture in the floor next to his seat.

"That was a result of your accident too, I suppose?"

"Yeah, but you get used to the noise eventually."

Bruno stepped out of the truck with Drake and looked him steadily in the eyes. "I know you came here in hopes of selling me this truck, but...quite frankly, it's a hazard to anyone driving it."

Drake couldn't believe it. After all the hope that had been built inside him, he was left standing right where he started. "But you said—"

"It's more than just the brakes and the hole in the floor. There were other things I noticed in the engine. Sounds, rattles...a lot of things I would have to go into detail in order for you to understand. Some of the parts are pretty much shot. It would cost me too much to try to fix it to resell. I'm sorry."

"I know it may not seem like much, but it really is a great truck," Drake countered, not willing to be refused this easily. "And there's only fourteen thousand miles on it!"

Bruno stared at him, his expression blank. "I was really beginning to like you, kid, but I don't respect liars."

Drake fell silent. He knew the odometer had been broken the day he bought it from that double-dealer across the road, and obviously Bruno had taken note of it too before he took it for a drive.

"Look, I'm sorry," Drake said, leaning against his truck in spite of the heat it brought to his back. "I'm just desperate. I need money." He lowered his head and stared down at the rubber strands peeling away around his shoelaces. *C'mon, think! Something...* "See...my grandpa's real sick, and I'm all he's got left. If he don't get a hospital bed in his home soon, I'll have to send him back to the nursing home again. All the loneliness and confinement nearly killed him last time. I can't do that to him again."

Drake began tearing up, and he turned away. *Man, I'm getting pretty good at this stuff.* He almost didn't even have to think about what he would say anymore; the lies just seemed to flow from his mouth.

Bruno's face softened as he heard the utter desperation in Drake's voice. "Well..."

"You're right, though," Drake said softly. "This truck...ah, I can see the years have taken its toll on it. But boy in its day, it was a pride just to drive it. It was my grandpa who gave it to me, you know. He's the one who sent me down here to...oh, but you know all that. Hey, sorry to cost you your time, sir. You're the car salesman, not me. If you say it's no good, I respect that."

Bruno gave the vehicle a once-over and checked his watch. Almost closing time. He nodded his head toward his office and said, "Come with me."

Drake followed the man inside. Bruno tugged his billfold from his back pocket and pulled six one-hundred dollar bills out. Drake nearly fell over.

"I'm not doing this because I'm going to make a profit, because the fact of the matter is, I probably won't after all the maintenance costs. I'm doing this because I believe that you're a good kid. Not only did I notice your truck out there, but I also noticed that there was no smell of alcohol or cigarette smoke in your breath as you talked to me. That made me doubt you wanted the money for beer or smokes."

Drake looked confused.

"Did you see my sign when you came in?"

"The thing about the chariots and horses? Sure, but what's it mean?"

"It's a Scripture. I like it because...well, because I'm a car salesman, and it's my way of reminding everyone who walks through that door that even though material things may fail us, God will never fail."

Drake raised his head slightly as if he understood, even though he was still clueless. *I don't think this guy's elevator goes to the top floor.*

"I'm a Christian, and I believe that God loves every one of us. I want you to know that Jesus is the one giving you this, not me. When

I see a brother or sister in need and begin to feel God tugging at my heart, I see it as my duty to help."

Is this guy for real? Drake raised an eyebrow and repeated, "A brother or sister?"

"Of course." Bruno placed the cash in Drake's hand and smiled.

Crisp and real. How strangely different it felt to be holding hundred dollar bills instead of a wad of ones. *As long as it's not counterfeit, this guy can talk to me about the migration patterns of Canadian geese for all I care.*

"I'm helping you because someone very special helped me," Bruno said. "His name is Jesus Christ, and a long time ago He died on a cross for us. It was the only way for God to take away our sins so we could live eternally with Him one day in Heaven."

Jesus Christ. Those words struck a wrong chord in Drake's heart. "Yeah, I've heard about Him," he mumbled, gritting his teeth. *He's the guy who got my mom killed. Thanks, but no thanks. I'm doing just fine without Him.*

"I'm glad to hear that," Bruno said. "A lot of young people these days don't even know who He is...But He's real, Drake."

Drake looked into the man's eyes and sensed those words really meant something to him.

"He's real and He loves you. If you have any questions, you know where to find me. Take care of yourself, Drake, and God bless you."

Drake nodded, but no words came out. He thrust the money deep inside his front pocket and walked through the door with a thousand new ideas.

Sucker.

Andrew Tavner didn't routinely go to bed this early, but he could tell Ronnie was tired and wouldn't go to bed without him in the room. "OK, but I have to warn you, I snore," he said.

"I know," Ronnie said, tugging on his socks. "I heard you last night."

Ronnie's words were about as matter-of-fact as if Andrew had asked him to describe the weather. "Whoever said honesty was the best policy forgot to mention how blunt it could be."

Ronnie grinned. "I still don't know what that word means, but OK."

Andrew threw a pillow at him and rose from the couch. "All right, time for bed."

Ronnie tucked his blanket under one arm and his stuffed panda under the other. "Arrow's tired too," he explained.

"Arrow? How'd you ever come to give a panda a name like that?"

"I had a cat one time I named Arrow because she had a spot on her head that looked like an arrowhead. She was my favorite. Black and white all over, even on the tips of her ears. After she died, Daddy bought me this bear to make me stop crying. The panda was black and white too, so I named my panda after Arrow."

"Ah, I see. That perfectly clears things up. Well, Arrow looks about as tired as you do right now, so I suggest we all get a good night's sleep tonight. Sound good?"

Ronnie held up Arrow and stared into his small, black eyes. "Does that sound good, Arrow?" He pretended to listen, and then turned to his uncle. "He thinks we should have one more ice cream before we go to bed."

Andrew put his hands on his knees and leaned down. "Tell Arrow he already had two today and a third might make his stomach hurt."

Ronnie gave him a sly look. "Oh, OK. Good night, Uncle Andy!" He reached up to hug him, and Andrew bent over to return the hug. "Good night—to the both of you. I'll be upstairs in a second."

Ronnie scurried off while Andrew followed him—at a much slower pace, naturally—up the stairs. Andrew crawled into bed and pulled the covers over his shoulders, hoping against hope that he would be able to get some rest tonight. It was only nine o'clock, and he wasn't the least tired.

"Uncle Andy?" Ronnie said, snuggling deeper under his covers.

"Uh-huh?"

"Do you have a job? Because you didn't work yesterday or the day before that."

Andrew smiled and gazed up at the obscure shadows darkening the ceiling. "That's because I'm retired, Ronnie. I don't have to work anymore."

Ronnie shot up straight. "You don't have to work?"

Andrew chuckled. "Well, I used to work a lot, but after many years at my job, I was able to retire."

"And they pay you? Just to sit around and do whatever you want?"

"Yep. That's the beauty of retirement, Ronnie."

"Wow. I wanna be retired when I grow up," Ronnie said, a new enthusiasm in his voice.

Not five minutes later, Andrew heard Ronnie's breathing getting deeper and knew he had finally gone to sleep. He closed his eyes and enjoyed the uninterrupted silence. *Jesus...thanks for giving Ronnie to me. He's such a wonderful kid. He's already added another ten years to my life. Always bright and happy, despite all the heartache and pain that ravaged his life for so long. Please let him always find peace here. Help me as I raise him, and draw him close to You. And God, as far as Kevin goes...*

He yearned to ask God to forgive his brother for the things he had done against Ronnie, but he couldn't find it in himself to get the words out.

I know it's wrong and I know You want me to forgive, but I just don't think I can. Not now. You were there at Kevin's house all the times I wasn't able to be there. You saw what went on and how he treated Ronnie. I know You forgive, but forgiving a lousy, drunken man for abusing a child seems way beyond even Your reach. I'm sorry, but not now.

A sharp rapping at the door broke Andrew's thoughts, and he instinctively sat up. "Kevin," he whispered to himself.

He threw his covers back and squinted in the darkness to see if Ronnie had heard the noise.

Still asleep.

He left the room and tentatively walked downstairs toward the front door. *No, it couldn't be Kevin. Not at this time of night. Anyway, he wouldn't dare...would he?*

He headed directly for the light switch and flicked on the porch light. Then he stepped aside to a nearby window and discreetly parted the blinds. He could only see the backside of a man, but from what he was able to perceive, he knew it couldn't be Kevin. *Thank You, God.*

Still guarded, he wondered if he should go get his gun—just to be safe. That would mean going back upstairs and probably waking Ronnie. Surely it was just the neighbor.

He cracked the front door open slightly and found himself face to face with a teenage boy. "Hello?" he said, glancing around his yard to make sure there was no one else.

"Name's Drake," the young man said, not bothering to offer his hand. He quickly removed his ragged cap and tried to appear as presentable as possible. "I, uh..." He looked past Andrew to the inside of his house. *Whew, what a place.*

"Did you need something, or..."

What're you doin' here, Drake? You're not even worth his time. Why don't you just leave and forget about it? Drake forced his pride behind him and said straightforwardly, "Do you know if there's a nearby shelter or anything around here?"

"A shelter?"

Drake wanted to roll his eyes, but decided against it. "Yeah, you know..." He broke off eye contact with the man and looked away somewhere to his left, never feeling more humiliated in all his life. "Where homeless people go," he said, so low that he could barely hear himself.

Oh, Andrew thought.

"Look, I ain't got no gun on me or nothin', if that's what you're thinkin'." He opened up the bag he was holding to show the man he was telling the truth. Then he lifted up his shirt to reveal that there was no handgun or weapon tucked away in his pants. "I don't have nothin' to hide. I just need a place to sleep for the night."

"Where are you from?"

"Missouri. I, uh...hitchhiked a ride up here from a man who had an Illinois plate and got dropped off here." *What a liar.*

"Do you have any family? Any relatives?"

"Nope. Only child, both my folks are dead, and as far as family goes, your guess is just as good as mine."

Compassion filled Andrew's heart as the words of his pastor came back to him. *I'm not saying that you give money to every person you see on the side of the road asking for it; God instructs us to use wisdom. Ask God to give you discernment, and let Him use you.* Andrew opened the door wide and asked Drake to come in and sit.

As short as the walk was from the front door to the living room, Drake took in every sight around him. A magnificent two-story house with a massive stone fireplace surrounded by armchairs made of smooth, mahogany wood and a glass coffee table in the middle of the room made Drake feel as if he were walking into the palace of a king. And the air conditioning...when was the last time he had been in a house that had that? "You have a very beautiful house," he said, unable to help himself.

"Thank you."

Drake stood in front of a chair padded with crimson fabric, but felt as if he would disgrace it if he sat in it with his filthy clothes. He set his bag on the floor and remained standing. "I don't mean to be in your way. All I came here for was to ask where a shelter was."

"Are you hungry?"

Am I ever. Drake nodded his head. He had been so preoccupied on the drive up here and during the whole episode with the car salesman that he had completely forgotten about food. The more he thought about food, however, the more he realized how hungry he felt.

"Good. Follow me."

Drake warily followed the man into the kitchen, where he watched him pull out a long, trim piece of steak from the refrigerator, put it on a plate, and heat it in the microwave. The smell overwhelmed Drake's senses so much that he considered pinching himself to make sure he wasn't dreaming. Then again, if this was a dream, he wasn't sure if he ever wanted to wake up. He didn't know what to make of a crazy, old man suddenly welcoming him into his home and treating him as if he were his own son. He was just glad he had picked this house to come to instead of the one across the street.

Andrew slid the sizzling plate of food over to him and sat. "Tell me about yourself, Drake."

"There's not much to tell," Drake said, careful to keep his food from dropping out of his mouth as he talked.

"So you were just going to find a shelter somewhere and what, live there until..."

"A job would be nice, but unlikely."

Andrew wasn't sure what he meant by that. "I'm not sure I understand."

Drake stopped chewing and faced the man expressionlessly. "What's not to understand? Just look at me and see if you can figure it out."

Andrew studied him and said, "I don't see anything—"

"You're right. You don't see anything. Neither does anybody else, and that's why I can't find a job. Even tattoo joints won't hire me, as filthy as they are."

"It can't be that bad."

Drake just nodded his head. "So what about you? Livin' in a big house like this, you must have kids."

"Oh, I'm not married. Never have been."

Drake snorted and said, "You don't have to be married to have kids these days, pal. This is the twenty-first century, remember?"

Andrew felt his face flush. "Excuse me?"

Drake swallowed his food and shook his head. "Never mind. So what's the big house for then?"

"I inherited it."

"No kiddin'? You know what my inheritance is?"

Andrew didn't know if he should even dare answer.

"A house that's falling apart and a refrigerator stocked with twenty-four cans of beer. That's all my old man leaves me with."

Andrew looked down. Saying, "I'm sorry" probably wouldn't be an appropriate response, so he decided it would be better if he said nothing at all.

Tiny droplets of juice from the steak still clung to Drake's fork, so he put it in his mouth and licked off what little was left, knowing that this would undoubtedly be the last time he ever tasted steak again in his life. Sure, he had six hundred and fifty-two dollars now, but he wasn't going to waste a cent of it on expensive food or hotel rooms. Five dollars a day on food would last him one hundred thirty days, meaning he would run out just before the cold months began. A hotel room would sure be nice then.

Drake set his fork on his empty plate and rose to leave. "Thanks. The steak was great."

"Are you leaving already?"

Drake shrugged. "Don't have no reason to stay."

"The nearest shelter is almost ten miles from here."

Drake looked outside into the blackness. "I guess I got a long walk ahead of me then, huh?" He tried to smile, but a frown exposed his uncertainty.

Andrew thought a moment, praying to God for wisdom. *God, You know I'm not one to let strangers into my home. Ronnie's here, and his safety is number one to me.* Andrew couldn't shake the feeling, though, that God was trying to tell him something. "Drake, wait," he said.

Drake turned, his hand clutching the doorknob. "What is it?"

"Why don't you stay here tonight? Ten miles is a long way, and seems even longer when it's night and you're tired."

Am I hearing this guy right? "You're asking me to stay here tonight? Here? In your house?"

"It's up to you. There's a bedroom upstairs I've never used. The bed sheets haven't been changed for over a year now, but they're clean and the bed's comfortable. At least more comfortable than the shelter's are, I'm sure."

Drake released his hold on the doorknob and stood with his mouth gaping open. "I don't know what to say."

"All you have to say is yes."

"If you're really sure about this..." Drake said slowly, "then I guess the answer's yes."

Chapter
7

ENTERTAINING ANGELS

Ronnie Tavner opened one eye slightly as he heard his uncle whispering to someone across the hall. He lifted his body off the mattress and moved a few feet toward the door, struggling to make out the words. An unfamiliar voice answered his uncle. Now his curiosity was aroused.

Someone was coming. Ronnie scurried back to his covers. The bedroom door opened and his uncle stepped into the room quietly, closing and locking the door behind him. Locking? That was strange. Ronnie wanted to peek through the door before it closed, but when his uncle shot a glance at him, he shut his eyes before he was noticed and pretended to be asleep.

Andrew breathed a sigh of relief and collapsed into bed, too tired to pull the covers over his legs. A satisfied feeling swept over him in knowing that he had made an impact on someone's life today. How long he planned to help Drake, he had no idea, but he was certain God was behind this. Was the kid dangerous? He doubted it. Would he take something of value and leave in the middle of the night? He doubted that too. God had laid it upon his heart to help him, so it had to be right. Whoever Drake was and whatever his background might be wouldn't determine how he would treat him. Everyone needed love, especially those who were hurting. He wasn't sure if Drake had told him the entire truth tonight—Andrew was remarkably good at being able to tell if someone was lying to him—but then again, what if Drake had a good reason for not telling him his whole story? Maybe he was ashamed of where he had come from and what his family life had been like. It sure sounded like that during some parts of the conversation.

Whatever the case might have been, Andrew was determined not to judge. If God had put it on his heart to help this young man, he was confident enough to trust that God knew what He was doing.

Drake tossed his duffel bag at the foot of the bed and surveyed his room for the night. Impressive. He couldn't believe how perfect the temperature was, how clean it smelled, and how the padded carpet felt beneath his feet. He longed for a deep, unbroken sleep, and for a few seconds, allowed himself to forget all the runaway plans and schemes and dividing his money into small portions so he could survive decently for a few months. *You got one night. Make it count.*

Drake sprawled himself on top of the covers and allowed his body to soak into much-needed rest. The mattress was comfortable; and for once, he didn't have to worry about rolling over and being assaulted by a cluster of broken springs during the night. The comforter, the pillows, the sheets—everything was fresh and soft. He wadded his pillow at his side and pressed his face against it, smelling the perfume from its last washing. And to think that this was only a guest room no one ever used. What about the other bedrooms? How much nicer were they?

Drake sat up on the bed and untied his shoes, feeling so tired that he let them drop to the floor.

His silver knife hit the floor. He saw its reflection in the glow of the moon and realized he had lied to Andrew about not having a weapon. He picked it up quickly and stuffed it in the hollowed-out heel of his shoe until it was once again out of sight. *Can't let him find that.* He hadn't lied on purpose. He only carried a knife as a protective measure, but Andrew still couldn't find out he had it. *It's not like it was really that important anyway.*

Along with the knife, hidden underneath the insole at the base of his heel, where he had carved out a narrow hole in the dense rubber, was his wad of money. Six hundred Benjamins. He had left his fifty-two dollars inside his wallet for easy reach in case he went into a gas station to buy food, but he kept his six hundred dollars tucked away where he knew it would be safe from being found or stolen. That too was something else he wouldn't tell Andrew or anyone else about, even though he figured that six hundred dollars would seem petty to a well-to-do man like him. Still, he couldn't trust anyone but himself.

Ronnie waited until he was sure his uncle was asleep before delicately lifting the covers off his body. With his panda under his arm, he tiptoed to the door, bit his lip as he looked over his shoulder at his uncle, and noiselessly cracked the door open wide enough to slip his body through. Now, he just had to figure out where that stranger was staying. He walked toward a room with an open door and peered inside.

Empty.

The next room down had a closed door. Ronnie thought about passing it up, but his curiosity just wouldn't allow it.

He turned the doorknob quietly. Inside, he saw a mound of covers gradually rising and falling, accompanied by the sound of labored breathing. He hesitantly sneaked over and tapped on the sheets.

Drake jumped like he had been shot. He wrestled his covers off his body and whirled around to find a little kid in Scooby Doo pajamas staring at him. He pressed a hand against his chest and exhaled. "What's wrong with you, waking a guy up in the middle of the night like this? Who are you anyway?"

"Ronnie. Who are you?"

Drake looked at him skeptically. "The man living here said he didn't have any kids."

"He's my uncle."

Drake raised an eyebrow and sank back down in his bed. "Look, kid, I am *really* tired and—"

"Are you an angel?"

Drake sat up slowly and squinted. "Am I a *what?*"

"An angel. The preacher said something about taking in homeless people who are angels or something."

Drake sat there, weary eyed and wishing that this little pest would leave him alone. "Do I look like an angel to you?"

Ronnie looked him over. "I don't know. Never saw one before."

"Well, I'm not. I don't know what kind of preachin' you've been listenin' to, but—"

"So what's your name?"

"What's it to you?"

"Huh?"

"Skip it."

"OK...then, where'd you come from?"

Oh, for the love of... "Around," Drake said dully.

Ronnie giggled. "That's a funny place to live."

Drake rolled his eyes. *Oh, I give up.* "Look, kid, whatever you said your name is—"

"Ronnie."

"Whatever. Look. I'm tired—as in very, very, very tired—and I want more than *anything* to go to sleep, so if you don't mind—"

"Why did you come here? Don't you have a family?"

Catch a clue, kid. I do not want to talk to you. "No, I don't have no family," Drake answered without any interest whatsoever, thinking that maybe after the kid was done playing private eye he would leave him alone.

"I live with my uncle because my parents didn't want me anymore."

I don't blame 'em, Drake thought. "Uh-huh. Well, I'd really love to sit here and talk to you all night long—"

"You would?" Ronnie said, perking up.

"—but I'm tired and I am *going* to get some *rest*. So leave me alone."

Ronnie looked down at his panda and handed him over to Drake. "You can sleep with Arrow tonight."

Drake shoved the stuffed animal away. "I don't need that stupid fuzz-ball in my face; I need sleep! Just leave me alone, OK?"

Ronnie scooped up his panda and dashed out of the room. Drake thought he heard sniffling before his door closed shut. *Yeah, good riddance.*

The front door creaked as Drake opened it and stepped inside cautiously. So dark. He tried a light switch, but there was nothing. Wait...someone was breathing. He heard it.

Drake reached inside his shoe for his knife. Never could be too sure. He crawled toward the back of the couch and heard the breathing more distinctly now.

But he knew he had killed him. He had seen the blood. Drake scooted to the edge of the couch and tried to see the fireplace through the hazy darkness.

He was gone. So was the blood.

A shadow swept across the wall. Drake clutched the knife more firmly in his hand as sweat and adrenaline chilled his body.

"Looking for someone, Drake?" Ben yelled, emerging from the shadows like a ghostly fog.

"You can't do anything to me!" Drake screamed, raising the knife. "You're dead!"

Ben pulled out a gun and aimed it at Drake's chest. "Yeah, and now it's your turn."

Drake gasped for air and threw his body in an upright position, beads of sweat clinging to his face. *He's dead. He can't do anything to me. It was just a dream. Nothing more. He's dead. He'll always be dead.*

A knock came at the door. "Drake? You awake yet?"

Drake put a trembling hand over his chest. No bullet. Just a violently beating heart. "Yeah, I'm awake."

"You like pancakes?"

"Uh...sure."

"That's all I needed to know."

Drake heard Andrew walking away and fell back on his pillow. *He won't find you. He can't. He's dead.* He closed his eyes and tried to forget his dream. *He's dead.*

Drake slipped his socks on and walked downstairs. He was still trembling, but found it was easier to ignore the feeling than to worry about it. Dreams were just dreams. What was happening in his life now was more significant than replaying his past a thousand times over and coming up with the same ending.

Ronnie was at the breakfast table chugging down a glass of chocolate milk when Drake walked in.

"Can I sit here?" Drake said, sliding a chair away from the table.

Ronnie shrugged without making eye contact.

"Pancakes are almost ready!" Andrew hollered from the kitchen.

Drake stared at Ronnie out of the corner of his eye, feeling ashamed though he knew he shouldn't. He felt out of place sitting here, like he should be moving along now instead of bumming another meal. When he realized the kid was purposefully avoiding him, he turned to face him. "All right, I'll bite. What's the problem?"

Ronnie looked at him for only a second before his eyes hit the table.

"You don't like me being here, is that it?"

"You threw Arrow down," Ronnie said, studying the clump of chocolate syrup stuck to the bottom of his glass.

Drake noticed the panda bear in Ronnie's lap and made the connection. *Didn't know the bear was so touchy.* But a rude remark wasn't worth it. Not in front of Andrew, as kind as he had been to him. It was a long shot, but maybe he could work on the old man's compassion some more and get another night's sleep in this palace. So the kid was sensitive. He could work around that. "I'm sorry, OK? Is that what you wanna hear?"

Ronnie sat with his arms folded. "You called Arrow a stupid fuzz-ball."

Drake scratched his head. "I said that?"

"You don't remember?"

Drake looked both ways and leaned forward. "Hey, want me to show you something?"

Ronnie scooted close. "Sure. What is it?"

"I saw there was a piano in the living room. Does it work? In tune, I mean?"

"Beats me. Why? Do you play?"

"About anything you wanna hear. I can show you after breakfast."

"Sweet. Think you can teach me?"

"Um...yeah." *More like in your dreams.*

Andrew emerged from the kitchen with a platter of stacked pancakes. "All right, you guys, a little black on the edges, but that's a proud trademark of us bad cooks, so eat up." The faint smell of hazelnut filled Drake's nostrils as Andrew slid him a hot cup of coffee. Did the goodness never end?

Drake's mouth watered as he forked four pancakes onto his plate, poured the syrup on thick, and shoved a large bite in his mouth. The flavor was phenomenal.

Andrew directed his attention to Ronnie and said politely, "Ronnie, would you like to pray over the food?"

Drake stopped chewing and looked at them both. Apparently, he had broken some kind of religious rule. He swallowed his bite and half-closed his eyes as Ronnie said a short prayer. *This whole town must be filled with religious nuts. Oh, well. If they wanna give me money for no reason and a place for me to stay, I can play along.*

Andrew lifted his head after the prayer was finished and said, "I don't want any leftovers, so let's eat!"

And boy, did Drake eat. For years, he had made a habit of skipping breakfast in the morning because of money issues. Then when he did get to eat, it was some stale, off-brand cereal that had cost practically nothing, and usually water had to be substituted for milk, because after all, "Water's better for ya and cheaper than milk, so why can't we just live with what comes out of the faucet and be happy?" his dad would say. Drake shook his head at the thought of it now. Beer had always been the exception for his dad.

Drake kept quietly to himself as Andrew and Ronnie talked. *If only he'll let me stay another night. Just one more rainy night and he'll give me a room again. I can't imagine anything better than this.*

Ronnie was piling food into his mouth almost as fast as Drake was. He forced a large bite down his throat and blurted, "Now can you show me?"

Andrew glanced at Drake. "Show him what?"

Drake sensed his face reddening. "Oh, uh...I couldn't help but notice your piano in the living room. If you don't mind, I'd kinda like to play it."

"You play?"

"I mean, every now and then. I don't own my own piano, but the hospital close to where I lived had a piano in the waiting room, and they let me play whenever I wanted."

"How did you learn?"

Drake wondered exactly what he meant by that. How did trash like him ever learn to play such a beautiful instrument? Or maybe he meant to ask how he could afford a teacher, especially if he were so poor. Drake didn't think the man intended to be impolite, but he was used to caustic comments and had to be on guard. "I taught myself. It really wasn't that hard. I heard a song one day, tried to play it, and bingo. Starting out was kinda bumpy, but over time I worked out the rough spots until I could play the whole song smoothly."

"That's amazing," Andrew remarked.

"It's really not that good."

"Why don't you play for us?"

"Yeah, uh...what's your name again?" Ronnie said.

"Drake," he said, suddenly feeling something strange happening on the inside of him. He actually felt important, like maybe something he did really had value and worth. These people had welcomed him into their home, given him food and a place to stay, and now actually seemed interested in what he did. Even if the kid did get on his nerves, and Andrew was one of those religious people, at least they hadn't treated him with contempt as so many others had.

"So are you gonna play for us or not?" Ronnie said, tugging Drake's arm.

Drake fought a smile. "Lead the way."

Drake was all over the piano, flowing gracefully in both the high and low keys as he stretched his fingers to hit every note perfectly. This was a breeze, but his audience of two acted as if he were doing something truly spectacular. Who knew? Maybe he was. But he didn't think so.

He ended the song beautifully and turned around to face Andrew and Ronnie. "I haven't played in a while, so it's kinda rusty."

"Drake, that was marvelous!" Andrew exclaimed.

Ronnie clapped loudly.

"Ah, it's really nothin'," Drake said, blushing at all the applause. "Just something I picked up a long time ago."

"Don't underestimate yourself, Drake," Andrew said. "You really have something there. Feel free to play the piano anytime. All it's been good for so far is collecting dust."

Drake laughed, but inside he was thinking of the possibilities. *Stay here and play...* Playing the piano was something he loved to do probably more than anything else, not to mention it was the *only* thing he had ever been good at. He loved listening to music, but being able to create and play his own music was even better. However, any chance of improvement had always been limited for him because the hospital was miles away. *Not anymore. Now, it's all right here. Everything's literally at my fingertips.*

Ronnie whispered something in Andrew's ear, and they both stood. "Excuse me, Drake," Andrew said, stepping into the next room with Ronnie.

A frown erased Drake's smile. *Already having doubts,* he thought. *Shoulda seen it coming before I got my hopes up.*

"What is it, Ronnie?" Andrew said from the other room.

"Is he going to stay?"

Andrew glanced at Drake, who immediately broke away from his gaze. "Why? Do you want him to?"

Ronnie nodded. "He's cool. I mean, he was a little grumpy last night, but—"

"Whoa, whoa, whoa," Andrew said, lifting his hand. "Last night? You *saw* him last night?"

Ronnie looked guilty. "Yeah," he said slowly. "I waited until you were asleep before I went in his room. Sorry if I did anything wrong."

Andrew knelt down and grabbed Ronnie by the shoulders. "Did he do something to you? Tell me, Ronnie."

"No, he didn't do nothin'. I just asked him a few questions, that's all. Honest."

"He didn't lay a hand on you?"

"No. I already said that."

A wave of relief swept over Andrew, and he let out a sigh. *He didn't hurt Ronnie. Thank You for watching over him, God.*

"But he *was* sorta grumpy," Ronnie continued. "I think it was because he was real tired. I was mad at first."

"How do you feel now?"

Ronnie smiled. "Now, I'm just happy he's here. I've never been around someone his age before...I think if I had an older brother like other kids, he would look like Drake."

Andrew found that amusing. "Oh, he would, would he?"

"He definitely would. So can he stay? Please?"

Andrew heard music begin to play and looked once more at Drake. "That's up to him, Ronnie. He may have somewhere he needs to go. He's looking for a job, you know."

"He doesn't have any family," Ronnie protested. "He told me that last night."

"I know, but still..."

Ronnie paused before saying, "I thought that's why you brought me here. Because my family didn't want me."

Andrew groped for words, but he was speechless. Ronnie was right. He could try to talk himself out of it, but every time he looked at Drake, he knew that if he let him go, he may wind up on the streets somewhere searching his whole life for a place to call home.

"Why can't *you* give him a job, Uncle Andy?" Ronnie said. "Something to make him stay."

Andrew thought about Ronnie's proposition. *Not a bad idea. The grass does need to be mowed every week, and the leaves all over the yard will be a hassle to rake up in the fall. Hmm...* "Drake!" he called.

Drake looked over his shoulder and saw Andrew waving him over. He scooted the piano bench back and ambled over to where Andrew and Ronnie stood. *Here it comes. Just buck up and prepare for it now so at least you won't look floored after he hits ya with the news.* "Yes, sir?"

"Do you know how to do yard work, like using a push mower and a weed eater?"

Drake shoved his hands in his pockets. "Guess so. Why?"

"Would that be a job you think you'd be interested in?"

Drake shrugged. "I dunno. When I learn how to operate 'em, sure. I'm just looking for a job. Nothing specific."

"That's great," Andrew said, clasping his hands together. "Now that it's almost summer and the grass is really starting to shoot up, I was looking to hire someone. If you want the job—"

"I'd love to have the job!" Drake said quickly. "You can show me now if you want."

"Drake, sit down," Andrew said, leading him to a chair.

"What's wrong?"

"Nothing, I'm just curious how serious you are."

"About the job? I told you, I'd love to—"

"Not just the job. I mean...your life. What are you planning to do with your life, Drake?"

Drake was taken off guard by the abrupt change in subject. He began to wonder if this conversation was really about the yard or about himself. "I don't know," he admitted. "Haven't really thought that far ahead to be honest with you."

"What were you planning to do once you got here? Earn enough money to find a home, go to college, or..."

"In time, I hope to buy my own place. That is, if I even get that far. I don't have a detailed plan laid out for my life, if that's what you're asking. I just figured I'd tackle the problems as they come."

"And you have no family at all? No second cousin somewhere, no long-lost aunt I could contact...no one?"

"Nope."

"How much money do you expect to make for a job of taking care of my lawn every week?"

Drake tilted his head sideways as he thought. "Twenty dollars, maybe. And even *that's* a maybe. You don't have a very big yard."

Andrew sat back and pursed his lips. "Tell you what. I think my yard's worth thirty dollars a week, so...you can either have your choice of thirty dollars a week, or you can have room and board here. It's completely up to you."

Drake leaned forward. "Are you serious?"

"Very."

"But...why? Why are you going out of your way to do a favor for me? You don't even know me, for Pete's sake."

Andrew searched for the right words. "It's because...well, it's not easy to put into words, but—"

"We want you to stay!" Ronnie blurted.

Drake looked at him warily. "I still don't get it. What would be your advantage?"

"I told you, I need my yard mowed."

"But—"

"If you would rather have the thirty dollars, then—"

"No, I just..." *This is crazy. No, it's more than crazy. It's insane. Something's just not right with this picture.* Drake had never been more confused in all his life.

"Please stay, Drake," Ronnie said, frowning to think he was considering otherwise. "I like to hear you play the piano."

Drake tried to think of a comeback—any possible excuse he could give, no matter how lame it sounded. But he had to ask himself, why was he trying to run away from such kindness? Was it because he was afraid it was a trap? Maybe the cops had a bounty on him and he was falling for a trick. Or was it because he simply felt as if he didn't deserve any of it? A nice house and good food was foreign to him. Was he afraid of the change? Of the love?

"I can help you with your room just like Uncle Andy helped me with mine," Ronnie offered, his voice now low and serious.

Feeling outnumbered and unable to present any further arguments, Drake gave in. "I still don't understand why you're doing this, and a simple 'thank you' seems so small. A home, a bed, great food to eat every day...wow. It's like an answer to prayer."

Andrew perked up at his choice of words. "Was that just an expression, or did you really mean it?"

"Of course, I'm thankful."

"No, I mean when you said that this was an answer to prayer. Do you believe in prayer? In God?"

Here we go. Drake didn't mean to disappoint the man, but his answer was and always would be a flat-out, irreversible no. "Actually, no," he said, studying the floor. It seemed like he was always looking at the floor or out of windows when a topic came up he didn't want to discuss. "My mom did, but...well, it just didn't work out for her." Drake watched as Andrew tried to cover his disappointment. "Nothing against you. It's just...not for me."

"But do you *believe* in God?" Andrew prodded.

Drake bit his lip. "I'd rather not talk about this, if that's OK."

Andrew tried to smile. "Of course, it's all right. Maybe some other time."

How about never? Drake wanted to say.

Chapter

8

AWKWARD ADJUSTMENTS

Drake had two pairs of blue jeans slung over one arm and five T-shirts over the other. He glanced back at Andrew and saw him waiting for Ronnie in front of the fitting rooms. Should he really get all this stuff?

It wasn't his money he was worried about. It was Andrew's. It had been his idea to take him and Ronnie to the mall to buy them both new clothes, shoes, and anything else he could think of that they might need. Drake wished he had thought to pack extra clothing in his duffel bag before leaving home, because now he felt like a deprived child as he constantly checked price tags and wondered if they were too high. Spending over twenty dollars on a pair of jeans was too much, he thought. Did he really have to buy them new?

He set one of the T-shirts down and decided not to mention it to Andrew, knowing he really didn't need five T-shirts when he could get by just as fine with four. It surprised him really, since it wasn't his character to act like this, but something in his gut made him want to behave differently toward Andrew. Here was a man—crazy and maybe a little too kind—who just wanted to give him something for no reason and expected nothing in return. It never bothered him before to take advantage of other people, but he couldn't bring himself to treat Andrew that way.

Drake's conscience was getting the better of him. He laid another T-shirt down. Three left. He didn't need all this, and yet all the while, Andrew kept pulling out his wallet and slapping down a wad of dollar bills at every checkout. Of course, he was probably wealthy enough to afford such purchases, but why should Andrew spend good money on him? Hadn't he given him enough already?

On the drive back to Andrew's house, Drake stared at the bags of new belongings that sat between his feet as they bounced and stirred with the movement of the car. *Enjoy it while it lasts. Remember what you're running from.* He moved his gaze to his hands. *You're fooling yourself. You think you're free now, but you're not. Not really. You're just as handcuffed as if there were metal chains on those wrists.*

But he had a job now and a place to live. The risk of being found out wasn't high anymore. He wasn't on the streets where he could be caught like all the other narrow-minded criminals. He had a plan, and he was going to keep it.

When Andrew looked his direction, he took the opportunity to ask again if he could be taught how to run the yard equipment before supper so he could get the mowing finished before nightfall. That way, at least if he got some work behind him, he wouldn't feel as bad about taking so much from Andrew without giving a little back first.

"Let the yard wait until tomorrow," Andrew said, slipping his driving hand lazily to the bottom of the steering wheel. "Don't sweat it."

"I just wanted to pay you back for some of this."

"Consider it paid tomorrow. I'm not worried about it. Really."

Drake fell silent. Andrew simply stared out the windshield, keeping his eyes trained on the road, but not paying much attention to it.

Why am I doing this? he kept asking himself. Was he taking it too far? A normal reaction—even for a generous person—might have been to give Drake a few bucks, a pat on the back, and a polite goodbye before shutting the door in his face, hoping in the back of his mind that he would forget the address and never come back. But Andrew's approach to the situation had been anything *but* normal. He had seen plenty of homeless teens walking the streets. What made this time different?

This time, God was in it. Andrew was certain of that. There had been no audible voice from above, no angels encircling him as a sign from Heaven; he just had that knowing feeling deep inside his heart that told him he needed to help this person. It had to be God.

One thing Andrew didn't have to be concerned about anymore was whether Drake was an alcoholic or druggie. If so, Drake would have gone straight for the money instead of staying at his home with no pay. Andrew had set the test, and Drake had passed it without even realizing it. That put Andrew's mind at ease and gave him one more reason to want to help.

Drake found it challenging to fall asleep that night. The air was too cold, then too hot. The ceiling fan was too loud, while at other times it seemed oddly silent. Shadows cast into the room from the outside began to sway as the breeze turned into a gushing wind that rattled the siding and made the house creak. *Leave me alone!* he wanted to scream. He pulled the covers closer to his body and shivered. So now the air was cold again. Whatever.

He rolled over on his back and tucked his hand underneath his smooth pillow, letting the gentle breeze from the ceiling fan drive back the black strands of hair from his sweat-soaked face. He was consumed with thoughts of his dad. *They must've found him by now. If nothing else, the neighbors probably phoned the cops about the horrible smell, if two days is enough to...I never meant for this to happen. It should have never gone this far. Too much time has gone by now. I'll bet the cops have my picture already and are combing the streets looking for me. I wonder how far news like that travels. Does Andrew know? Will he know?*

Drake couldn't shake the gnawing feeling that all this strange kindness being offered toward him lately was all somehow part of a setup. A sting operation, perhaps, set up by the police knowing that he would be just the type to fall for it. But could he afford to leave now and toss an opportunity like this out the window just because he got scared and decided to run? He wasn't stupid. He knew his chances of finding a job with benefits as good as Andrew had offered him were one in a million, especially in a big city like this where most jobs demanded more than a high school education to make a living. If he left now, it was over. Done. No turning back.

But then again, if he stayed, it could still be over. *Let's look at my options. Leave and live the rest of my life on the streets and probably sell drugs just to get by when the money runs out, or stay here, get caught, and likely get thrown behind bars for the rest of my life.* Just thinking about either one gave him a throbbing headache.

Ah, Drake, why'd you have to go get yourself into such a mess? You had a life—maybe not the greatest in the world and filled with more bad than good—but at least you had something. Now, you may just lose everything. He closed his eyes. Tired. So tired. If only he could sleep, he would fall into a deep, long sleep. He wasn't even sure if he would ever want to wake up. As long as he had peace.

The bright glow from the rising sun roused Drake from a sound sleep. He lay there for a while, just breathing, thinking. It was still early if the digital clock beside him was right, so he was in no rush.

Why did he have to dream so much? When he was younger, all he dreamt about was scuba diving in the Pacific ocean, climbing trees, playing baseball, or riding ostriches—mainly because he had watched so many re-runs of the *Swiss Family Robinson*. But now...now all he dreamed about was getting into fights—his dreams were filled with knives and guns that were more often used on him than the other way around.

Dreams were stupid, only meant to scare. And the scenes didn't come from movies anymore, even from the horror movies he had dared to watch occasionally. No, these dreams were the result of a scared, tortured heart that refused to heal.

Drake shuddered as the memory from last night's dream came back to him in blurry fragments. This time, he saw the blood. He saw his dad lying motionless on the floor, cold and lifeless, just as he had left him. There was no gun aimed at his chest and the shadows were empty. His eyes were completely focused on the wound on the back of his dad's head that continued to pour blood—blood now more black than red.

He was a murderer. And the dream was all too real.

What're you doin', Drake? Think this is something you just run away from and eventually forget? This is going to stay with you for the rest of your life. People are looking for you, and when they find you, it's bye-bye world and hello iron cage. This house may seem great and all now, but you better have a backup plan somewhere in the back of your head if you find they're on your trail.

Drake eventually mustered up enough strength to rise from bed and turn the blinds upward to deter most of the sunlight. The carpet on his bare feet felt warm and soft where it had stayed in the sunlight for so long, so he sat on the edge of his bed with his feet touching the floor. *So what's it gonna be, Drake? Leave or stay?* He studied the room. Not particularly large or elegant, but remarkably clean and neat for a room that had rarely been used. White curtains, a muted-green bedspread, a dresser with a round pearl mirror above it, and a few devotional books along with a Bible stacked atop the nightstand made the room simple yet impressive all at the same time. Drake couldn't recall if the books had been there the night before or if Andrew had recently placed them there in hopes that he might pick one up. *Yeah, fat chance.*

Drake stared down at his feet and exhaled. There he was doing that same routine again—looking down while all his emotions eroded away more of his soul. He looked up at the ceiling just for the change in scenery. *It's your choice, man. Your gamble. Your life.*

He wished it weren't so difficult to decide. He had all he could ever hope for here, yet he was trying to find something that would make him give it up. Why was he doing this to himself? Couldn't he just be content and put his mind at ease?

He decided he was too tired to answer that age-old question. After considering the pros and cons of both options, he concluded it best to stay here and lay low until he actually had some tangible evidence to make him leave. *I'll stay here for now, but if I start suspecting anything—even so much as a second glance from anyone—I'm outta here.*

After lunch, Andrew led Drake outside to the shed and showed him the equipment he would be using to do the yard work. "It's really not that hard once you get used to the way it runs. I will tell you, though, the back left wheel doesn't roll as smoothly as the other one, so you may find at times you have to pull harder toward the right to keep it straight. Got it?"

"Yeah," Drake said, trying it out for himself while the engine was off.

Andrew showed Drake the steps to start it, stop it, and shut it down. "Now you try," he said, stepping out of the way.

Drake double-checked the throttle level and handle bar switch before slipping his finger through the metal loop. He yanked the cord back three times until he heard the engine rev up and felt the machine vibrating under his grasp.

"Good!" Andrew shouted over the noise. He waved his hand and motioned for Drake to turn it off. "And that's basically all there is to it. I'll fill up the gas for you before you mow every time, so you don't have to worry about that."

"And I start the weed eater up the same way, right?" Drake said, already beginning to sweat as the blistering sun bore down on him. He wished he hadn't chosen to wear a black shirt.

"I'll go over the weed eater separately with you, but basically, yeah, the same steps," Andrew said. "But don't worry about using that until you've had at least an hour of rest after mowing."

"Why's that?"

"You'll see soon enough," Andrew said, shading his eyes as he peered up at the sky. "This may look like a small yard, but it's no picnic to mow. Watch out for tree roots above the ground, flowers, bushes, and especially rocks, though I haven't seen that many in the yard lately."

"Lately? Wouldn't they be out of the yard by now? I mean, if you've been mowing—"

"You'd think that, wouldn't you? But my neighbor—" Andrew raised his arm and pointed to the right, "has a child who loves to play cars in the dirt near the fence and, for some strange reason, throws any rocks he finds over his shoulder—"

"Which wind up in your yard," Drake said, finishing his sentence for him. "Just go over and tell the little brat to stop, then."

Andrew would hardly call the child a brat. "I've mentioned it to his father, but I see no real harm in it. It's good to see kids having fun."

Drake just nodded, not really understanding Andrew's reasoning but hardly caring anyway. "At any rate, I'll be careful and watch out for the rocks."

Andrew patted Drake's shoulder before walking away. "Don't wear yourself out!" he called over his shoulder.

Drake rubbed the palms of his hands together. *Here goes nothing.*

Drake had the front yard mowed in less than twenty minutes, but already his shirt was soaked with sweat and the palms of his hands rubbed raw. The smoke from the engine kept blowing in his face every time the wind changed direction and made the yard and everything else around him seem blurry. Back at his old house, his yard was nothing but hard dirt and rock with the exception of a patch of thorns and weeds at the end of the driveway, and neither he nor his dad had even touched a mower in all the time they had lived there. *Well, I'm touching one now, and it feels like it's glued to my fingers from sweat.*

Drake pushed the mower around to the back of the house, his mouth parched and forehead sticky. At least back here he would have some shade under the trees. As he guided the mower to the right, he noticed Ronnie sitting on the bottom step on the back porch, almost as if he had been waiting for him. *Lucky me.*

Drake ignored him, or at least tried to, and went on mowing as if he never even noticed Ronnie's presence. He couldn't put a finger on why the kid bothered him so much. Andrew was easy to get along with for the most part, but Ronnie was someone he did *not* like and couldn't explain why. He had never liked kids to begin with, but sharing a house with one who was always in his face asking questions only heightened the issue.

He pulled the mower left, wishing he didn't have an audience. Maybe it was Ronnie's age that hassled him. Maybe it was his undying curiosity of anything and everything around him. *Maybe it's because he's staring me down like a hawk watches its prey before it goes in for the kill.* He quickly pushed the mower past Ronnie without making eye contact. He didn't even blink, for that matter. Still, he sensed that Ronnie was following him with his eyes. *What could possibly be so interesting about a sweaty guy pushing around a half-broken lawn mower?* he wondered.

In his peripheral vision, he saw Ronnie stand up and move to the other side of the yard where he reached down and picked up something. *Good grief, what's he doing now?*

Ronnie reached down again and took hold of something in the grass.

Drake killed the mower and marched over to where Ronnie was standing. "What're you doing?" he said irritably. "Inspecting my mowing or hunting for last year's Easter eggs?"

Ronnie looked up and opened his hand, revealing two small rocks. "Just trying to help. Sorry."

Drake gulped. He had completely forgotten about what Andrew had told him concerning the rocks. Looking around him now, there were probably ten or twelve more still buried in the grass. If he had mowed over them without remembering, he might have damaged the mower's blades and possibly even sent a couple of rocks soaring toward the house. Feeling like a complete idiot in front of a 7-year-old, Drake said meekly, "Oh, uh...thanks."

Worst part was, Ronnie didn't even try to rub it in or make a smart remark back. He simply bent over and began picking up more.

Drake waved awkwardly at Ronnie as he took a few steps backward and started the mower again. Just a little longer, and he would be done. He just hoped the kid wouldn't come back out to watch when he used the weed eater later. What a thrill that would be.

Drake ran the mower over the last strip of grass and paused to survey the work he had done. Not bad, minus the few chewed geraniums he hadn't seen until it was too late. But that was on the backside of the birdbath and would doubtlessly even be missed. Besides, he had managed to cover most of the ravaged petals by bending some of the untouched flowers toward the front. Couldn't even tell the difference... sort of.

He shut down the mower and walked it inside the shed, noticing for the first time how tired and wobbly his leg and arm muscles felt. Overall, it was a good feeling, though. Hard work felt like medicine to his blood, just what he needed. He locked the shed door behind him and turned to see Ronnie holding a glass of iced water. He pointed at the glass and said, "That for me?"

"Yep," Ronnie said, handing him the water.

Drake, with Ronnie trailing behind him, walked to the back porch and slowly lowered his sore body down on the steps. Wood had never felt more comfortable in all his life. Andrew had been right—this may have been a small yard, but when he was the one pushing the mower over every inch of it, it suddenly became noticeably bigger. He could feel the nerves in his legs bouncing as he nursed the cool glass in his hands.

Ronnie sat down beside him and rested his chin in his hands. "Tired?" he said, letting a yawn escape from his mouth.

Drake gulped down the icy water, ignoring the sting it brought to his parched throat. He exhaled forcefully through his nose and wiped his mouth with his sleeve. "More'n you know."

"Still like it here?"

"Absolutely."

Ronnie bit the inside of his cheek. "You don't talk much, do you?"

"Ah, you just don't know me that well yet." Drake glanced over at him and could tell that he didn't buy it. "What do you do in this yard anyway?"

"Not really anything yet. I just moved into Uncle Andy's house a few days ago."

Drake looked at him curiously as he fanned his shirt. "Is that so?" He tossed the rest of his water in the grass and stretched his legs out in front of him. "I figured you'd lived here awhile."

"Nah."

Drake suddenly remembered that first night he had spent here when Ronnie had said something about his parents not wanting him. He hadn't paid much attention to it then, but now he found himself filled with concern. It was then he realized what a jerk he had been. "You OK? I mean, you wanna talk about anything?"

Ronnie pursed his lips and bent over to tie his shoe. "Not really. I'm fine."

Drake stared out into the yard again, wondering why he even cared about the kid's past. So the kid had problems. Who in this world didn't? A broken heart and shattered life was no new concept to Drake. He had been there and done that, but you didn't see him crying or whining to anyone about it. He had to remind himself, though, that Ronnie was only 7 years old. He had a reason to be upset.

Trying not to let the conversation get too silent or depressing, Drake changed the subject. "So, back to the yard. What do you plan to do out here? Build a tree house? Plant a garden? What?"

"I'd like to have a dog," Ronnie blurted.

"A dog? I thought you just liked panda bears."

Ronnie frowned and looked away.

OK, *cut the sarcasm.* Drake nudged Ronnie's shoulder. "C'mon, man. I was just kiddin' ya. No, really, a dog? What kind of dog?"

Ronnie looked back at him undecidedly, fearing that Drake would only make fun of him more. "A beagle," he answered faintly.

Drake whistled loudly. "A beagle? From what I've heard, beagles are a lot of money, pal."

Ronnie stared down at the grass. "Yeah, I know. I asked Mommy for one before, but she said no."

"Well, hey, your uncle's got a lot of money, right? I mean, just one look at his house says that much. He could buy you a beagle."

Ronnie tried to smile. "I dunno."

"What do you mean you don't know? Have you asked him?"

Ronnie shook his head. "He's already done so much for me already. It doesn't feel right asking him for anything else."

"Yeah, I see your point."

"I have about twelve dollars so far in my piggy bank, though," Ronnie said, his intonation rising. "I probably have close to enough, huh, Drake?"

Yeah, like a few hundred dollars short. "Maybe you could ask for one for your birthday," Drake suggested.

"It's still eight months away," Ronnie said miserably, resting his chin on his knees.

"You could sell lemonade."

Ronnie made a face and shook his head.

"OK, maybe as a Christmas present, then."

Ronnie took Drake's glass from his hand and stood up to leave. "Yeah. Maybe."

All the yard work was behind him. Flecks of grass clung to his legs and shoes, and his skin felt like it had just been baked in a hot oven. Drake wanted to collapse as he walked through the front door, but as soon as he caught sight of the beautiful grand piano in the adjoining living room, he headed straight to it in spite of his fatigue and sat down on the smooth, glossy bench. He couldn't let this day pass without his fingers feeling these keys again.

Only at this specific time in the afternoon did the sunlight permeate the delicate curtains and strike the piano at a certain angle, making the polished wood glisten like refined gold and giving the keys a light orange tint. He lightly ran his fingers over the ivory keys as a song slowly trickled into his head. He found the right key, positioned his hands, and began playing softly. The delicate music was a much-welcomed change from the harsh, grating sound of the lawn mower, and for a few moments, he forced his mind away from the subject of his fears.

After the song ended, Drake continued to play his own made-up melody. He could never remember the same tune the next day and had never even thought of writing it down to play later, but the wealth of ideas stored within the deep recesses of his brain never seemed to run dry. Besides, he couldn't read music off a sheet because he had never been taught that way. He merely heard the song from inside his heart and let it come out through his fingers. It wasn't difficult for him to play, though some people seemed fascinated by his skill. It was just something he did—almost without thinking sometimes. Andrew called it a God-given ability. Drake called it a song. Nothing more.

"Whatcha playin'?" Ronnie said, ambling up to him from behind.

Nosey again, I see. "Oh...a song I made up just now."

"Does it have a name?"

"Nope."

"Oh...sounds sad."

Drake continued playing, gradually moving into the lower keys for a greater effect. "Story of my life, kid."

"Is that its name?"

"Sure. I don't care."

Ronnie watched him intently. "What's the story about?"

Knowing that he would get nothing done this way, Drake gave up and faced Ronnie. "It's a story about a guy who lives a lousy life. It stinks. He hates it. *Comprende?*"

"Huh?"

"Forget it."

Ronnie sat on the edge of the bench with his back to Drake. "Why don't you like me?"

"What are you talking about?" Drake said, though he could have answered that question in one sentence. "I just got through talking to you out there."

"You didn't act like you wanted to talk."

"Well, I did, didn't I?"

"I don't mean to make you so mad. I just...sometimes I talk too much, don't I?"

"You didn't want to say two words outside, and now when I'm trying to play, you wanna carry on a conversation. I just wanted a few seconds alone to think, that's all."

"Yeah," Ronnie agreed, tilting his head down. "That's what Mommy and Daddy always said. That I talked too much, I mean. I think that's why they got mad at me a lot. I'm sorry."

Drake fell silent, wanting to kick himself for being so stupid and inconsiderate. It hurt him to see the kid hurt. "Don't say that. You didn't do anything wrong."

Ronnie stood to leave.

"Ronnie, just...stay. You don't make me mad."

"I don't?"

"Course not. I'm just not used to the company, I guess. No one ever really talked to me before now."

"Really? I would have thought you had a lot of friends."

"Why's that?" Drake said, now somewhat amused.

"Because you're cool."

That got a laugh out of Drake. "Cool? Hardly."

"I think so. You can play almost anything on the piano, and you can mow the yard out there faster than anyone I know."

Drake grinned and shook his head. "I'm probably the only one you've watched mow a yard, so how could you compare me to anyone else?"

"Well, still. I'm glad you're here. And I'm glad you don't think I talk too much."

Chapter
9

PHONE CALL

Drake Pearson went to bed early that night after complaining of a headache. After a lingering evening of grilling hamburgers and watching Alfred Hitchcock's *The Wrong Man* starring Henry Fonda—which Andrew had to pause several times to answer Ronnie's unending questions about the plot—Ronnie brought up the bright idea of playing a board game. Ronnie sped Drake through the rules, which basically consisted of taking all the marbles around the board and back home again by rolling a pair of dice. Pretty lame concept to Drake, but Ronnie seemed to love it. And on top of that, it took over an hour before the game finally ended—Ronnie being the winner, of course.

Drake couldn't remember the last time he had played a board game. The more he thought about it, he wasn't sure if he had ever even played one at all. Most of his memories as a kid had to do with the outdoors; but as he had grown into his teenage years, he had spent nearly all his time watching television and playing video games at a friend's house or browsing the Internet at the library. Some days, he actually found himself missing the small things again, like listening to the rope creak around the branch overhead as he rocked slowly in the tire swing, or shouting "Pow! Pow!" at the invisible bad guys he relentlessly harassed in his backyard. Spending time around Ronnie seemed to dredge up all those forgotten memories. He had been so consumed with the bad side of his life lately that he had neglected to remember the good, innocent child he used to be. Kind of like Ronnie.

Drake's legs felt like lead as he staggered up the stairs. He dreaded the nightmares that would invade more of his precious sleep tonight. He was tired of hearing the muffled noises in his head, seeing the surreal images every time he closed his eyes, double-checking the shadows because he thought he saw a face, fighting the darkness that seemed to threaten his very sanity. One false move, and his entire life had catapulted itself into an abyss that could never be escaped. His dad had taken his mom's life, he had taken his dad's life, and now he was slowly snuffing out his own. Maybe it would be better if he were dead. That was a new concept. He wanted to live, to fight his way out of this mess he had created and start a new life, but he wasn't kicking out suicide entirely yet. He wondered if life was really worth living if this was what every second of his would entail.

Drake pushed the bedroom door closed behind him, listened to make sure Andrew and Ronnie were still chatting downstairs, and pulled out his shoes from underneath his bed.

The money and pocketknife were still there. Good. Andrew and Ronnie may have seemed like nice people, but he could never be too sure.

Drake didn't really have a headache; he had just told Andrew that so he could have some quiet time alone. He had almost convinced himself that the beads of water rolling down his cheeks while he had been mowing earlier were only sweat droplets from his forehead. But they weren't, even though he wasn't quite ready to admit that to himself yet. They were tears. All the time he had spent mowing, he had been thinking of his mom. He hadn't really allowed himself to cry since that day he found out the truth at the library. He had cried in his car, but his heart had been so blackened by hate that it had suffocated the love he felt for her. Then he was driving again, had rushed home to his father, and yelled and screamed and threatened. The next thing he knew, his father was dead after a single, seemingly insignificant blow to the back of his head.

That night didn't even seem real to Drake anymore. It had all happened too fast for him to grasp what he had done. He had just swung his fist at his father; he hadn't calculated in that short amount of time that his father would fall backward and crack his skull on the stone of the fireplace.

But how could he tell the police that? *Hey, I know what it looks like, but I really didn't mean to kill him.* Yeah, right. They'd laugh in his face and throw him in jail so fast he wouldn't know what had hit him. So whether he wanted to be a fugitive or not, that was his new title. The guys in the action/adventure movies always got away with stuff like that and somehow ended up as heroes, but Drake was living real life, not performing on a movie set. If the police were able to piece the clues together and pinpoint his location in Springfield, then it was just a matter of how long he could hold out until they found him.

But he could never tell Andrew that. If push came to shove, he would have to find someone else—someone who understood what he was going through and would hide him.

Andrew didn't realize how tired he was until his body hit the mattress. Ahh. Such a long day for someone who was supposed to be retired. He still couldn't believe Ronnie had chosen to sleep in his own bed tonight. Maybe the newfound independence would be good for him.

Andrew closed his eyes as a verse from Psalm 68 came to his mind. Somewhere in between dreamland and reality, he recited the verse in his mind. *A father of the fatherless, a defender of widows, is God in His holy habitation. God sets the solitary in families...*

That's what he and God were doing now. A heavenly Father and an earthly father to two people in the world who needed a family the most. Andrew wondered if Drake really did have a family. Perhaps he could find the words to ask him someday.

God sets the solitary in families. Andrew listened to the soft patter of rain against the window as the ceiling fan weakly rippled the bed sheets. Yes, sleep would come easy tonight.

Bacon, eggs, and biscuits were the alarm clock the next morning. The sound of spitting grease and the fragrance of blackberry jam were just too much to ignore. Drake usually slept in until sometime after lunch every Saturday, but the mixture of the overpowering scents quickly made him reconsider.

As would be expected, breakfast was delicious. The bacon was crunchy, the biscuits peeled off in buttery layers, and the eggs were running with Velveeta. The only thing that curbed Drake's appetite was when Andrew once again felt the need to go through his little routine of bowing his head and saying a prayer over the food. *Please. As if anyone is out there listening anyway.*

Ronnie was talkative throughout the meal, rambling on and on about how he wished it could be summer forever, or at least something along those lines. Did the kid never shut up? Stress was choking the life out of him right now. Could they not see it on his face? If they could only feel half that kind of pain, maybe they would be shaken out of their perfect little worlds for two seconds and show some consideration. Drake was genuinely trying to maintain his patience throughout the prayers and endless babble coming from Ronnie's mouth, but with a death-penalty convicting murder on his conscience, he sensed that his patience barrier was wearing thin.

After he was certain he could eat no more, Drake set his plate and silverware in the sink. He was hesitant at first to ask, but eventually mustered up enough courage to say, "Mind if I watch some television?"

Andrew chewed his food unhurriedly as he thought. "All right. But let Ronnie have the remote at twelve."

"That's when the Saturday cartoons start," Ronnie explained.

Drake shrugged in agreement and walked into the living room. He crashed on the sofa and pushed an exotic-looking table plant aside so he could elevate his feet on the coffee table. After he thought a moment, he withdrew his feet and moved the plant back into place. *Don't push it, Drake. You don't own the place. You're only a guest.*

He snatched up the remote and scrolled through the channels until he spotted a movie he remembered watching years ago. He hit the enter button, but instead of displaying what he had selected, the television went dark and showed a small, blue box at the bottom of the screen. "Parental controls locked," he read aloud. "Please enter pass code... what?" He tossed the remote aside and walked back into the kitchen. "Hey, uh, I think your television's messed up. Says something about a pass code. Do you know it?"

Andrew breathed slowly and set his fork down. "Mm-hm."

"Great. Then do you mind puchin' the numbers in real quick? Movie's started and—"

"I'm afraid not," Andrew said straightforwardly, as if he had already anticipated this conversation beforehand. "Sorry, Drake. I created that pass code for a reason."

Drake stared at him blankly. "Meaning...?"

"I didn't want Ronnie to accidentally see or hear something he shouldn't, so I locked all programs with a PG rating and up. If I know there's nothing wrong with one of the PG programs, however, I'll unlock it."

"Oh, well, as long as Ronnie doesn't come in there while I'm watching, you won't have to worry."

Andrew didn't know how he could possibly make what he had already stated any clearer to Drake. "That goes for all members of this house, including myself. I'm not letting anything get into my spirit that could potentially harm it."

Drake couldn't help but raise an eyebrow. "Your *spirit?* What does that have to do with watching—"

"Because I'm a Christian and I have Jesus living on the inside of me, I refuse to listen to anyone speak out against His name or curse Him. Any cursing. And if people don't wear modest clothing on television, then I'm not gonna stoop to their level and watch that either. I like television as much as anyone else does, Drake, but I have certain boundaries I set, and what I set I follow."

"It's just a movie. People cuss all the time, so what's the difference?"

"I can't help it if I walk by someone and hear them use bad language, but I *can* stop it from coming into our home, and that's what God holds me accountable for. Anyone living under this roof has to follow those boundaries."

"Not everyone in this house is a Christian," Drake said edgily, knowing as soon as those words left his mouth that he was stepping on dangerous ground.

Andrew pondered that statement for a moment and finally said, "Then as a Christian, that puts an even greater responsibility on me to watch out for you too, doesn't it?"

Drake turned around and stormed into the other room. He had a few choice words for that man right now. He reluctantly turned off the television and shook his head. *I can't even watch any good movies anymore? This ain't gonna work.* Maybe he could figure out the pass code himself.

Yeah, that's what he'd do. He would just go through every combination possible until he got it right. *0001, 0002, 0003, 0004*...OK, so down the drain with that idea. The movie wasn't that great anyway.

Drake spotted a DVD rack beside the television and quickly scanned through the titles. *It's a Wonderful Life, North by Northwest, Casablanca, The Don Knotts Classic DVD Collection.* He rolled his eyes and stood up. *Oh, brother. He's one of those types.*

Since watching a good movie wasn't an option, Drake retreated to his room and turned the radio in his digital clock down to a low volume. At least the radio didn't have a parental lock on it. Music was probably the one thing Andrew had forgotten about in his big book of "spirit-harmers," so Drake made a mental note to keep the music down to a safe volume. He certainly didn't want that freedom stolen from him too.

Da...Da-da...da-da-la-da...storm the gates for refuge...da-da and betray the innocent mind...da-da-da...listen for an answer...la-da in the life you left behind...

Drake took his hands off the piano keys and scribbled the words down on the page in front of him. For the first time in his life, he dared to put lyrics to his chords. The melody was deep and somber, unlike anything he had played before, and they deserved more than just the sound of a blank song.

Emptiness now dares to speak...darkness holds the gun...da-da-da...breaking through the–

The shrill ring of the phone disrupted his thoughts. He stopped playing and listened for a second, waiting to see if anyone would pick up. Ronnie was up in his room starting on a new puzzle, and Andrew had stepped into the shower about ten minutes ago.

Drake looked across at his half-empty page and frowned. *Might as well answer the phone,* he thought. He walked over to the caller ID and saw the name Tavner, Kevin displayed. *Hmm. Must be a member of the family.* He picked it up. "Hello?"

The speaker on the other end was silent for a moment before saying gruffly, "Who's this?"

"Drake."

"Drake? I don't know no Drake," Kevin said irritably. "Is this Andrew's house?"

Drake moved to the bottom of the stairs and looked up, hoping to see Andrew emerging from the bathroom. The shower wasn't running, but the door was still closed. "Yeah, this is his house."

"Then who are you?" Kevin badgered.

Drake leaned against the stair handrail. "I work for him."

"Oh," Kevin said, though he still sounded confused. "Well, I need to talk to 'em."

"He's busy right now. Could I maybe take a message?"

"Is Ronnie there?"

Drake glanced up to the top floor again and saw the light on in Ronnie's room. "Workin' on a puzzle, I think. Why?"

"I'm his father. Tell him to come answer the phone."

Drake remembered Ronnie's words about his parents not wanting him. He wondered if Ronnie had only been exaggerating or if his father really was the problem. "I don't know. I..."

"Who are you talking to, Drake?" Andrew said as he descended the stairs, hair dripping and smelling of shower gel.

Drake covered the mouthpiece with his hand. "Some guy named Kevin. Wants to talk to Ronnie."

Andrew's expression altered at the mention of Kevin's name. "Give me that," he said. He snatched the phone from Drake's hand, the old anger he had wrestled to subdue now fully aroused in him again. "Hello? Kevin?"

"Andrew?"

Andrew's hand stiffened around the phone. "What do you want?"

"I wanna talk to my boy."

"You know what the judge said!" Andrew said in a raised voice. "Don't push me, Kevin."

Drake wrinkled his brow. *Judge? So it ended up in court...Ronnie wasn't lying when he made it sound like a big deal. His parents must be worse than I thought.*

"They said no visitation rights!" Kevin said heatedly. "They never said I couldn't call!"

"How easily my visit to your house slips from memory."

"And how quickly you forget whose blood runs through that brat's veins! Now put him on the phone!"

"If you think you can threaten me—"

"Let me talk to my boy!"

"I don't think you have anything worthwhile to say."

"If you don't give him the phone—"

"I'm not making the decision. It's Ronnie's choice whether or not he wants to talk to you."

"Stop wasting my time and ask him then!" Kevin demanded.

"All right. I will ask him." Andrew covered the mouthpiece and called Ronnie downstairs. "Ronnie, your dad's on the phone," he said softly.

Ronnie shook his head and backed away, his eyes fixed on the phone. The look on his face exposed his inner terror of the monster waiting on the other end to talk to him, to bruise him deeper. "I don't wanna talk to him," he said in a shaky voice. "Please don't make me do it."

Andrew put the phone back up to his ear. "He doesn't want to talk to you, Kevin. Leave him alone."

"You can't refuse me! I'm his father!"

"You were never a father. Goodbye, Kevin. Don't even try to call this house again, because no one will pick up." Andrew moved the phone away from his ear as Kevin let out a string of curses, and hung up. He sighed and hesitantly turned to Ronnie. "I'm sorry, Ronnie, but I wanted to ask you first."

Ronnie walked back up the stairs and into his bedroom without saying a word.

Drake looked at Andrew, speechless at the sight he had just witnessed. "I wouldn't have answered the phone if I had known."

"I know," Andrew said, still wearing a frown. "It's not your fault."

"If you don't mind my asking, what happened between Ronnie and him?"

Andrew made sure Ronnie was occupied in his room before taking Drake over to the couch and sitting down beside him. His eyes searched the room as he tried to begin. "Kevin was never a real father to Ronnie," he started, wrinkling his brow as all the awful memories he had tried to forget flooded back into his soul again. "He drank all the time, gambled away his share of Dad's inheritance one week after it was given to him, and did a whole lot of other stupid things I'd rather not say. When he lost a gamble, he got himself stoned out of his mind, then took all his anger out on Ronnie. It was like a chain reaction every time. Ronnie never told anyone, never talked about the abuse he suffered night after night. Still doesn't, for that matter." Andrew wiped a tear away from his eye and clasped his hands together to keep them from shaking.

Drake knew what it was like living with a father who drank regularly, but he had never once been beaten. "Man, I hate that for Ronnie. I never realized." *No, I sure didn't. No wonder he talks so much. He never had anyone to listen to him before.* "What are you gonna do about his dad? From what I heard of your end of the conversation, he sounded pretty angry."

"I'm going to keep him away from Ronnie," Andrew said, his words precise and matter-of-fact. "He doesn't care a thing about seeing or talking to Ronnie. He's just looking for a fight because now he's got no one to beat up. He doesn't scare me, though. I doubt he'll even try to call again."

Drake folded his arms and noticed the serious concern in Andrew's eyes. "Hope you're right. For Ronnie's sake, I mean. I saw the look on his face. He seemed scared when you mentioned his dad."

Andrew sighed and turned his gaze elsewhere. "I can imagine."

"Is there anything I can do to cheer him up?"

Andrew lifted his head and looked at Drake. "Why don't you ask him?"

The floor creaked as Drake walked up to Ronnie's room. He approached the already opened door and stood silently in front of it for a few seconds, hesitating. He wasn't good at stuff like this, but tapped lightly on the door anyway. "Can I come in?"

Ronnie glanced up from his sitting position on the floor and set down the puzzle piece he was holding. "If you want," he said indifferently.

Drake walked in and sat down beside him. "Your uncle told me about your dad," he started slowly. "He thought it would be better if I knew."

Ronnie shrugged and looked away.

"Anything I can do?"

"Not really."

"C'mon. Nothing?"

"Being here with you and Uncle Andy, I almost forgot about him." Ronnie looked into Drake's eyes for some form of comfort and brought his knees close to his chest. "Now it just hurts again."

Drake picked up a puzzle piece and inserted it in the top corner of the puzzle. "Let me know if there's anything I can do, OK? I know I've been a jerk at times—especially that first night—but I really do wanna help." He nudged him gently, hoping to get a smile. "Now it's my turn to say I'm sorry."

Ronnie teared up but managed to hold it back.

"Hey, things won't stay bad forever. They can't. Believe that." Drake rose from the floor and turned to leave.

"Wait."

Drake faced him. "What is it?"

"There is one thing."

"Yeah?"

"Can you come to church with Uncle Andy and me tomorrow?"

Drake opened his mouth and froze. "Oh...well, you see..."

Ronnie shook his head and turned his attention back to his puzzle. "Never mind."

Drake took a deep breath, knowing what he was about to say went against every desire inside of him. "All right, Ronnie. I'll go. But only for you."

"Really?" Ronnie said excitedly. "'Cuz you'll just love it there. And the pastor's real nice. He even shook my hand after the service."

Drake literally had to force himself to smile. *I can hardly contain myself.*

Chapter

10

A STEP AHEAD

Drake Pearson didn't exactly look dressed for the occasion. A slightly wrinkled button-up shirt that might as well have not had any buttons, a gray tee underneath, faded jeans, old shoes with six hundred dollars and a knife buried inside, and a hemp-string necklace with a lizard engraved on a wooden bead roughly sized up his apparel for Sunday morning. He was comfortable, at least, and maintained a sense of pride that he didn't walk around as if his clothes had been soaked overnight in starch—like "church folk."

Ronnie was chipper, as always, on the way to church that morning. He filled Drake in on the praise and worship, what the preaching was like, and even offered to give him a tour of the church before the service began.

"No thanks, little man," Drake mumbled, hoping to catch a short nap before they arrived. Why did church have to be so early in the morning? And why did he ever agree to put himself through this humiliation in the first place? He stretched his sore arms and yawned. Then another yawn. Did he say humiliation? No, this went beyond embarrassment;

this was sheer agony. "I guess it would sound rude if I asked how long service is," he said, directing his statement to Andrew.

"It usually ends sometime around twelve," Andrew said. "But then again, the pastor isn't on a time schedule, and if people start closing their Bibles or checking their watches too soon, that usually seems to make him want to continue even longer."

"Great," Drake moaned, leaning his head back. "My stomach will be rolling by that time."

"Can we order pizza afterward?" Ronnie piped up.

"Sure," Andrew said. "You like pizza, Drake?"

"I could probably eat five pieces right now," Drake said. If he hadn't been so rushed this morning, he wouldn't have forgotten to eat breakfast, and if he wouldn't have forgotten to eat breakfast, he probably wouldn't have a headache right now—this one for real. He hoped today was one of the pastor's shorter messages. Or maybe he had caught a cold and was home sick today. Before he knew it, he was dreaming up a fantasy of ideas that might have happened to the pastor between now and the short time span of five minutes before they reached the church.

"Have you ever been to church before, Drake?" Andrew said.

"Sure," Drake said, trying to restrain another yawn. "Plenty of times. Went there with my dad to get food from the food pantry."

"Oh," Andrew said despondently.

"The church started making people attend the morning service, though, then gave 'em food afterward. That meant everyone had to wait and hear the sermon before they got anything to eat. Dad and I stopped coming after that. There were a few other churches in the area to bum off of for a while, but eventually they closed their pantries or did the same thing as the first church. So in a way, I guess church has helped me. Kept me fed for a while, anyway."

Andrew pulled into the parking lot, which was already half full of cars. The second Drake stepped out of the car, Ronnie began begging to show him around until Drake finally gave in. "OK," he agreed, "but I don't see what's so special about a concrete building."

Ronnie walked Drake past the doe-eyed greeters at the front door and rushed him into the sanctuary. "That's the stage up there," he explained, as if Drake hadn't already realized that for himself. "Over there's a guy who plays a sweet-looking guitar, and the drums are awesome."

Drake surveyed the stage and was saddened to find that there was no piano. What a shame. A piano might have been the only thing he would have found interesting here. Everything else had been fairly predictable so far. Pews lined up perfectly, air smelling of recently sprayed air freshener, and everyone smiling unnaturally at him whenever he walked by. Church just creeped him out, period.

Ronnie tugged at his hand. "C'mon, I'll show you the kids' class."

The children's class was downstairs, and the theme on the wall appeared to be of some man with a boat and a crowd of animals around him. "Who's the old guy?" Drake said, nodding toward the painting.

Ronnie squinted as he thought. "I think he's Noah. He was the guy who built a boat and brought all the animals inside before a big storm came and flooded the whole world."

"How do you know all this stuff? Thought you told me you've only been to church once."

"I have, but Uncle Andy's been reading to me at night."

Drake raised his eyebrows. "At night? Why?"

"So I can learn more."

"That's what Sundays are for. To learn when you come to church."

"Oh, no," Ronnie said quickly. "Uncle Andy tells me lots of exciting stories every night. I know a lot of them already."

Drake looked at the painting again. Eerie that kids actually took an interest in this stuff. "Exciting. Right," he said doubtfully.

"No, really, they are. I can't wait to learn more."

Drake simply nodded in his confusion. *Poor kid, he's been brainwashed.*

Ten minutes later, Drake and Ronnie found a seat by Andrew just as the praise team emerged from a side door and walked onto the stage. After a brief prayer and a warm welcome to the congregation, the music began. Ronnie and Andrew stood during the songs, but Drake pointedly stayed seated with his arms folded close to his chest and eyelids drooping. The music was OK, but he had heard better. The instruments impressed him somewhat, but what was the point of it all? To sing to someone who may or may not be listening?

Drake wasn't sure where he stood on the whole "God" issue, and considered himself at most to be an agnostic. He simply didn't know. Who could ever know? The belief in evolving from a chimp or a blob of slime from the ocean had always been lame to him; but on the other hand, the belief in a God who magically created the entire world in a matter of days made no sense either. But what did it really matter? Maybe he would get serious about his life and eternity once he got into his 70s or 80s, but his life was just too full and messed up right now to try to juggle something else.

Drake was beginning to get fidgety. The fourth song had ended, yet soft instrumental music still played as the pastor rambled on about salvation and something called an altar call. And most of the people were still standing. Drake peeked at his watch and rolled his eyes. *Sit down already. You're encouraging him to go longer.*

"If there's anyone in this room today who has not made Jesus Christ the Lord of his life, please do so immediately," Pastor Don Bauer said. "Don't leave here today without knowing for a fact that your life is right with God. All you have to do is repent of your sins and believe that Jesus

Christ is the Son of God and that He died and rose again. Give your heart to Him. He doesn't ask anything in return except your love."

Ronnie tugged on Andrew's shirt and stood on his tiptoes to whisper something in his ear.

Tears welled up in Andrew's eyes, and he embraced Ronnie.

Ronnie whispered something else to Andrew, and Andrew nodded his head. Then Ronnie sat down and scooted close to Drake. "Can you come up front with me?" he said quietly.

Drake looked at the stage, then back at Ronnie. "What? Why?"

"I want Jesus in my heart," Ronnie whispered, wondering why Drake hadn't already understood.

Drake glanced up at Andrew, who was beaming proudly and on the verge of tears. *Oh, brother.* He sighed and said finally, "Why do I gotta go up there?"

"I don't wanna go by myself."

Then ask your uncle, Drake wanted to say. *He'd be more than thrilled to walk you up there.*

"Anyone at all?" Pastor Don said, searching the crowd for any raised hands.

Ronnie bit his lip. "Please, Drake," he pleaded.

"Ronnie, don't..." But Drake couldn't pull himself to say no. He grudgingly gave in to the pitiful look on the 7-year-old's face and sheepishly made his way up to the front behind Ronnie. *I can't believe I'm doing this. And in front of all these people! Me and my brilliant, backfiring ideas. Thank you once again for your stupidity, brain. I look like an idiot.*

Pastor Don smiled at Ronnie and Drake as they ambled toward the front where he stood. "Thank You, Father, for these two people who have come forward in their desire to know You."

Minus one, Drake thought, pushing his legs onward to keep from freezing on the spot.

The music droned on as people all around continued to worship God with their eyes closed, but Drake felt as if a huge red target was on his back and everyone was staring at him. He felt himself begin to sweat as the pastor stepped in front of them and asked them their names.

"Ronnie!" Ronnie answered instantly.

"Uh, I'm just up here for the kid," Drake said without making eye contact. He clamped his mouth shut. *I feel sick.*

Ronnie turned around and gazed up at Drake. "You mean you don't want Jesus to come into your heart, too?"

Drake bent over and said in a hushed voice, "Look, you just do what you gotta do and I'll do what I gotta do, so make it snappy."

Ronnie turned back to face the pastor, but the joy, it seemed, had almost completely wiped off his face. He prayed the prayer after the pastor, and all the while Drake's cheeks were growing redder by the second. Finally, Ronnie said "Amen" and walked back to his seat while Drake headed directly for the back door.

Andrew hugged Ronnie again as tears streamed down his cheeks. "I'm so happy for you, Ronnie. You were so brave."

Ronnie tried to smile, but his attention was turned toward the back of the church. He pulled away from his uncle. "Why did Drake leave?"

"I don't know, Ronnie."

Ronnie scooted to the end of the pew and stood. "I'm gonna go find him."

Ronnie found Drake outside leaning against the side of the church, driving the heel of his foot into the soft dirt. "Whatcha doin'?" he said, slipping both hands in his pockets.

Drake glanced at him for only a second before shifting his eyes back to the grass. "Don't ever make me do that again, understand?"

"Do what?"

Drake snorted and rammed his foot deeper in the dirt. "You know what."

"Because I wanted you to be with me when I asked Jesus in my heart?" Ronnie said, kicking a pebble away just to show Drake he wasn't the only one upset. "Sorry."

Drake sat down on the cool dew and wrapped his arms around his legs. "Don't say that. I know you meant well, but it's just different for me, that's all."

"That doesn't make sense."

Drake shrugged. "Does to me."

"Why would anyone not want to go to Heaven when they die?"

"I guess for the same reason teenagers don't sit in Santa's fat lap. You grow up and stop believing what every dim-witted person tells you."

"Nobody made Uncle Andy believe it. He just does."

"Fake is still fake. I don't care who believes in it." Drake noticed the edge in his voice. Always angry, wasn't he? Maybe he could tone it down a bit, just for the kid. *Ah, so what? Let it stay. You know it feels good to release it.*

"But what if God is more than fake?" Ronnie pressed. "What if He's really out there?"

Drake looked up at the cloudless sky and then back at Ronnie, as if to say, *Where?*

Ronnie accepted defeat. "OK, sorry, but I still say it doesn't make sense."

I never asked your opinion.

"But I'm not sorry for caring," Ronnie continued. "I could never be sorry for that."

Drake reconsidered toning down his anger problem. Maybe it would be better to give the kid a break. Save the anger to blow up on someone who really needed it. Anyway, he might need the extra ammo someday. "I was just spouting off, Ronnie. Nothing serious. It's better to ignore me when I get that way."

Ronnie pursed his lips. "Thanks. I'll remember."

"Yeah, well...I think it's great you feel like things are good between you and God now."

"You do?"

"Yeah, but see, not everyone's the same. Some people find comfort in God, some people find comfort in family, and some people even find comfort in a high. No one's really right; it's just whatever they feel. Right now, the only thing I find comfort in is having a place to sleep at night and food to eat. Nothing more. I've done just fine without a family, and I can do without God, too."

Ronnie pulled apart a blade of grass and let it fall to the ground. "Does that mean you don't wanna be around me anymore 'cause I have Jesus in my heart?"

Drake finally allowed himself to smile. He ruffled Ronnie's hair and said, "As long as it's not contagious, pal."

The drive home was silent—which ironically spoke louder volumes than if the three of them had all carried on regular chatter. Drake knew the stunt he had pulled was likely the prominent topic in the back of Andrew and Ronnie's minds, but he *had* warned them, so anything they could say would only be a repeat of what he had already told them. Andrew didn't ask where Drake had been during the sermon, and Drake wasn't offering any explanations. Ronnie had likely told his uncle what had happened once he went back inside the sanctuary, so what was the point in rehashing it all? Oh, well. At least now, everyone knew where he stood.

When they got back to the house, Andrew followed Drake up to his room and closed the door behind him. He waited to see if Drake would voluntarily speak to him first or if he would have to prod it out of him.

No response.

Andrew cleared his throat. "Uh, what's up?"

Drake threw his shirt to the floor and dug through his dresser drawers for something more comfortable. "What, is it your turn to quiz me now?"

Andrew hadn't expected an attack this early. "I just asked a simple question. A simple answer is all I'm looking for."

Drake rolled his eyes. "I don't like church," he said flatly.

Andrew nodded his head and considered that. "OK."

Drake stared at him skeptically. "That's it? You're not gonna hound me for leaving church early, or—"

"I never said you had to come. You gave your word to Ronnie, not to me."

Drake looked away. "Then why did you come up here?"

"Because I care." Andrew leaned sideways and tried to see Drake's face. "Are you sure there's nothing bothering you?"

Drake tried to act nonchalant about it. "Not that I know of."

Andrew wanted more of an answer than that, but Drake had dropped the ball and cut that part of the conversation off without any hope of reviving it. If he pressed him about it, he would only come across as prying and suspicious. "If you say there's nothing wrong, then I believe you," he said.

"Good."

Andrew debated whether he should leave now or attempt to talk to Drake more. *I can't just walk out on him now. All we've done is exchange words, not had a real, personal conversation.* He glanced over at the loose, tangled mess of covers on the bed and the wad of dirty clothes quickly piling up in the corner. He took a deep breath. *You can address that later. Right now, Drake needs someone to talk to.* "I want to be your friend, Drake, not your enemy," he started. "Now, I know there's a bit of difference in our age—"

Drake raised his eyebrows and pursed his lips together as he slowly nodded his head.

"All right, so there's a vast difference," Andrew admitted, getting Drake's silent message. "But that doesn't mean we can't communicate. I want you to feel like you can talk to me." He paused before asking, "What do you think about Ronnie's decision today?"

Drake turned away from Andrew and moved toward the window, even though the blinds were still closed. "Beats me. If he's happy, that's all that matters, right?"

"He looks up to you, you know."

Drake whirled around. "What are you saying? You worried about me being a bad influence on his soul?"

"I never said that."

"Yeah, well, I know what you must think of me," he said, turning back to the window.

"You wanna know what I think?" Andrew said, taking a step closer. "I think you're a teenager who's struggling to find a place to call your own. A place where you feel like you fit in and belong. I'm not trying to push you out, Drake. In fact, I hope you stay. So does Ronnie."

"Whatever." Drake didn't know why he was on the defensive today. Every little thing someone said or did seemed to set him off. Was it because he was more scared than he had ever been? Time was ticking, and he found himself jumpy and nervous more than ever before. Nothing had turned up with the cops yet, but he had the nagging feeling that back in his hometown they were putting the pieces together. Sooner or later, they would track him down. But exactly *when* they would find him was the part that kept him on edge.

After a couple hours of on-and-off dozing on his bed, Drake wandered downstairs and found Ronnie sitting on the couch watching television. He stretched his arms in the air and looked around for Andrew. Good, maybe he was upstairs. The last thing he needed was another sermon.

Ronnie seemed engrossed in some program about penguins. Since Drake had nothing better to do with his time, he decided to join him. "Whatcha watchin'?" he said, grabbing a pillow.

Ronnie's eyes barely left the screen as he replied, "A story about people who go to Antarctica to help penguins."

The narrator's voice droned on, nearly putting Drake back to sleep. "You *like* this kinda stuff?" he said, wincing.

"'Course. I wanna be a vet when I grow up."

Drake snorted, knowing he didn't have enough fingers on both hands to count how many times that phrase had come out of his mouth when he was Ronnie's age. "I remember when I used to say that."

"Used to say what?"

"I wanted to be practically everything when I grew up. First, I wanted to be a mailman."

"Really?"

"Oh, yeah. Taking people's mail to their house while listening to the radio *and* getting paid for it sounded like a one-of-a-kind deal to me."

Ronnie laughed. "So what happened?"

"I grew out of it, that's what happened. Wanted to be a director next and make it big in the movies. Then I thought space sounded pretty sweet and decided to be an astronaut. The list went on and on."

"So which one do you wanna be now?"

"Be?" Drake forced a laugh and said, "I threw all those ideas out the window a long time ago. They were just dreams, kid. Nothing ever happened to 'em. They were just kinda there, a passing thought."

"But you could still be those things. Gosh, you could even add being a piano player to your list."

Drake smiled. "Nah, it's a little too late now. I mean, it was cool for me to think about what my life would be like when I was lying in bed with nothin' to do but soak up the heat. I was in my make-believe world for anywhere between thirty minutes to several hours—whenever I finally got tired of pretending and fell asleep. Eventually, I knew I could never be any of those things, so I decided that trying wasn't even worth the effort."

Ronnie absorbed his story, but the effect it made on him was little to none. "Well, no matter what, I'm gonna be a vet."

"More power to ya," Drake said, really meaning it.

Ronnie stared down at Drake's shoes and scrunched his brow. "Man, do you ever take your shoes off? I like wearing socks better."

Drake glanced down at his ragged black shoes. All the money he had to his name was hidden in there. "Only when I sleep," he said, content to leave it at that.

The telephone rang. Drake stood, but then heard Andrew coming from his bedroom to take the call. A simple move maybe, but something about it didn't feel right.

Second ring.

Drake groped for the armrest and lowered himself back down on the couch. Weird. His hand was shaking. Somewhere in between a tainted mixture of dread and uncertainty came the lurid feeling of being trapped. Caged.

Wonder who was calling?

Third ring. Drake glanced over his shoulder just as Andrew looked strangely at the caller-ID. He picked up the phone, answered it with an uncertain, "Hello?" and then walked into another room.

Overcome with a looming concern, Drake left Ronnie and walked over to check the caller-ID for himself.

Wrong move. All the thoughts, terrors, nightmares, warnings he had seen coming but foolishly ignored—the very thing he had dreaded was now upon him, breathing down his neck like a starved monster. Fear milked the last drop of boldness from his heart as he read the words POLICE DEPT on the tiny screen.

They had found him. Life was over. He was trapped. Duped. Caged.

Game over.

Get out.

Adrenaline gushed through Drake's veins, quickening his heart and alerting his mind to give every defensive instinct top priority. Still, he gave no thought of running...not yet, anyway. Not until he figured out their plan and foiled it with his own. The survival, save-your-hide part of him begged him to use his legs to run until his body crumpled underneath him in fatigue. But the revengeful, swear-on-my-life-I'll-pay-you-back part of him that refused to be destroyed commanded full obedience—and that obedience would be served.

But this is real life, not a game of cops and robbers! a thought arose. *What if they catch you?*

They won't, he argued with himself.

You're a fool.

Maybe.

Electric chair...

Drake clenched his teeth as a new fury arose in him. *I'm not dead yet.* He noiselessly walked toward the door Andrew had closed behind him and put an ear against it. Andrew must have been close to the door, because his words were unmistakably clear.

"You know it's him?" Andrew said solemnly. "How?"

Drake's pulse accelerated. He wanted to run away, but he had to be sure first. There had to be a logical explanation for all this. *Of course there is...me. Why else would they be callin'? To invite me over for teacakes?* He held his breath and listened.

"You traced the license plate number, huh? Yeah, I figured that would come in handy."

Oh, no, my truck! That salesman must've been working with them the whole time and reported my license plate number. How could I be so careless?

"Mm-hm. I understand. But what did he use?...A baseball bat? That makes sense."

Drake had heard enough. He was out the door in a flash. For once, there were no questions and too many answers. *Run. Just run. As far away as you can. They're onto you, but you're still a step ahead of them. Remember that. Don't let them catch you or even come close to finding you this time. Just keep running.*

Drake cursed the police, cursed Andrew, cursed his father, cursed himself for falling into this unwanted ditch that had taken his life so far off course. Life shouldn't have to be like this. It wasn't fair. Nothing was. *Well, if they want to set traps and lower bait in front of my face, I can play dirty back. Bring it on.*

He cut through yards and weaved his way through mazes of buildings, staying away from the roads and sidewalks as much as possible. Where was he going? He wasn't even sure himself. Being traced to Andrew's home so far away from his own hadn't fully registered in his mind yet. One thing he was sure of, though. He was through with trusting people. Oh, Andrew had sounded sincere and genuine, but he knew now that it had all been a façade.

Buying me clothes, giving me a bed to sleep in, telling me I was welcome in his home, and even applauding me on the piano...all that was his way of keeping me there until the cops showed up. He thought he had me, but he'll get the surprise of his life when he ends his little, secretive phone call and finds out I'm long gone. What then, huh? He tricked me once, but I swear he'll never do it again. I hate him. If I had a gun in my hand, I might even be tempted to go back and shoot him.

Chapter
11

NEW ACCOMPLICE

Drake Pearson's legs were stiff and aching, and he wasn't sure if he had gone one mile or five. He had run so far that he was no longer in the wealthier part of town, but had somehow wound up in the middle of an extremely poor neighborhood. He had thought his hometown was rough, but this place gave him chills.

Most of the windows had bars in them; that is, if they weren't already boarded up with scrap wood or flattened car hoods. Dehydrated trees with gnarled branches hung suspended over the road like groping arms, the fallen leaves and peeling bark the only substance available to fill cracks and level potholes in the deteriorating road. Most every ditch he saw was littered with smashed aluminum cans and empty potato chip bags—an occasional paint can or mangled toy beneath the garbage added a splash of color to the dirty streetscape. This was not where he wanted to be.

Drake took a left down a narrow road and spotted several mailbox posts wound tightly with oxidized barbed wire—a silent threat to trespassers. A Rottweiler strained against his chains and pawed the ground, baring his teeth and snarling viciously at Drake's uninvited presence. Drake turned and walked back down the shaded street from where he had come, not doubting for one second that if he continued any further, he would see a grizzly-looking man cradling a shotgun who looked more fit for a cave in the B.C. era than on a front porch. His luck, the man would probably use the shotgun on him just for the demented thrill of it. Nothing would surprise him anymore. Not even the sight of the giggling kids he saw in the distance pouring dirt and algae water down a crumbling chimney. *I just had to pick this place.*

With every dog coming unglued at his presence and eagerly joining the barking crusade, Drake sensed he was beginning to attract an audience—mostly nosy people with nothing better to do than peek through their windows and wonder what this daredevil was doing on their turf... or dirt, or cracked pavement, or whatever this hole in the ground was supposed to consist of.

Drake felt the fingers of fear grazing against his heart. He jogged through the streets, wanting to run but fearing that might give the snoopers the wrong impression. He wanted to look innocent; he didn't need more people calling the cops on him. Then again, these people didn't exactly look the type to enlist the help of a police officer. If there was a problem, they would probably deal with it themselves—two shells and a shotgun, then a shovel to bury the remains. Just a wild guess, purely speculation, but it was probably more realistic than Drake dared to admit.

The people he passed stared enviously at his clothes, looking over their shoulders and whispering. Drake kept his eyes straight ahead and urged himself to keep moving, knowing that if he displayed the smallest ounce of fear they would be all over him. He could only guess what they were saying.

"Look who just blew in."

"Who's he think he is?"

"Gonna get himself hurt if he's not careful."

Drake kept jogging. *Don't worry. I'm being careful. I didn't exactly pick this place off a list.* Still, in spite of his efforts, he couldn't help but meet the faces of those he passed. Some of the men and women carried bags over their shoulders, few rode bikes, and others had nothing but the ragged clothes on their backs. Every bleak expression was sagging with a frown and paired with criminal eyes. *Where am I?* he wondered.

Drake slowed his pace to a walk, trying to blend now. He couldn't afford to appear suspicious. As he walked, he took in all the sights and sounds around him. Other than the dotted pink clouds in the sky above, he found nothing beautiful about this place. The range of odors in the air assaulted his senses, almost to the point where he had to hold a hand over his nose. Homes were rotting, an abundance of graffiti made up for the lack of color, and he could have sworn he smelled a hint of marijuana in the light breeze.

Though it was three o'clock in the afternoon, it would only be a matter of hours before it would be getting dark—and Drake still didn't know where he was or if he would stay here for the night. He looked for any signs along the side of the road, but there were none. It was then that he began to feel uncomfortable.

As he continued walking aimlessly down the lonely street he had stumbled upon, he glanced to his left and saw an older couple sharing a tattered couch on their front porch, smoking cigarettes. Drake briskly strode by without so much as a quick glance or nod of the head. He had no idea what kind of people lived here, but their faces were far from friendly.

Drake detected the smell of burnt grease as he walked by a place called Miller's Diner. Surprisingly, even the smell of unpleasant food made his stomach churn with hunger. Maybe he should go inside and sit awhile until he got his strategy together. He had to get off these streets anyway before he got mugged.

A heavy fog of cigarette smoke engulfed him as soon as he pushed open the door. Cigarette smoke had always detested him, even when he was the one doing the smoking, so being in a small room where the air was concentrated only made it worse. Though he was glad he had kicked cigarettes, he hated the fact that now even the smell gave him a pounding headache and teary eyes.

The place wasn't too crowded. He had to conserve his energy before nightfall, and since there was nowhere else to go, it seemed this would be the best place to stop and get his bearings. He scouted out a table in the corner of the small room and sat with his hands crossed over his face. *Oh, here we go. You lived it high. Now it's time to taste life from the bottom again.*

A man with a braided black goatee asked him from behind the counter what he'd like to eat.

Drake turned and patted his pockets. "I ain't got no money. Just came in to sit, if that's all right."

The man frowned and gave Drake a once-over. "Sure, sure," he mumbled.

Drake stared out the window and traced his eyes over the colorful graffiti on nearly every building wall. Some were just markings, but most were real talent. What really surprised him was a painting on one side of a two-story building across the street of a burly man with a cane in his hand climbing up a black and purple rainbow. He rubbed the chills on his arms and looked down at the table.

"Hey," someone said behind him.

Drake didn't move. *Someone talking to me?* He turned and saw a young man maybe a couple years older than him staring back at him. "Hey," he replied guardedly.

The man waved him over.

Great, he wants me to sit with him. Drake stood up and walked stiffly over to the table where the man sat. "Yeah?"

"Sit."

OK. Drake sat across from him and surveyed the room to make sure no one was lurking in the corner waiting to jump him. So far, no shotgun—a definite plus. He faced the young man again and waited. "What?" he said finally.

"Nice clothes."

Drake glanced down at his shirt and jeans. "What about 'em?"

"Name's Ivan. What's yours?"

Kinda forward, aren't ya? "Why do you care?"

"Hey, chill, bro. Don't be so jumpy."

"I'm not jumpy," Drake said, his voice strict and affirmative. He tried to ignore the fact that blood was rushing to his face, making him appear guilty.

Ivan held up his hands. "OK, OK. So why are ya here?"

"I wanna know why you're asking."

"What? Mommy said you can't talk to strangers? I just asked what you were doin' here."

Drake noticed a strange tattoo on the side of Ivan's neck. "Just passin' through," he answered, trying to figure out where all this small talk was headed.

Ivan laughed. "Nobody just passes through here. Especially a rich boy like you. Bad things could happen if you turn your back for only a second." Ivan heavily peppered what was left of his hamburger and shoved it all in his mouth at once.

Drake looked away as grease trickled down the side of Ivan's mouth. "Believe me," he said, "I'm not rich."

"Oh, right," Ivan said sarcastically, making little use of the napkin he held wadded in his fist.

"I'm not!"

Ivan eyed him. "So where'd you get the clothes? Steal 'em?"

Drake felt uncomfortable under Ivan's glare. "I worked for a man who lived in a nice house. Mowed yards for him."

"What's his name?"

"Why do you wanna know everyone's name?"

Ivan leaned back. "Just like to know who I'm dealin' with. I may know him and I may not, but that's up for me to decide, not you. So spill. What's his name?"

"Andrew," Drake said, still not seeing the point in all this. "Last name's Tavner, in case you wanna get that detailed."

"And this Andrew is a fairly wealthy man, is that correct?"

"You've got the idea."

"He fire you?"

"Fire me?" Drake said, a hint of pride in his voice. "Hardly. I quit. He was a slave driver, and that bratty kid of his drove me nuts."

Ivan smiled and shook his head. "You're a bad liar, you know that? Listen, pal. You ain't foolin' me. What are you runnin' from?"

Drake shoved his chair back and stood to leave.

"Fine, run away," Ivan said, stirring his drink with his straw. "If you don't want any help from me, that's cool."

Drake turned and glared at Ivan. "Help? Help from what?"

Ivan glanced at the chair.

Drake huffed and unwillingly sat. *Why am I listening to him? He can't help me. I can't even help me.*

Ivan looked at the man behind the counter and glared at him until he walked into a back room.

Drake noticed how deep his breathing was getting. OK, so maybe he had been wrong about this guy.

Ivan turned to face him, satisfied at the tension he had created. "I'm trying to help you, but if you don't tell me everything I wanna know, I'm useless to you."

"What makes you think I need your help?"

"I'm pretty good at reading people, and believe me, you're easy to read. Why were you running?"

"I wasn't running. I was walking," Drake said, knowing he had stopped running long before he reached this place. Ivan couldn't have possibly seen him.

Ivan took a sip of his soda. "Your face is awful red."

Drake felt his heart pick up speed. "It's hot outside."

"No, it's not."

"Then I give up," Drake said, exasperated. "I'm tired of this game. If you know all the answers before you ask them, then you tell me."

"Never said I was a mind reader."

"Well, I wouldn't put it past you."

Ivan chuckled. "You know, I like you. I think we could get along."

Don't flatter yourself.

"So, back to my question. Why were you running?"

Drake finally conceded. "Why do you think I was running? I was being chased."

"Cops?"

Drake rubbed his forehead with both hands. "Yeah," he said miserably.

"Figured. What'd ya do?"

With his head still buried in his hands, Drake mumbled, "I murdered my dad."

Ivan let out a low whistle. "Wow, capital felony. I'm impressed."

"I'm not."

Ivan thought a moment before leaning close—close enough to make Drake feel uncomfortable—and said quietly, "I can help you if you want, but you have to help me first."

"How can you help me?"

"I can hide you."

Drake snorted. "Yeah, sure. I tried that, and it doesn't work."

"You think I'm playing you?"

"C'mon, get real. How can you hide me?" Drake shook his head angrily and clenched his teeth, despising everything his life was becoming. "No criminal can ever really hide from the cops. Sure, maybe some, but ninety-nine percent of the time, you get caught. I'm smart enough to know that much."

"I've been holed up for nearly two years now and the cops have never once come close to findin' me."

Drake stared into Ivan's dark brown eyes. "What dirt do the cops have on you?" he said, almost too afraid to ask.

Ivan smiled smugly. "Two murders. One was connected to a kidnapping and rape, and the other involved a strategically planned armed robbery that left me with thousands. The only thing that went wrong was that the money didn't last as long as I had hoped. Now, your name please."

162

Drake waited, hating himself already for what he was about to do. "Drake," he said slowly.

"The rest."

Drake wanted to throw up. "Pearson," he said through an exhale. "But I still don't think I fully understand your plan yet."

Ivan scooted his chair away from the table and rose from his seat. "Follow me, Drake Pearson."

Ivan led Drake around the back of Miller's Diner through heaps of old tires, discarded twines of barbed wire, jagged pieces of scrap wood, and a tangle of thorns and poison ivy. Drake welcomed the shade beneath the cover of the massive white oaks, but the coolness reminded him that evening was coming. Soon, darkness would resume control, and he knew how the night enjoyed muddling with his thoughts, dictating his mind, torturing him to no end. He glanced at Ivan's sweat-soaked muscular body and thought, *There's really no difference between him and me, is there? Both murderers. Both running. Both scared to death, though we've managed to mask the pain.*

Drake's insides began to writhe in pain. How could he have not seen this day coming before now? Why did he ever open himself up to Andrew's scheme, just to end up walking through this unfamiliar place with a murderer who promised hope? Ivan could be packing heat right now for all he knew and have ulterior motives for bringing him here.

Drake looked over his shoulder, yearning to go back. He could do this on his own. He didn't need Ivan, and he sure didn't need to keep walking like this unarmed.

Ivan stopped. "And here we are," he said, pointing to a small shack half hidden beneath the trees that shockingly reminded Drake of what used to be his own home.

"Wow," Drake remarked. "This where you live?"

"Well, it ain't no subdivision, but it's the best we've got."

Drake shot him a look. "We?...As in me and you, right?"

"Oops, did I forget to tell you about the others?" Ivan said, acting surprised. "My bad. I'll introduce you to the gang."

Drake gulped as he followed Ivan up to the old structure. *What have I gotten myself into?*

Ivan hammered forcefully on the door and yelled, "Open up! It's me, Ivan!" He shook his head. "Bunch a cowards. Leave 'em alone for two seconds and already they got the place bolted up like Fort Knox."

The man on the inside went through a lengthy process of unlocking, unchaining, and more unlocking until he eventually cracked the door open. "Who's that?" he said, staring daggers at Drake.

"Relax, Lomas. He's gonna help us." Ivan forced his way through the door and held it open for Drake. There was something sinister about the way his cold smile suddenly curved downward as he said, "Welcome to my castle, Drake."

Drake took one step inside and found himself staring into the faces of eight hard-looking men. He would have preferred wrestling with that Rottweiler he had seen back on the road than taking on one of these gorillas. If Ivan gave the command, they would turn his body into a sack of bones so fast he'd be dead in a heartbeat. *This was your idea, stupid. You play with a murderer, you get the whole package.*

On a rickety table in the middle of the room lay a soupspoon that had been charred black by heat. Beside it were four discolored needles, stained mostly by blood. Drake stared at the sight, suddenly feeling way in over his head.

"Drake here's a wanted man," Ivan explained, shoving Drake in front of him so everyone could get a good look. "Cops want him for murder. We're gonna help him in return for a favor." He looked sideways at Drake and said, "That is, if he decides to cooperate."

"Of course," Drake said, almost too quickly. "But you still haven't told me what it is you want me to do."

"Ever smoke?"

Drake shrugged. "Yeah, who hasn't?"

All the men laughed.

Ivan rolled his eyes exhaustedly. "Hilarious. I'm talking about weed and crack, brainless, not cigarettes."

Drake tried to hide his embarrassment. "Oh. No, I never smoked it."

"Then I guess you don't know how expensive it can be to buy."

"No, I don't, but I have a clue."

"Hershall died a few months back," Ivan said abruptly, cutting his eyes to the other end of the room. The other men seemed to have their entire attention glued to him as he paced the room. "The chemicals he was working with blew up in his face and set his whole house ablaze. He never made it out."

"Um...OK," Drake said, not knowing where Ivan was going with this.

Ivan stopped walking and turned to him. "He was our supplier," he said solemnly.

Oh, Drake thought. "No one else sell around here?"

Ivan snorted. "The others want more cash. A lot more than Hershall ever asked for. We're goin' broke faster than we ever planned with the new guy, and we never have enough cash. Can't keep up."

Drake was beginning to understand why Ivan had brought him here.

"That's where you come in, Drake," Ivan said, resting a calloused hand on Drake's shoulder.

"The old man you worked for had wads of cash, right?"

"Right, but—"

"Do you mean anything to him?"

"What?"

"C'mon, kid, cut the stupidity. Would he give up something of value if he thought his little hired hand was in trouble?"

"He would now, but not for the reason you're thinking. I heard him talking to the cops before I took off. He was trying to lead 'em to me."

"Perfect," Ivan said, his eyes dancing with ideas as he began to put a plan in motion. "This'll be easier than I thought."

Morning came, yet did little to erase the darkness in its early rising. The tall, orange lights surrounding the backside of the grocery store gave the wet pavement an eerie tint, as if it had been veiled in evil from every descending shaft of the light's glow. Ivan slowed to a stop and parked his truck against the windowless backside of the building just as he finished giving Drake his directions. "I want you to do this right, understand? You ain't got no second chance, so make it sound real."

"I hope this works," Drake said.

"You do what I told you and it will."

Drake glanced around the building skeptically. "How do you know there aren't any cameras?"

Ivan chuckled and killed the engine. "Man, we been doin' drug deals for years behind this building and never got caught yet. Why? You ready to bail out already?"

"Hardly," Drake retorted, hating it when people laughed at him. "Just give me the money and point me in the right direction." He snatched the quarters from Ivan and kept them clutched tightly in his fist as he stepped out of Ivan's truck and made his way up to the pay-phone. The air chilled him, but he knew his fear was to blame for most of the goose bumps on his skin. *Forget about it. You want revenge, don't you?* Did he ever.

Drake slid the coins in the machine and, with a trembling hand, punched in Andrew's number.

It rang twice before it was picked up. Those two rings felt like an eternity.

"Hello?" Andrew said tiredly.

Drake's voice was weak and raspy as he said, "Mr. Andrew? Is that you?"

"Drake! Where are you? I've been looking all over for—"

"Please hurry. I was beat up real bad and my...my head's bleeding a lot. You have to come."

"I will, Drake! I will! But where are you?"

"They dragged me behind a grocery store after they mugged me, and—"

"Grocery store?" Andrew said hastily. "Which one?"

"I don't know...beside a Blockbuster, I think. Please, you have to come quickly. I...I don't think I can hold out much longer. I feel so..." Drake let the phone fall from his hand and hang there.

Revenge was so sweet.

Andrew dropped Ronnie off at his mother's house after a very brief explanation and sped off toward the grocery store. He was driving way over the speed limit, and he prayed he wouldn't be stopped. He had to get to Drake as quickly as possible. "God, whatever trouble Drake's in, however hurt he may be right now, I thank You that You will protect him and keep him safe from all harm." He curled his fingers around his trembling chin and breathed deeply. "Let him still be there when I arrive."

Andrew swerved in front of the grocery store, applied his brakes, and surveyed the front of the building for any payphones. He saw one, but it was currently being used and Drake was nowhere in sight. Knowing Drake probably hadn't used that one when he had been attacked, he drove around the backside of the building.

Andrew slammed on the brakes. "Oh, no," he said under his breath.

Underneath the dangling phone lay Drake's body in a heap. Unmoving.

Andrew left his keys in the ignition and wrestled out of his seatbelt. *I'm coming, Drake.* He jumped out of his car and rushed toward the pay phone.

"Not so fast," someone said, emerging from behind two large garbage bins waving a Glock 9mm in his hand. Six or seven others stood behind him like stone images.

Andrew lifted his hands in the midst of his confusion. *They must be the ones who jumped Drake,* he thought. He knew there were people around the other side of the building, but he wouldn't dare call out for help with a loaded gun pointed at him. "I don't need trouble," he managed to say calmly. "I just came to get him." He nodded toward Drake.

"Get up, Drake. The act's over," Ivan said, aiming his gun at Andrew's chest.

Andrew looked warily at Drake. "What is this?"

Drake stood up and brushed himself off. "A setup. Only this time it's turned around on you."

"Drake, I thought you were—"

A heavily tattooed man with a thick stick stepped behind Andrew and gave a solid blow to the back of his head.

Andrew's vision went black. He collapsed to the ground and heard a loud ringing in his ears just before he lost consciousness. It was all Drake could do to stop himself from rushing toward him.

"Load him up in the trunk and cover him with the blanket," Ivan ordered. "I'll meet you back at the hideout with his car. Oh, yeah. Nice work, Drake."

Wooziness. A throbbing pain. He couldn't move...wait, yes he could, but barely. Andrew raised an eyelid. A thousand thoughts flashed through his mind but not one of them made sense. Something rough was scratching against his wrists, keeping them locked in place behind him.

Then it hit him. *Drake.*

Andrew lifted his head weakly and discovered he was tied to a chair with his hands fastened behind him. The room was dark. Drake was sitting in a chair across from him. He struggled against the ropes tying his hands and said, "Drake, what is this?" His voice sounded as weak as he felt.

"Don't talk."

Then Andrew realized Drake was holding a gun. He held his breath and said slowly, "I thought you were hurt."

"Yeah, and I thought a lot of things about you, too," Drake said, his voice betraying his bottled rage.

"What is this all about?"

"Quit acting like you don't know!" Drake exploded.

"But I don't! You—" Andrew stopped, wincing at the sudden pain in his head. He wished his hands were free so he could make sure his head wasn't bleeding from the blow he had received earlier. "Drake, I don't know what's going on, whether you believe that or not. All I know is that I got a phone call from you saying you were hurt, and then I come to find you had arranged some kind of ambush. Why, Drake?"

"Better your tail than mine."

"What?"

"Just shut up, OK!"

Andrew squirmed in his rickety chair. "Do you have to point that gun at me? It's not like I'm going to try to hop my way out of here on this chair."

Drake looked at Andrew, noticing for the first time the tiny beads of sweat that formed in the deep lines of his face. He bit his lip and set the semiautomatic high on the shelf beside him.

Andrew seemed to relax a little. "Thanks, though I suppose I really shouldn't be thanking you for much of anything right now."

"I plan to keep it that way."

"Mind telling me who tied me up like this?"

"I did."

Andrew let his head fall back. "Yeah, I might have expected it from you," he murmured.

Drake raised his hand to him and shouted, "I told you to shut your mouth!"

"Who do you think you are talking to me like this?" Andrew yelled back, strengthening what little energy he had left in him. "I welcome you into my home and—"

"Don't start giving me that. You never cared about anyone but yourself. I shoulda known you were up to something all along."

"Drake, I honestly have no idea what you're talking—"

"Just stop, OK? Just stop the stupid game!"

"I can't help it if you don't believe—"

"Quit playing the innocent victim and own up to what you did! You brought this on yourself."

Andrew suppressed his anger and said calmly, "Can I at least finish my sentences?"

Drake huffed and looked away.

Andrew peered around the small room, realizing that pursuing his viewpoint on this issue would never amount to anything but more shouting. Instead, he said simply, "Where are the others?"

"The others?"

"Look, I may be nothing more than an old man to you, but I'm not blind. I saw the others before I was knocked out."

"They're in the other room."

Andrew relaxed in his chair and swallowed. "Plotting my murder, I suppose. Why aren't you in there helping them? You've pretty much done everything else there is to do against me."

"I wouldn't be making jokes if I was you," Drake warned. "Remarks like that could get you killed around here."

Andrew sighed and studied the room again. "Where exactly *am* I?"

Drake squinted at him. "You think I'd tell you that?"

"OK, then. *Why* am I here?"

The door opened. Ivan poked his head inside and nodded toward Drake. "The boys and I need to talk to you."

Drake looked at Andrew, then back at Ivan. "You want me to leave him here alone?"

"I doubt I'm going anywhere," Andrew said.

Drake left Andrew and locked the door on his way out.

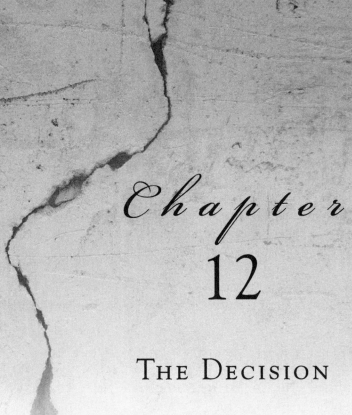

Chapter 12

THE DECISION

Ivan had the contents of Andrew's wallet spread out on a small table. All the men were gathered around it as Drake entered the room.

"How much cash he have on him?" Drake said.

"Not enough." Ivan replied. "And he must be anti-credit cards, 'cause he ain't carrying any."

"Nothing at all?"

"Isn't that what I just said?"

Drake took the clue and shut up.

"All I found were a bunch of dumb pictures, a gas card, and..." Ivan glared at Drake. "A gun permit. Little detail you forgot to mention to us."

The stares from all the men felt like heat to Drake's body. "How could I have known he—"

"Don't let it happen again, Drake. Lucky for you, he wasn't armed tonight. Otherwise, you would have taken the bullet."

Drake looked at the floor. *It feels like I've already taken a bullet.*

Ivan smiled and said, "But that doesn't really matter, considering what I have planned. I need you to do one more thing for me, Drake."

Drake knew the look on his face was one of shock, but this time, he didn't try to hide it. "I thought you said that that was it," he said, his voice on edge. "I already did my part of the deal, Ivan. You got your money."

"Two hundred and somethin' odd dollars ain't enough," Ivan said, matching his stare.

"I can't control how much he decides to carry. Tough luck."

Ivan's eyes turned evil. "You're forgetting your place, Drake. I don't like people who step out of line. Or haven't I made that clear enough?"

The others crowded around closer. Behind him, a man with a stained, white tank top stepped up and wrapped his bulging arm around Drake's neck with lightning speed.

Drake inhaled and gripped the man's arm. It felt like steel.

Lomas, the one Drake had met earlier at the door, stepped out from among the others and stood before Drake. Without warning, he gave a martial arts-style kick to Drake's midsection.

Drake clamped his mouth shut as burning waves of pain coursed through his body. No sound of broken bones, but his stomach would almost certainly go into permanent shutdown after that ruthless blow. But he wouldn't scream. No way was he going to give Ivan the satisfaction of hearing him in pain.

Another kick. Same place. Worse pain.

It felt like his internal organs were exploding.

Drake clawed and kicked in a desperate attempt to break free from the man's unyielding grip around his neck, but his efforts were useless. For a fleeting moment during his turning and bucking, he thought he saw Ivan's derisive grin. *You snake.*

More pain was inflicted—this blow landed severely close to his ribs. His abdomen throbbed in incessant agony. He tried to move, to escape somehow, but his body felt feeble and numb, and the biting sting inside him remained a lingering sensation. He clenched his teeth and closed his eyes, expecting another attack. Instead, the man behind him loosened his hold. Drake crumpled to the ground, heaving up blood and vomit all over the floor. He wiped his mouth with his sleeve, nearly throwing up again at the bitter stench the vomit left on his clothing.

A hand clamped onto Drake's shoulder and squeezed hard enough to make Drake's pulse race. "You better do as Ivan tells you, boy, unless you want that mug of yours rearranged," Lomas warned.

Drake stopped breathing to keep from inhaling the man's putrid breath. It was then he realized what breed of humans he was dealing with. "Just tell me what you want me to do," he said weakly.

Andrew's eyes were fixed on the top shelf. Specifically on the gun. Drake had left it there without realizing, but it was too high for him to reach while strapped down to his chair. He struggled and tugged against his ropes, causing him to sweat more profusely. *God, get me out of here. You can't leave me here like this.* He closed his eyes and thought of Ronnie smiling up at him. He thought of his mother and what she would do if something awful happened to him.

Then he thought of Drake.

Oh, God, what's happened to Drake? I was so sure this was what You wanted. Was I wrong? Did I slip up somewhere? Was church the trigger to all his resentment and anger? God, You have to help him. Help me too. If I make even the slightest noise, they'll come charging through here and do who knows what. I have to reach that gun before Drake or one of the others comes back. Please help me. If I could just somehow get free...

Ivan laughed and broke a smile that sent shivers down Drake's spine. "I figured you would reconsider. Know where the bank's at?"

Drake nodded. Words didn't seem possible at the moment.

"Ever use one before?"

"No," Drake said, having trouble pronouncing a one-syllable word.

"Well, there's a first time for everything."

There sure is, Drake thought. *Like now.*

"I want you to drive to the bank I pointed out to you on the way back here."

Drake wanted to argue, but his bruised insides begged him to keep his trap shut. "How do you know that's the one he uses?"

"Says so on his ATM card," Ivan said, shoving Andrew's wallet into Drake's hand.

Drake swallowed and tried to force the lump down his throat.

"Take Andrew there and have him withdraw twenty grand."

Drake's mouth fell open. "Twenty?" he said, trying to catch his breath. "What if he don't have that much?"

"I'm goin' by what you told me, Drake," Ivan said, his voice thin and detached. "He's a rich man. Twenty thousand won't break him."

Drake's mind was spinning. "Why do I have to take him there? Can't you do it? I mean, you're the one who's pulled off an armed robbery before, not me."

Ivan stared at him dumbly. "Do I look stupid to you? There's cameras out there, genius. My face is already broadcasted all over the cops' wanted list, but not yours. 'Sides, you wouldn't back out on us now, would you? Not after you've already tasted a dose of our treatment."

Treatment. He had tasted it all right—blood, acid, and anything that happened to be in the middle of digestion when he had puked it up. Thanks, but no thanks. "I didn't say that," Drake mumbled, hating every minute he was forced to endure this humiliation.

"I thought not. Now remember, keep the Glock in your pocket at all times, even when you enter the bank. Trust me, the old man won't try anything if he's convinced you'll really use it."

"But I won't have to use it, right?" Drake said it as more of a statement than a question.

Ivan chuckled and said coldly, "Wouldn't you?"

Drake took a step back and collapsed in a chair. "The way you say it makes it sound so evil."

"That's my language."

"I don't wanna kill him."

"Aw, the murderer has a heart. You'll get over it."

Get over it? He couldn't get over an accidental murder. How could he possibly go through with intentionally firing a gun on someone like Andrew? He pressed his hands against the sides of his head. "This is crazy. What if we get caught, Ivan? What if it doesn't work? This plan isn't foolproof, ya know. If something goes wrong—"

"Nothing will go wrong, will it?"

Drake didn't know why everything had to be a question with Ivan. Ivan felt safe—and for a good reason. He wasn't the one about to risk his neck. What kind of a deal was that?

"You'd be safer if you crouched down in the backseat most of the ride. Can't twist the gun out of your hand that way while he's driving. Just have your gun on him at all times and he won't budge."

No, duh. Give yourself a pat on the back, Ivan. Really had to brainstorm that one, didn't you? Drake could feel the anger heating up inside him. "And after that?"

"Make him get the money and slide over to the passenger seat, then you take the wheel. Drive him a good distance away from any pay phones or stores...a nice quiet area. Then drop him off."

Drake wasn't about to ask what "drop him off" really meant in Ivan's so-called language. He knew the man standing before him was the type who would put someone to death without the slightest hesitation.

"Is that clear?" Ivan pressed.

Drake looked up. "Sounds like you've got everything figured out, huh? Completely foolproof. At least, from your standpoint it is."

Ivan smiled thinly. "It's only what you make it, Drake. Do it right, and you won't ever have to worry about those cops following you again."

It was three thirty-nine P.M. when Drake led Andrew outside blind-folded. Because he followed the path Ivan had instructed him to take to the car, they were seen by no one. Even the buildings they walked between had no windows facing their direction. Drake didn't know why that really mattered, though. He assumed that most of the people living here were probably tied in with Ivan and his gang in some way, so it wasn't as if they would report any suspicious activity to the police.

Still, Ivan had planned their exit strategically so there would be no problems.

The temperature steadily plunged as the wind picked up speed and the clouds formed into one large, saturated mass of gray across the sky. An occasional raindrop hit Drake on the nose or cheek, sending a rushing chill through his body. It felt more like fall instead of summer. He listened as chimes played an unbroken melody across the street and shot a glimpse at a white-breasted nuthatch scurrying vertically up a black walnut tree. So much excitement, so little time. He cleared his mind and focused only on Ivan's instructions: Get to the car, get the money, get out, and...well, the last part he could figure out later.

The wind broke out into a gust, rocking the trees and sending a whooshing sound through the leaves. Andrew stopped and tilted his head up, as if wishing to see.

"It's just the wind," Drake told him. "Keep moving."

Andrew walked stiffly beside Drake, keeping a tight clutch on his arm to guide his steps. Once Drake reached the road where Andrew's car was parked, he helped Andrew lie down in the backseat. He gripped the semiautomatic with a shaky hand, aware that he didn't need it, but it made him feel safer nevertheless.

"Where are we going?" Andrew said, his throat tight and constricted.

"Tell you later, but don't worry. You'll get to see again soon and even get a chance to drive. Just don't want you to see where you are right now."

Andrew thought of a thousand things he could try to do to get out of this, yet for some reason he resolved not to take any action. This wasn't just about him anymore. Something was drastically wrong with Drake. "Have you found what you're looking for, Drake?"

Drake took a quick glance toward the backseat before averting his eyes back to the road. "What's that supposed to mean?"

"I'm simply asking a question. You don't have to answer if you don't want to."

Four miles down the road, Drake found a secluded parking lot behind a convenience store and parked the car. "I'm happy here," he answered finally.

"Are you?"

Drake reached behind him and cut Andrew's hands free before untying the blindfold over his eyes. "Your turn to drive." He took the keys from the ignition and stepped out of the car before making Andrew climb to the front. Drake found a comfortable position on the floor and held his gun up just high enough to let Andrew know he was ready if he tried anything. Then he tossed him the keys. "Drive."

Andrew placed his shaky hands on the steering wheel. It was streaked with sweat. Hmm...so Drake was more afraid than he admitted.

"What are you waiting for? I said drive!"

Andrew tried to balance his thoughts. "Where am I going?"

"The bank," Drake said, feeling the car slowly lurch forward as Andrew pulled out onto the road. He had never remembered feeling more nervous in all his life.

"The bank," Andrew repeated to himself. "You don't have to explain the rest. I think I know."

"Ivan told me to tell you to take out twenty thousand and put the money in the bag beside you."

"Old Western style, huh?"

Drake rolled his eyes. "You should know with all those old black-and-white movies you call thrilling."

"Touché."

Drake stared at the side of Andrew's face. "Why are you even talking to me?"

"Well, despite your being armed to the teeth, I don't feel scared of you in the slightest. Therefore, I talk."

Drake glanced at the 9mm. "One gun doesn't qualify for being armed to the teeth."

Andrew shrugged. "One's enough for me."

"You sure are making light of your situation."

Andrew pursed his lips. "What else am I supposed to do? Get angry and hold an innocent person at gunpoint?"

Drake started to say something, but closed his mouth instead. *Touché.*

Andrew arrived at the bank in less than five minutes, but instead of pulling up near the entrance, he drove a little further and parked in a separate parking lot.

Drake sat up higher and lifted his gun. "Hello? You know the orders. The bank closes in less than an hour, so we don't have much time."

Andrew checked the time. "We got fifty-two minutes."

"Don't try me."

Andrew stared at the gun and smiled slightly. "Why did you bring that?"

"Safety. Now let's get going."

"So you'd be willing to shoot me if I refused?"

"Just get the money and no one gets hurt." That was strange. For a second there, Drake thought his voice sounded almost identical to Ivan's.

"You're wrong, Drake. I'd be hurting you if I did what you told me."

Drake called him a foul name and swore. "Look, don't press your luck. I know you don't think I'd use this thing."

"Would you?"

"In a heartbeat."

"Then do it," Andrew said, unblinking. "There's no one here to stop you. No one watching."

Drake didn't know what to make of this man. He gripped his gun firmly and stared directly into Andrew's eyes.

"You won't, will you?" Andrew said after a long moment of silence between them.

"Not until I have what I came to get. I can't afford getting rid of you yet."

"It's all about the money, isn't it?"

"Yup."

"And you expect to get a cut of this money?"

"That's what they told me," Drake responded, his face as solid as stone.

"And you believe them?"

"I trust them."

"Trust them? You just met them today."

"I trust them with my life. That's more than I can say of most people. Namely, you."

Andrew drew out a long breath. "Would it be too much if I asked again for an explanation to all this? Am I missing something? I looked for you for hours upon hours yesterday. Then, out of the blue, I get this call from you saying to come down here because you were hurt. Where has all this anger and hatred toward me suddenly come from?"

"I know what you're trying to do," Drake said with a smirk. "You're trying to buy time, but it's not gonna work. Get the money now, or else."

"Or else what?"

"I told you what this gun is for."

"And I already told you, Drake. I'm not giving you the money." Andrew swept the bag beside him to the ground with his hand as a way of showing him that his decision was final. "So I guess that leaves you with a decision, doesn't it?"

Drake's blood was boiling now. How would he explain losing the money to the others and still expect them to hide him? "Are you mad? Don't think I won't shoot you."

"Sorry, but that's exactly what I think."

"Then you're signing your own death sentence."

"And you're gonna sit there and pretend like you're not signing yours?"

"I'm not signing away anything."

"You signed me and Ronnie away. And for what? To live like this? To shove other people around in the daytime and hide like scared animals at night? Because that's what you're joining, I hope you know. A pack of wolves that eventually gets so starved they rip at each other's throats."

"And what were you supposed to be? Anything different?"

Andrew shook his head. "If you can't see the difference...I don't know what got into your head, Drake, but I'm still willing to offer you my help if you're willing to accept it. You ought to know that by now."

Drake stared at him for the longest time, clenching his gun securely with one finger curled back on the trigger. *What're you doin', Drake? Have you become nothing more than a murderer now every time you run into a problem? He may have set you up, but you don't have to kill him.* He gritted his teeth and thrust the gun away furiously. "Just leave me alone," he said, turning away.

"Drake, what's wrong?"

"I said leave me alone! Go! Do anything! Just get outta here before I change my mind." Drake covered his face in his hands, struggling to hold back tears. What a lowlife he had become. Had he stooped so low that he would be willing to kill someone just because he was afraid of getting caught? Andrew may have betrayed him, but he had to remind himself that he deserved it. He had killed his father, and now he felt like a caged lion lashing out at anyone and everyone who threatened his freedom.

"What are you going to do?" Andrew said gently. "Just stay here like this until they come find you?"

"What does it matter?!" Drake screamed, picking up the gun again. He turned it on himself and pressed it against his heart. "My life is over! I'm tired of fighting it!"

Andrew unbuckled and crawled between the front seats into the backseat beside Drake. He laid a hand softly on his back. "Your life is far from over. Don't fight yourself like this."

"I told you to leave!" Drake fumed through clenched teeth. "I don't want to live anymore."

Andrew pried one of Drake's hands open and put something hard inside.

Drake looked down and blinked twice. "A magazine?" He stared down at the gun he was holding and realized it wasn't even loaded. "But it wasn't like this when they gave it to me," he said in amazement.

"I know. I unloaded it while you and the others were in the other room."

Drake gawked at him. "You? But how did you—"

"Let's just say you didn't learn how to tie knots from Boy Scouts. I was able to untie myself and reach your gun in less than a minute's time. I tied myself back up before you came back."

Drake stared blankly out the window. "You could have killed me when I walked back in the room. Why didn't you?"

Andrew gazed out the window with him, finding a world almost as dark and lonely as the one inside the car. "Because this was more important to me. Talking to you so we could work out what's wrong."

Drake looked at him in disbelief. He had pointed a gun at the man who could have easily pointed the same gun at him only minutes earlier. "Why are you doing this to me?"

"Because I care. And I believe in you."

"Stop it! Your words don't mean nothin' to me. Don't think I don't know what you're up to. I heard you talking to the cops, and that's why I took off. Well, you can't have me, you hear? I'm not goin' back with you, even if it means loading up this gun again and killing myself!"

Now Andrew was thoroughly perplexed. "What? Is that what this is all about? You thought I was talking to the police about *you*?"

"Who else?" Drake retorted.

Andrew shook his head. "Drake, the police called to tell me they found the man who's been going around at night beating up people's mailboxes—mainly, my mom's. It had nothing to do with you. Why would you even think such a thing?"

185

Drake felt blood rush to his face. "Oh. Well, I just...I don't know. I guess I figured you got suspicious of me or somethin' and called the cops," he said, not even making sense to himself.

"It had nothing to do with you. I reported the mailbox-smasher to the police after Mom told me about her busted-up mailbox, and I made them promise to call me back as soon as they heard anything. The police traced the license plate number and apprehended him yesterday. That's why they called."

And that's where the baseball bat comes in, Drake thought. *To smash the mailboxes.* The pieces were finally beginning to come together now. "I thought you were telling them about me," he said, still reeling from the news.

"Why would I tell them about you, Drake? I've never suspected you of a single thing."

Drake turned back to the window, feeling like the biggest idiot alive. Andrew had explained his side of the story, but Drake's side—that is, what he had told Andrew—didn't add up at all. Andrew had never once suspected him of anything, yet that was the only excuse Drake could give. *What a loser. What a self-centered, shallow guy I've turned out to be. I've been so worried about myself and so focused on my own fears that I've ignored their concern. What was I thinking getting myself mixed up with Ivan and his gang? All along, I was safe at Andrew's home, but tonight I put both my life and his in danger.*

And in his pathetic attempt to keep away from the cops, he had just given Andrew a reason to take him straight to them. He tore his mind away from his endless stream of stress and turned to Andrew. "So, what are you going to do to me now? Turn me in?"

"For what?"

"For attempted robbery while armed," Drake said dejectedly.

Andrew climbed up to the front seat and started the car. "You didn't rob me, and I can't honestly say you were armed. That would suggest the gun was loaded, and it wasn't."

Drake couldn't understand this guy. He thought he had Andrew all figured out, but the man never ceased to amaze him. What Andrew saw worthwhile in him was a mystery even to Drake.

Andrew pulled into his mother's driveway, thoroughly exhausted. He glanced in the rearview mirror and felt the weight of the day settling in. "You coming inside?"

"No thanks," Drake mumbled, sitting slumped in the backseat. Those were the first words he had spoken to Andrew since they had pulled out of the bank parking lot. He felt ashamed and still slightly confused, but his dignity refused to confess that he had been wrong. OK, so he had had a little misunderstanding about the whole phone call ordeal. So far, Andrew hadn't pressed him about it, so why should he feel so badly? What he did was just a natural reaction. Anyone with brains would have done the same thing.

The front door flung open suddenly and a small figure bounded down the porch steps and ran up to the car. "Drake!" Ronnie threw open the car door and jumped in beside him.

Just what I need to top off my day.

Kara embraced Andrew as soon as she rose from her chair to meet him. "Where have you been?" she said, trembling as she held him.

You wouldn't believe me if I told you, Andrew thought. Instead, he answered, "Everything's OK."

Kara took a step back and looked into her son's tired eyes. "I've been so worried about you. I tried calling you and calling you. How's Drake? Is he hurt?"

"He's fine, Mom, and so am I. Stop worrying about me so much."

"Where were you? What took you so long?"

"It just took a little longer than I expected, but Drake's all right. It was all a mistake. Drake was fine. He just needed a ride back home."

"But you said he called you and told you he was badly hurt. Andrew, you're not making sense."

Andrew breathed deeply. Obviously, it didn't make sense. All he wanted to do was go home and put this day to rest; instead, he felt like a piece of barbeque chicken being grilled on both sides. "I know, I know. I said a lot of things, but come to find out, he was never in any danger after all. It was just a misinterpretation of a phone call." Here he was, covering for the young man who had just lied to him over the phone and had the intent of taking a large sum of money from him.

Yet somehow, he knew what he was doing was right. Andrew had to admit he had considered driving Drake straight to the police and turning him in. His actions needed to be punished. Andrew knew what sin could lead to in Drake's life, and he wanted to break it before it had the chance to grow in his heart.

But was it what God wanted him to do? That was the most important question that had no easy answer. For some bizarre, outlandish reason, Andrew couldn't seem to give up on Drake. And he had the feeling that Drake wanted—and needed—his support, too.

Kara seemed to relax only slightly at Andrew's response. "Well then, why didn't he come inside? I would have liked to meet him."

Andrew shot a glimpse through the screen door and saw Drake's unmoving silhouette in the backseat of his car. "Oh, I don't think he's up to it today. Maybe some other time." He continued to stare at Drake, scared of what the future held, but in spite of everything, still prepared to take the risk. It was hard to see at times, sometimes growing and sometimes fading, but there was something worth believing in that kid. He just had to find it.

"Would you like some hot chocolate, Andrew? Coffee?"

Andrew smiled. "Could I get it to go? Coffee with two spoonfuls of sugar and a little of that Italian Sweet Crème you got me addicted to."

"I'd give you just the coffee grounds to drink if I thought it would wipe that tired look off your face."

"You just mix it up, and I'll drink it." Andrew watched her walk off into the kitchen. What a crazy day. What a crazy life.

"Uncle Andy told me you were in trouble," Ronnie said, out of breath. "Are you OK?"

Drake pretended to be interested in something out the window and tried not to look at Ronnie. "Sure."

"What happened?"

"More than I could tell." Drake eventually peered past Ronnie and saw Andrew hugging his mother through the open door. "You've got a great uncle, you know that?"

Ronnie grinned proudly. "Yeah."

Chapter

13

"YOU'RE TRASH..."

The atmosphere was tense when Drake was back in Andrew's house again, even with Ronnie in his room upstairs. For once, he could hear the clock on the mantle ticking. The floor creaked a little as he stepped across the room. If it was up to him, he would just go to bed now and call it a night. But Andrew said he was coming back down to talk.

Drake was ready to defend himself against any accusation Andrew might throw at him, but he was running out of excuses—and fast. How far would he go to avoid telling the only person who seemed to care about him that he was fleeing from a murder and needed help? He couldn't hold out like this much longer. His soul screamed to be freed from the weight that jerked and wrenched at his heart like venomous fangs; it was killing him slowly—death was always like that, never merciful. Dreams were cruel, a smile only sent a shock of pain, kind acts were twisted into bad motives...face it, the world just wasn't the same anymore.

What he said earlier was true. He wanted to die. He should have loaded the gun and got it over with when it was still in his hands. As much as he relied on his own strength and fast thinking, even he was smart enough to know that he couldn't get himself out of this pit on his own. His dad had warned him of this, repeating the wounding phrase over and over until Drake found himself saying it in his sleep. *You're trash, just like me. Everyone knows it, so you might as well get used to the idea while you're young, OK?* Bad thing was, he was starting to believe it.

Andrew walked in from behind him. He moved over to a lamp and clicked it on before sinking into his favorite chair. He allowed a few seconds of silence before he began. "Drake, I don't know how to say this..."

"Spare me. I already know what you're going to say. I'll have my bags packed in ten minutes."

"That wasn't what I was going to say."

"Fine, then I'll leave now."

"Sit down, Drake."

Drake sat, combating every emotion he felt that told him to run away as far as he could and never look back. However, after all Andrew had suffered from him, he at least deserved to be heard out.

"I still feel like there's more you're not telling me," Andrew said, studying Drake's facial expression closely as he spoke.

Drake slumped in his seat, wishing he could sink to the floor and ooze through the hardwood. His internal organs still felt like jelly after the brutality they had suffered by Ivan's hired ninja, so that idea might not be too far-fetched. "What else am I supposed to say? I'm sorry. I just acted on impulse and it was a stupid decision. I know that now, and it'll never happen again." He snorted and added, "'Course, I don't blame you if you don't believe me. It's hard for me to even trust myself anymore."

"I'm not talking about what happened today," Andrew said. "I noticed a change in you long before this ever took place. You've been bothered by something. I can tell by the way you've lashed out at people here lately. It's like you're always nervous about something, but I can't put my finger on what the problem is. Every time the phone rings, you jerk your head in its direction. At meals, you act like you're sick and stare down at your food. What's up, Drake? You can tell me."

"No, I can't."

"Why?"

"Because you wouldn't understand."

"Don't give me that. Families tell each other things."

"I'm not family."

"Ronnie and I consider you our family."

"Well, I hate families. If there's anyone that's gonna look out for me in this world, it's me," Drake said, jabbing a finger in his chest.

"Drake, I don't mean to pry, but—"

"Then don't."

"I deserve answers, Drake. Since this morning, I've been knocked out, tied up, held at gunpoint, and now you're giving a big spiel about all the things you hate while you choose to keep all the things that really matter locked inside. What are you holding onto? Can't you just trust me?"

Drake nervously ran a hand through his hair and glanced at the clock. It was late. He needed sleep, though he despised the very word. "Not now."

"What do you mean 'not now'? Then when, Drake? When another incident like this one takes place? I'm sorry, but I'm not taking that risk."

"It's nothing against you or Ronnie. Gah, can't you understand that? I got something I have to deal with myself. Nothing of it's related to you. It's all me, and I don't want to talk about it."

"That's why I'm here. To help."

Drake stood and paced to the other end of the room. "You can't help me outta this one. Anyway, what would you know about problems? You're living in a big house with a nephew who loves you to death. What have you ever had to deal with? Your life is perfect. Mine just stinks."

"A house and a lot of expensive things don't make a person. I've had my share of trials and fears and doubts, believe me."

"Whatever," Drake muttered.

Andrew rose from his chair but restrained himself from walking over to Drake. "Let's not go through another conversation arguing about the same old stuff again. It's time to talk this thing out once and for all and get everything out in the open."

Drake shook his head and ran up the steps briskly. He slammed his bedroom door shut behind him.

Andrew sighed and looked up at the ceiling. *Help him, God. Right now, he seems so far away.*

No matter how much he tossed and turned and fluffed his pillow, Drake found it impossible to stay asleep for more than thirty minutes at a time. And when morning finally came, after what seemed like a lifetime, he refused to get up. Even after the clock struck twelve, he was still lying there with his eyes focused above, trying to see what figures he could create by connecting the tiny, white dots on the ceiling.

I must be going crazy, he thought. *I feel so numb and detached from life that it's affecting every part of my body, especially my state of mind. I know I was never much to begin with, but I had hoped for a better life than this. I was going to make something of myself, but I threw away every chance of that happening when I let anger take over my better judgment. I've been telling myself ever since that day that the whole thing was an accident, but was it really? Didn't I go into that house from the very beginning with every intention of killing him? I know I told him that's what I was going to do, but it never really registered in my mind until after it happened. None of it had been an accident, had it? Hadn't I realized how hard I planned to strike him before I did it? Hadn't I seen the hearth behind him and known in the back of my mind that he would hit it?*

It hurt to think about it. That part of his life felt so far away now. He wasn't sure of all the details behind his father's murder, but one thing he was certain of: He had killed him, and that's all the police needed to put him behind bars.

What does it really matter anyway? Why do I care if I killed him on purpose or on accident? I can't change what happened, and even if I could, I'm not sure I would. All I know is that I'm getting what I deserve. I'm a murderer, and I'll live with that till the day I die, accident or no accident. I took another human's life and put another one's in danger yesterday. So what's next, Drake? Is there another victim in your path? Will it be Ronnie's life you put in danger next?

Drake heard the clang of utensils against plates and detected the aroma of fried chicken in the air, but food didn't appeal to him as it had before. How could he eat? After all he had been through yesterday, and then having to deal with the fact that he had been wrong all along, he felt wasted. All the events that had taken place yesterday seemed like a vague memory every time he thought about it. The meeting with Ivan, the walk to the hideout, and the conversation he had with Andrew in the lonely bank parking lot was almost hard for him to picture anymore.

Maybe it was just because he had seen so much junk in his life that nothing stuck out to him any longer. Just days ago, he had discovered that his mom had drowned, his dad had killed her, and then out of rage, he had killed his father. Now this. He had put an innocent man into the hands of thieves and murderers yesterday just so he could protect his selfish self. How could he ever face Andrew again?

Drake searched the drawers for a pen and paper. He realized he couldn't stay here any longer no matter what Andrew said, and he would tell Andrew that. Well, knowing the coward he was inside, he would most likely write a note and sneak out without ever having to speak to Andrew's face. Then what? Anywhere, he guessed. Or he might even turn himself in. At least that way he could finally get rid of this baggage.

He found a pen stuffed away in the back of the bottom drawer of the dresser, but there was no paper in sight. He caught a glimpse of the devotional books on top of his nightstand and decided to rip out one of the back pages that had no words on it. *Now, what to write?*

A light knock came at his door. Drake instantly jumped up from what he was doing as the door cracked open.

It was Andrew. He was holding a plate of food in one hand and a full glass of iced tea in the other. "Thought you might be hungry," he said, briefly scanning the room to see if Drake had packed up his duffel bag. "I let you miss breakfast because I heard you sleeping, but I didn't think you should miss lunch too."

"I'm not hungry," Drake said brusquely. Truth was, he actually wasn't. With all the sleep he had lost last night, the desire to eat must have vanished along with it. Even if he *were* hungry, he doubted he would've had an appetite with everything he had running through his mind.

Andrew's lips were tight and his eyes tired as he set the food down on the dresser beside him. He was trying so hard to develop a friendship between him and Drake, but every time he took a step closer and thought he was making progress, Drake put his foot down and seemed to fight back all the more. Calmly—mustering up all the coolness and composure he had left inside of him—Andrew said, "Well, just in case you get hungry later—"

"I won't."

"You're trash…"

Andrew bit the inside of his cheek. "You have to eat something."

"I have a lot more to worry about than filling my stomach right now."

"It's your decision if you choose to keep it inside, Drake. I can't make you want my help."

"I don't need your help."

"How do you know? We haven't had a friendly conversation ever since we got back yesterday."

"Gee, wonder why?" Drake said, not restraining any bit of his sarcasm.

"Then why are you mad at *me*? Just talk to me about whatever it is that's eating you up, and I'll help you."

"I said I don't need your help," Drake said, not knowing how he could possibly stress that statement more.

Andrew folded his arms, on the verge of letting his frustration loose. "So what are you gonna do? Sit up here and mope for the rest of your life? Refuse to eat? I don't know why I'm suddenly taking the blame for all that took place yesterday, but it's not fair to me to be treated this way, Drake."

"Oh, I know. It's my fault again just like everything else that goes wrong in my life."

"That's the problem! The biggest part of forgiveness is admitting that you're wrong and learning to drop the issue. Instead, you wanna keep bringing it up without ever telling me the real reason for your anger. You're angry with yourself, you're angry with the people around you…I don't want that life for you and neither does God. You'll never heal with that kind of attitude."

"I don't expect to heal. And I certainly don't expect church-lovers like you to make my life perfect. That's a joke."

"You hate church that badly, don't you?"

Drake saw his mom in his head, just as clear and unblemished this time as if deep creases had never scarred the picture he carried of her. "No, I hate God." He sounded just like his dad when he said that. "I hate the kind of life He dumped on me. I hate Him for coming into my family and ripping it apart. We were happy and normal before He ever came in."

Andrew listened quietly before saying, "Are you sure it's God you hate and not your real enemy? If a family is sick, Drake, whose fault is it? The doctor's or sickness's?"

"The doctor's, because a real doctor—if that's your way of talking about God—should never let them get sick in the first place."

"But the people still have to open their door to the Doctor. He won't force Himself in."

Drake gritted his teeth and felt a burning sensation flare up in his chest. "He sure forced Himself into mine. If there is a God, then I've got a lot of questions for Him, starting with this one, 'Why did You give me such a miserable life?' Where's that at in your Bible? Oh, yeah, I forgot. All you people care about is yourselves."

"Whoa. When did I ever say—?"

"Outside of your little circle, everyone else is just dirt to you. Filthy little sinners who are going straight to hell. I'm not good enough for Heaven, and I know it. I'm not exactly looking forward to hell either, but it's what I deserve and I'm not going to try to get myself out of it." He stopped and breathed deeply as Andrew stood there, watching him rant in his anger. "Just give me some time alone," he said quietly. "That's the best way you can help me right now."

"I don't know what I'm doing wrong, Mom," Andrew said over the phone that afternoon. "Nothing works anymore."

"I thought you told me everything was fine," Kara said, concerned.

Andrew straightened a few scattered items on his computer desk as he talked. "That was just because I didn't want to go into it all yesterday. Truth is, I don't know what to do anymore. I've never been a father before. I feel like I'm doing the best I can for Ronnie, but he's easy to get along with. A frustrated teenager who clams up at the slightest remark is an entirely different story. I mean, I thought I was doing the right thing at first, but I can tell his heart's far from this place."

"What about Ronnie? How is he handling this?"

Andrew opened a drawer and tossed a handful of pencils inside. "That's another thing I can't understand. Even though Drake's eighteen and Ronnie's seven, Ronnie seems to love the fact that there's someone a little closer to his age he can talk to. You outta hear the way he talks about Drake."

"Does Drake talk back, or does he ignore him?"

"Sometimes I think Ronnie gets on his nerves, but he's talked to him. In fact, Ronnie is the only reason Drake came to church."

"But now you're saying it's different?"

Andrew sat down slowly on the armrest of his chair and glanced at the picture of him and Ronnie on his desktop. It felt like he was looking at something that took place years ago, though it had only been days. "Very. Now he doesn't want to talk to anyone. He hasn't left his room all day, and when I came to get his plate, I found he hadn't even touched his food. Something's wrong, but I can't figure it out. It's like that call from the police just set him off, and now he won't listen to what I say anymore."

"Andrew, I admire you for what you've tried to do for Drake."

"But you think it's a bad idea?"

"I didn't say that. But what you need to realize is that before you can expect him to trust you, you have to show that you trust him first.

199

You have to remember, Andrew, that you don't know his background or where he came from. He may just have a lot of stuff in his past that he's ashamed of, so don't try to figure it all out at once."

"You mean I should *let* him keep it inside?"

"For now, yes. Otherwise, he'll feel like you suspect him if you try to pry too much. Once he feels like he can trust you, then either you can bring it up gradually or he may willingly come to you."

Andrew didn't know what to say. Show Drake that he trusted him? But he didn't trust him, did he? How could he ever trust someone like that again after what he had done? Drake had betrayed his confidence in *him*. He hadn't reported him to the police, but he could never find it in himself to completely put his faith in him again either. Hadn't that been enough trust shown on his part already?

"I don't know if I can do that, Mom. Like you said, I don't know anything about his past. How can you trust someone you hardly know anything about?"

Kara was silent for a moment before saying softly, "Why don't you try asking Ronnie?"

That statement stunned him. "Oh, come on, Mom. That's different and you know it. Ronnie's family. He already knew me before I took him in, and I knew him."

"If anyone had to learn how to trust again, it was Ronnie. He had been hurt too, Andrew, just as I'm sure Drake has had his share of hurts. He may not have the same story as Ronnie, but I know from what you've told me about him that he needs you just as much as Ronnie needs you."

"He sure has a strange way of showing it."

Kara laughed. "Raising kids is never easy, Andrew, but I have to say, if anyone could take care of Drake best, it's you."

Andrew tried to smile despite his fears. "Just pray for him, Mom. And me too."

"I will."

"No, I really mean it. I have a feeling he's in a major battle right now."

"With you?"

"No, with himself. That's the worst kind."

Drake had never been one to formulate words easily, so he gave up before he even got started with the note and packed his things instead. *I'll just wait till he's in the bathroom or something before I sneak out of here. Who cares if I give him an explanation or not? It's not like he won't know why I've left. That isn't too hard to figure out.*

Drake heard the enormous grandfather clock downstairs strike four o'clock. Where had the time gone? *If I'm gonna leave, I need to do it now.* He wasn't spending another night in a strange place without first scoping out the area—preferably one with no Ivans, drugs, or devious plans. With only five, maybe six more hours of daylight left, he knew he needed to leave now whether Andrew saw him or not.

That familiar feeling of doubt settled in his gut as he wriggled his shoes on and flung his dirty duffel bag over one shoulder. It was good-bye easy living and hello street life again for him. Only this time, he wasn't coming back. He would never make that mistake again.

Andrew hung up the phone just as Drake was descending the stairs. "Where are you going?" he said, eyeing the single bag Drake was carrying and noticing his shoes were on.

"Leaving."

"Leaving?"

Drake stopped and stood there. "Why are you lookin' at me like that? I thought you would've been expecting it."

"I had expected you to stay, not leave."

"Oh, well. You know now."

Andrew stepped in front of Drake just as he reached the bottom of the stairs. "No one wants you to go."

"I do."

Stubbornness isn't helping your case. "It's raining hard outside now, so—"

"I've walked in the rain before. I'll get used to it."

"Well, I won't, so you're staying here until it passes, understand?" Andrew said edgily, wishing that every time he and Drake spoke it wouldn't end up in a fight.

"You can't stop me."

"We'll be eating supper soon and you're welcome to a meal. After that, you can do whatever you like."

Drake sighed loudly and threw his duffel bag in a chair. "Fine." He was actually glad Andrew had mentioned food, because by now he was starving. Plus, this may be the last decent meal he tasted in a long time, if ever again.

Ivan remembered details. People were only pawns for getting the information he wanted, and Drake had been the perfect candidate because he was desperate. Their conversation had all been an act on Ivan's part, a manipulation of words that was meant for his own gain. Using Drake was supposed to be easy, just another game of chess where he picked apart his opponents until they were forced to either forfeit or face the penalty—never a pretty sight from six feet under. The setup and kidnapping were flawless, and while the wallet contained little, Ivan's plan promised cash. Everything was going smoothly until...

Ivan cursed. He knew he shouldn't have trusted Drake. He could practically feel the money leaving his hands every time he imagined Drake conning him at his own game. Andrew Tavner may have slipped from his grasp once, but Ivan had a way of getting what he wanted, due to a little more information Drake had spilled without realizing its far-reaching consequences. But Ivan remembered. Oh, yes. He remembered well.

"Was that the house?" Lomas said, turning in his seat to check the address on the mailbox they had just passed.

"Missed it," Ivan said, abandoning his thoughts to muse over some other time. "I'll turn around." He slowly drove past the mailbox again.

"That's the one," Lomas said, unable to break his gaze from the antique white, Victorian-style home trimmed in chocolate brown and accented by a winding stone walkway. "Just look at that house. I'll bet the inside's filled with all sorts of expensive stuff."

Ivan ignored his drooling. "Lots of windows means most likely all alarm-protected. That goes for the doors as well."

Lomas tossed his cigarette out the window and faced Ivan. "Whadaya think? We never tried breakin' into a house this big before. Could be more of a gamble than it's worth."

"Nothing's worth more than the money," Ivan snarled. "Drake has a debt he owes us for standing us up." He surveyed the area for any busybody neighbors who might be lurking behind the protection of their curtains, watching them. "Coast appears clear, but I still don't want you actin' suspicious. We'll meet up behind the fence in his backyard. If we're gonna get in, it's gonna be through the back where there's nothin' but trees and thick brush. Is that clear?"

"Sure."

"Good. You go first. I'll park the car and meet you in ten minutes."

For once, supper was dead silent. The only sound came from the occasional crackle of garlic bread; too bad spaghetti noodles could be eaten noiselessly. Andrew could feel his body tensing up as he shot another glance at Drake, who stirred his food as if he were prepared to do so until he made pudding out of it.

"What's wrong with everybody?" Ronnie finally said, looking at them both.

Andrew glanced up and caught Drake staring back at him. "Do you want to tell him, or would you rather I told him?"

"Might as well get it over with now," Drake said jadedly, slapping his fork down with a clang. "I'm leaving, Ronnie."

Ronnie furrowed his eyebrows. "What? But you can't—"

"I'm not staying here anymore. My mind's made up."

Ronnie's eyes fell to the table. "So you don't like us anymore?"

"Nothing personal. I just think it's time I move on."

Ronnie bit his lip as his eyes blurred over with tears.

Oh, no. Not the tears, Drake thought.

Andrew reached over and rested a hand on Ronnie's arm. "Ronnie, don't get upset. It's Drake's decision."

Ronnie furiously shoved his chair away and darted from the room, blubbering words no one could understand. Drake heard the back door dramatically fling open, then bang shut. *Knew I should have left a note.*

His appetite now completely lost, Andrew stood to go after him.

"Wait," Drake said. "I caused this. I'll go find him." He wandered through the living room, past the piano and all the beautiful things he knew he would soon miss, and opened the back door slowly. "Ronnie, c'mon, man. Don't do this." As tough as he was trying to be, it hurt him deeply to see the kid cry, especially after knowing he was the one who had caused it. "Ronnie?" he said louder. He shook his head and stepped out onto the porch.

"Help!" someone shrieked.

Drake searched the yard but didn't see anyone. *That sounded like...*a stick snapped. He jerked his head in the direction of the noise.

In a flash, Drake saw Ivan clamp a hand over Ronnie's mouth just before he shot out of sight.

Chapter

14

KIDNAPPED!

Drake Pearson rushed through the door, nearly knocking Andrew over. "Ronnie's been kidnapped!" he blurted, out of breath.

Andrew's face turned ashen. "What?!"

"No time to explain!" Drake pushed past him and took the stairs two at a time.

Andrew wanted to follow him, but ran outside instead and searched the streets. There wasn't a single car on the road. *No, God,* he pleaded, his knees threatening to buckle underneath him. *God, not Ronnie. Anyone but him.*

Drake yanked open Andrew's dresser drawers and hysterically searched for his car keys. Stamps, no. Envelopes, no, not there either. Good grief, what was this, the post office? *Hurry up! Hurry up!* He heard Andrew sprinting up the stairs and yelling, "Who are they, Drake? Where are they taking Ronnie?"

Drake ignored him and tried another drawer. *Bingo.* He snatched up the keys in a numb fist and turned to leave.

Andrew appeared in the doorway like a pale phantom, eyes wide and frenzied with panic. "Tell me, Drake!" he demanded. "Tell me where they've taken him!"

Drake wanted to scream. His mind was playing games with him again, confronting him with an evil he wasn't ready to face. He knew he was to blame for this disaster; was his mind resolute on beating him down with that truth until he fell apart in self-destruction? A guy could only take so much pressure before—

"Drake!"

Drake shook in anger. He could kill Ivan for this. "Call 911 and tell 'em he's probably been taken to a shack behind some diner called Miller's!"

"Where's that?"

"I don't know! I didn't take notes about the place! That's all I remember!"

"Well, show me! Drive me there...do *something!*"

Reminded of every wasted second by the rapid pumping of his heartbeat, Drake rammed past Andrew. "I'm going to get him!"

Andrew spun. "Drake, you're not leaving without me!"

"I'm going alone!" Drake hollered back, racing down the stairs.

Andrew tried to catch up, but Drake was out the door before he reached the bottom stair. "Drake! Drake, do you hear me?!" he screamed.

An engine started. Andrew looked out the window just in time to see Drake peel out of the driveway and accelerate down the street. *Dear God...Don't let them hurt Ronnie.*

Drake was flying through the streets with the hazard lights on, trying desperately to remember exactly where it was he had been yesterday. He had taken so many side streets and cut through countless back yards that more than once he had to back up and retrace his steps. Some things looked familiar, but every time he thought he was on the right track, he came to an intersection, forcing him to rely on what little information he had stored in his memory. Everything had taken place in one huge blur yesterday as he ran down lonely alleys and sidewalks that he was surprised he could remember anything.

Drake could feel something stirring inside him, and even though he was angry and frustrated with himself, he found himself crying out to the only one who could help him now.

God.

"Oh, God..." he started, his bottom lip quivering with fear as he felt warm acid creeping up his throat. "God, if You're real...if You can even hear this...I promise I'll go back to church if You'll only protect Ronnie. I'll even get a Bible to read. I'll go to church every week and get my life right if You just promise me that You won't let them hurt Ronnie. I promise I'll change. Just give me another chance."

"Say something, you stupid brat! Where's Drake?" Ivan yelled, slapping Ronnie hard across the cheek for the fifth time.

By now, Ronnie was so much in tears that he could barely speak. "Please don't hit me again," he whined.

Ivan knelt down and shook Ronnie's shoulders brutally, clenching his teeth to keep from losing it. "Tell me now, or so help me..."

"I don't want you to hurt him!" Ronnie cried, releasing a new flood of tears. He lifted his head slightly, then cowered at the sight of Ivan's frozen glare. He reminded him too much of his father.

"Maybe he don't know where Drake is, Ivan," Jameson, one of the eight, said. "Drake obviously wouldn't still be livin' with 'em after what he done, so how could the kid know where he's at?"

"You got somethin' better in mind?" Ivan hissed. He raised a hand to slap Ronnie again.

"Leave 'em alone, Ivan!" Jameson said, pulling his arm down. "He's just a kid."

Ivan's body tensed. "Yeah, and I'm just a guy who lost out on a lot of dough, so *shut up!*"

A loud bang shook the door. Everyone snapped to attention.

Ivan secured a hand over Ronnie's mouth and slowly drew a finger across his neck to accentuate his warning. "Don't think I won't *kill* you," he mouthed, his lips curling at the word *kill*.

Ronnie swallowed and tried to keep from bursting out in tears again.

"Put the kid in the back room," Ivan whispered to Lomas. "I swear, if he makes the slightest peep, it'll be your life."

Lomas moved Ronnie into another room and closed the door.

Ivan pulled a handgun from his pocket and moved tentatively toward the door. "Whatdaya want?" he hollered.

"It's Drake! Open up!" Drake yelled back, banging more fiercely.

Ivan unlocked the door and flung it open. He met Drake with a crooked smile. "Decided to come back and fling yourself on our mercy? What happened? The old man get away from ya? Or was the money just too tempting to give up?"

Drake wasn't smiling. He matched Ivan's stare and stepped up close to him until they were nose to nose. "Where's Ronnie?" he said sternly.

Ivan casually leaned against the doorframe. "Who, the brat? Perfect timing. I was just askin' him about you, but now that you're here, you can join him." Ivan held his gun on Drake and turned serious. "Walk."

The sight of a gun was no scare to Drake anymore. He more than happily walked inside and made eye contact with every one of Ivan's low-quality friends as Ivan led him toward the back room where Ronnie was being held.

"Ronnie!" Drake exclaimed, running to him. "Ronnie, have they hurt you?"

Ronnie's face was pale as he stared helplessly up at Drake. "I'm OK," he said, his timid words barely discernable.

Drake caught sight of a thin trickle of blood at the corner of Ronnie's mouth and red marks on his cheeks, evidently due to slapping. He looked over his shoulder and glared at Ivan. "Is this your idea of payback, you animal? Does it make you feel like a big man when you hit a little kid?"

An indescribable fury rose in him. He didn't have a thought-out plan to go by or even a clue about how he would escape, especially now. All he knew was that Ronnie was in danger, and if he were there only to offer comfort until hopefully the police arrived, that was a good enough reason for him.

Ivan twisted Drake's arms behind him while one man—Drake guessed it was Lomas considering the size of those swollen pieces of flesh some might call hands—frisked him to ensure he was carrying no weapons. "Drive here?" Ivan said after the pat down was finished.

Oh, how he craved to kill this man. "You tryin' to be funny, Ivan? If I didn't have no money yesterday, I sure ain't got none now." He was glad he had thought to park several blocks away, just in case they decided to check.

"You woulda had wads of cash to buy whatever you liked if you'd followed through with our plans. Then again, maybe you did go through with it and kept all the cash for yourself. But surely you wouldn't have done that to us. Not your pals."

Drake continued staring and pressed his tongue against the roof of his mouth. Ivan thrived on information. This time he would retain his self-control and use his words only to twist Ivan's.

"What happened? Grandpa jump ya?" Everyone roared with laughter. Ivan just stood wearing a repulsive smirk.

Drake half-smiled. "Nah, I just realized what an idiot I must've been to ever trust dirty scum like you."

Ivan's smile quickly faded. "Just what *did* you hope to accomplish by comin' down here anyway?"

Drake glanced at Ronnie. "To get him. You don't want another kidnapping on your record, do ya, Ivan? Armed robbery is one thing, but no jury in their right mind ever goes soft on kidnapping a seven-year-old kid. And don't think they won't find you, either. You let us go, and nobody gets hurt."

Ivan gave a soft clap. "Oooh, big man. Just listen to him talk. Thinks he's got it all figured out."

Drake sensed his hands tightening into concrete fists, turning his knuckles white and not helping much with his self-control. Fear slinked to the background as guts rammed its way to the forefront, embedding in him a hatred for such a revolting evil. Ivan had no purpose in life other than to slither through the dust and search for new victims to wrap his alluring coils around. *But not Ronnie,* Drake thought. *I'll die before I see him hurt that kid.*

"Just get this through your skull, snake. You came to me once with the smooth talk and I bought into it, but I'm not going that route again."

"You came back. That only makes my plan all the more superior."

"You thought your first plan was secure and it crumbled. I don't see a lot of good plan-making on your part."

"You're wrong." Ivan's words felt like an icy sting to Drake's heart. "The difference is you won't be leaving my sight this time." He nodded his head sideways at Ronnie and told one of the men, "Tie him up with the kid. Make sure their backs are to each other so they don't try anything."

Drake's hands were fixed behind him with a grayish, abrasive rope before being tied to the one binding Ronnie. It scratched, it itched, it sawed against his flesh like fine razors, but he refused to acknowledge the pain just to keep from adding to Ivan's gratification. Then, if that weren't enough to hold them, a rope was wrapped around their waists several times to prevent them from moving. Drake could feel how cold and numb Ronnie's hands were as they trembled lightly against his. He could only imagine what kind of panic the kid must have gone through before he showed up.

Once Ivan was convinced that neither Drake nor Ronnie could escape, he turned off the light and left them tied in the dark room on the cold floor. There was a faint murmuring outside, then the heavy thud of a lock bolting in place. *Cla-clank.* The whispering stopped, the footsteps faded, and the regulated sound of breathing continued— somewhat. Drake's body warmed over with sweat. And so began a new nightmare.

Drake waited until he saw Ivan's shadow disappear from underneath the door before saying, "It's OK, buddy. Try not to worry, huh?"

"Why are they doing this, Drake? What do they want?"

Drake struggled against the tight ropes and discovered them to be sturdier than he had thought. "I dunno," he said. Another lie. How could he not know? He had no one to blame but himself. "But your uncle's calling the police right now," he added quickly, trying to offer some ounce of comfort to Ronnie. "I'll bet they're on their way already."

"I'm glad you came," Ronnie whispered back, trying to blink his tears away.

Drake couldn't believe the guilt piling up a mile high inside of him. He had never planned on Ronnie being involved in all this. If his life was screwed up, then that was his problem and his headache. Ronnie didn't deserve this. If he was destined to ruin, why couldn't he just go through his punishment alone like everyone else? *Because that's what selfish people do. If they're going to fall, they always make sure to take a crowd of people down with them.* Somehow, those people always turned out to be the ones who cared the most. That's what caused the real hurt.

After minutes of silence between them, broken only by an occasional deep breath or jeans brushing back and forth across the floor to regenerate blood flow, Drake managed to say, "You still mad at me? About wanting to leave, I mean?"

Ronnie squirmed a little. "Made me sad. I just wanted you to stay."

Drake couldn't understand what Ronnie saw in him that made him bond with him the way he had. Right now, Drake wanted nothing but to die. Well, not now. Not until Ronnie was safe first.

"Why did you wanna leave?"

"Because I've done a lot of bad things," Drake said, detested by the person he was forced to look at in the mirror of his conscience. He could only avoid it for so long before it came back to him in wave after wave, crashing into his heart and leaving a deeper slash every time it hit. Sure, maybe he wasn't serving time in prison or being punished by any federal court, but he was suffering. He knew what he had done, whether in light or in secret, and those memories could never be erased. Though he wasn't the worst person in the world, there were times he sure felt like it. He had carried enough for a lifetime, and now all he wanted to do was let go. Even the fighter in him got scared sometimes.

He felt himself letting go. The very flame that had remained ignited in his soul was now flickering weakly, fading gently. The smallest breath of air could blow it out now. But he wouldn't fight it. Why hold on to a life that was deteriorating? His soul wasn't at peace, and his mind was in a constant state of unrest. He had never been one to quit, but now he was relinquishing his very life. Abandoning everything he had lived for just to sleep in quiet blackness, never to wake again. *Why try if you're just going to fall down again? I'm through with fighting the world. The game's getting harder and I quit.*

Now, he sensed the burden to let it all out to someone before it formed into something worse, even if that person was a 7-year-old. "Ronnie, you're a great kid. I hope you know that. I know I've been mean and rude and selfish sometimes, but that's nothing against you."

"I know, Drake."

Drake felt more blood rushing to his red-hot face. "I just had to leave because every time I see you and your uncle, I'm reminded of what a jerk I am. Maybe choosing to leave is just another selfish decision... I dunno, but I can't take it anymore. I've lied more times than I can count, I've stolen before, I've tried alcohol and drugs, and I...I hurt someone really, really bad in a way you probably wouldn't even understand if I told you. You don't want me, Ronnie. I'm no good."

Ronnie thought about that for a while. "Uncle Andy told me once that in the Bible it says that no one is good. Not even one person, except Jesus."

Drake nodded weakly. "Won't argue with that."

"I've done bad things too. But when I ask Jesus to forgive me, I feel better again."

"Yeah, well, I can understand overlooking the small sins. You got nothing to be ashamed of, Ronnie. You just don't know the real me. My bad outweighs my good so much that if there was a God out there, there's no way He could ever forgive a past like mine."

The conversation ended there. Ronnie had no further words of encouragement to offer, and Drake wasn't willing to accept any. This was his life, and he knew every little dirty part about it. Ronnie was just trying to be nice, and he knew that. Part of him even wanted to believe what he had said, but Drake was too smart to know otherwise.

There was no hope for him; people had told him that. His own father had told him that. He had scoffed at them then, but now as his life was unfolding in a way he had never expected, his future looked just as they all had predicted long ago. Failure, job-seeker, theft just to get by, unstable husband and father, alcoholic, druggie—he had heard it all too many times to remember. Of course, it had hurt then, but it hurt even more now as he realized how true those statements were.

Ronnie believed in him, and that was at least encouraging, if not slightly amusing. But Drake didn't even believe in himself. Never would again. He had done plenty of bad things in his life, but being responsible for an innocent child's kidnapping beat all. He had simply gone too far this time.

The wind died down outside. For the first time, Drake overheard Ivan discussing with the others the idea of waiting until midnight before calling Andrew and demanding a high-priced ransom. "That way," Ivan told them, "it'll give him plenty of time to worry and stress. By the time our call comes, he'll be so desperate that he'll agree to anything we demand."

It turned Drake's stomach hearing them talk, mostly because he knew that ultimately he was to blame for all this. The only way they were able to come up with this plot was because he had ignorantly supplied all the information they needed to pull it off. He had given away Andrew's name, told them Andrew had a nephew living with him, and basically led them to Andrew's house without even realizing it. Why couldn't he have just clamped his mouth shut or at least lied to Ivan about Andrew's name? Because he always did stupid things without thinking, that's why. And where did it get him? Tied up in a dark room wondering what would happen next.

Drake observed the room around him. This was where he had sat only yesterday, holding a gun on Andrew. *Had that really been just yesterday?* The room was small and empty except for a built-in shelf on the wall and a couch that appeared to have been knifed several times from top to bottom. The air was filled with the smell of dust and old books—maybe blood, but nothing could be certain to a person sitting in pitch-black darkness with an over-alerted mind.

His eyes darted toward the sound of rustling in the corner. A small creature with a slithery tail scurried under the couch. Drake swallowed and inspected every square inch of floor that was visible to him, suddenly realizing how much he appreciated the light.

Drake had a watch on, but with his hands tied behind him, he would never really know when midnight came. *It must be getting close, though,* he thought as a soft, blue glow cast its light on the floor through a small window near the ceiling. He was grateful for the narrow strip of moonlight on the floor since he could now kick at any mouse that might happen to sneak up to them for warmth. *They'll be making the call soon. Man, I feel like such a fool. Making Andrew pay several grand when I should be the one they charge. How could I ever pay him back for something like that?*

Ronnie scooted his feet close to his body. "I'm scared, Drake. I think I saw something over there."

"We'll be all right, little man. I'll think of a way outta here."

"That man tied the knot right over my stomach. If I could reach it, I could untie it and get us both out."

"Don't beat yourself up about it."

"Are we gonna die?"

Drake stared straight ahead, finding it strange that tears were stinging his eyes. "No," he said solemnly. "I won't let them touch you, Ronnie. I swear." In a way, Drake felt like an older brother to Ronnie, and he assumed it his duty to protect him. *How ironic,* he thought. *I get him into this mess, and then I tell him I'm gonna protect him from something I created. Oh, well. As long as he buys it. I don't like seeing him afraid.*

Ronnie had been annoying at times, and often Drake had wanted to plug his ears and walk away. No, the kid didn't really talk that much. In fact, it was probably considerably less than a normal 7-year-old typically talked, and he knew why. His dad had made a habit of beating up on him, and being here in this place getting slapped around again was probably only rehashing old memories for Ronnie.

"Ronnie..." he started, his voice trailing off. *Just shut up. Don't try to get him to talk about it.*

"Yeah?" Ronnie said.

Drake could feel Ronnie's small shoulders nudge up against his as he strained to turn his head, trying to see behind him. "Do you like living with Andrew?"

"A lot."

Drake swallowed. This wasn't going to be easy. "I guess what I'm really trying to get at is...does it still hurt thinking about your folks?"

"You mean my parents?"

"Yeah, but...never mind. None of my business anyway. Sorry for bringing it up."

"No, it's OK. Sometimes it feels better to talk about it. When I don't, it makes my stomach hurt, and I sometimes get nightmares."

Drake grimaced. "That bad, huh?"

"I don't know why he did it. He got mad, and then he just started hitting me."

Drake closed his eyes. "Makes me mad just thinking about it. Did he hurt you like that a lot?"

"Slapping me wasn't the worst part. After he slapped me, he sometimes pushed me against the wall and grabbed my neck, like he wanted to kill me. He screamed and hit me a lot too, mostly in the stomach. Sometimes I threw up."

Drake held his breath and pushed the images out of his mind. How could Ronnie not hate a man like that? "Ronnie, I...I'm so sorry. I never knew."

"I still feel mad at him sometimes, but Andrew is real nice, and that makes me feel better."

Drake was hesitant at first to ask, but eventually forced himself to say, "Did Andrew tell you what happened yesterday?"

"Before he left me at Grandma's, he said something about you being in trouble."

"No, I mean after that," Drake pressed, fishing for more. "He didn't say anything else?"

"Nothing except that you were OK."

What had he done to deserve that kind of forgiveness? Nothing, that's what, and that's what was bothering him. He knew that if he were to place himself in Andrew's shoes and vice versa, there would have been no second chance. In fact, if he were to be completely honest with himself, there would have been no second *glance* that first day he showed up on Andrew's doorstep.

Now, he had forever ruined his chances of any further kindness because of another one of his stupid ideas. The good food, the warm bed, and even the grand piano was good while it had lasted, but he had always known in the back of his mind that it wouldn't last forever. Nothing good ever did for him, especially with the way he always seemed to mess things up. Everything always started off seeming like a good plan, but without fail, something went wrong and it ended in disaster.

Like the day he had murdered his dad. One decision had forever cost him, and being tied to a little kid only made him despise the person he had become even more. *Eighteen years old just a couple weeks ago. Happy birthday, Drake.* Instead of becoming a responsible adult, the only thing he had done successfully was screw up his life even more.

When I get outta here... He cut his thought short and refused to continue. The familiarity of those words stung. He had said them too many times before, and every time he had broken his own promises.

When he had smoked his first cigarette at age 9, he had told himself, "I promise I'll change." When he had taken his first shot of alcohol and experienced his first real hangover as a preteen, he had said, "I promise I'll change." After he had gotten a girl pregnant, only to find out later that it had ended in abortion, he had again said to himself, "I promise I'll change." He had made so many promises to himself that over time he just lost count.

Now recently, he even made a promise to God and included the words, "I promise I'll change." But they were just words filled with a lot of emotion that he never really meant in the first place. He knew that when he made one wrong decision, it was like a chain reaction for all the others following.

Andrew didn't know what he was getting into when he welcomed him into his home, and if there was a God somewhere, He must not have known what He was getting into either when He created him. Why would any loving God, as Ronnie depicted Him, ever create such a sinful person and then allow him to be shown a kindness he didn't even deserve? Everything that had happened to him from day one was just a mistake that a kindhearted old man had made, thinking he could somehow influence a homeless teen's messed-up life by showing love and providing a home.

Well, kind and thoughtful as it may have been, and even if Andrew were in some strange way still willing to give him another chance after this, Drake found it his responsibility to put a stop to it before the monster inside him got any worse. If not for himself, he would do it for Ronnie.

Chapter 15

CLOSING IN

"I can barely feel my legs anymore," Ronnie said, restlessly trying to find a comfortable position. "Wish I could walk around."

"Try stretching them," Drake suggested.

"I have, but they still feel tingly. And my feet hurt too."

"Can you kick off your shoes?"

Ronnie grunted as he pushed one shoe off, then the other. He sighed. "That feels better."

Drake decided to kick off his shoes, too, and was amazed at how good it felt to be able to wiggle his toes again.

"Now if we could just get this rope off like we got our shoes off," Ronnie said. "Too bad it's not that easy."

Drake looked at his shoes and remembered the money. *What am I doing?! I can't let them find that. It's all I have left.* He extended his legs and pulled his shoes close to him. He wriggled one foot in and felt a smooth object beneath the thin layer of padding in the heel of his shoe. He could hardly contain himself from gasping, "Ronnie!"

"What?"

"There's a pocketknife in my shoe! If I can reach it, I can cut us loose!"

"Really?"

"Yeah, but shhh." Quietly and cautiously, fearing now that at any moment Ivan or one of the others would unlock the door and burst into the room, Drake and Ronnie scooted around the shoe until it was at their fingertips. Drake leaned back slowly, blindly groping for the knife. The pressure caused the rope to creak and constrict tighter around Ronnie's waist.

"Have you reached it yet?" Ronnie panted.

Drake stretched down just a few more inches and wiggled his fingers underneath the padding. He touched the pocketknife and snatched it up. "Got it!" He traded it to his other hand and unfolded the blade. "Don't move your fingers, Ronnie. I don't want to cut you."

Ronnie just nodded and closed his eyes as Drake began sawing against the thick rope. Drake kept the blade close to his own hands facing his back so he wouldn't accidentally cut Ronnie if he happened to miss and slip. *Careful,* he told himself. Sweat rolled down his forehead and stung his eyes.

"Feel anything?"

"Not yet, buddy. Almost..." He sucked in another breath of cool air. His hands were shaking now and his heart pumping faster to supply the needed strength and adrenaline to his bloodstream. He should have cut through the rope by now. It had been too long. *Don't try to rush it. Just slow, easy motions. That's it.*

The rope slackened, then crumpled to the floor. That soft thump was the most wonderful sound in the world.

He had done it. It was only after he held his quivering hands in front of his face that he realized he had really freed himself. He was surprised, however, to see numerous slashes on his wrists seeping with fresh blood. Apparently, his hands had grown so numb that he hadn't felt the blade as it had sawed against his bare flesh. He was thankful his hands were still deadened; it would be best if the numbness were prolonged. He had more important things to worry about right now, like what their next step toward freedom was.

He turned and saw that Ronnie had already freed his hands and was working on untying the knot in front of him.

"Got it!" Ronnie said in a hushed voice.

Drake finished unraveling the rope and laid it silently on the floor. No noise, no mistakes, and still no Ivan. *So far, so good.* He slid the knife back into its hiding place and slipped his shoes on. "Now to find a way outta here," he whispered, searching the dark room uncertainly.

Ronnie investigated the walls until his eyes came to rest on the window. "What about there?"

Drake studied the window. Would he even be able to fit through something that small? Well, whether he would be able to or not was out of the question. Ronnie could squeeze through, and his safety was priority.

Drake went over to one end of the worn couch in the middle of the room and slowly picked up the side, gradually rotating it sideways as he took small steps toward the wall below the window.

"Need any help?" Ronnie said, watching from a distance.

Drake quietly set the couch down, and then moved over to the other end and repeated the same process. "There," he said, positioning the armrest directly underneath the window. He stepped onto the couch and bent over. "Here, hop on my back."

Ronnie mounted Drake's back about as gently as a rider mounts a bull in a rodeo. He wrapped his arms around his neck so forcefully that it endangered Drake's air supply.

"Maybe not so tight," Drake said in a strained voice.

Ronnie let up—which was realistically no more than an inch slack.

Unintentional payback. Drake ignored it and took shallow breaths instead.

"How am I doing?"

Like you're bracing for an earthquake. "You just tell me how close you are to the window."

"Right now, a long ways."

Splendid. That meant tackling the armrest. *Oh, man. Here goes nothing.* Carefully, Drake steadied one foot on the armrest, then quickly raised the other and balanced himself. He came close to falling forward, but he threw Ronnie's weight back just in time to keep him from tipping. *Easy,* he thought. *One wrong move and you'll fall, and then you'll have the entire gang in here in an instant.* He tried to look up, but was afraid that if he tilted his head back any further, he would throw himself off balance and fall backward. Instead, he asked Ronnie, "Now can you reach it?"

Ronnie stretched his hands up as high as he could and barely felt the latch on the bottom of the window. "Almost."

Double splendid. To come this far only to miss the perfect escape by a few inches. Drake wasn't about to let that happen.

"What are we gonna do?" Ronnie whispered.

"Shhh." What could he do other than put Ronnie on his shoulders? It was the only way to reach the window. Drake placed the palms of his hands against the frigid concrete wall in front of him and slightly bent his body forward. "Climb up on my shoulders," he said, taking another deep, labored breath. This kid was heavier than he looked.

Still keeping a steady hold around Drake's neck, Ronnie wriggled his legs up until they too clung around Drake's neck. "Sorry," he whispered.

Don't worry about me, Drake thought, while a rushing, erratic feeling of anxiety was charging like voltage through his body. *I just can't breathe, that's all.*

Once Ronnie was certain he was in a position where he wouldn't fall, he again reached up. This time, he was high enough to see out the window.

"Open the latch," Drake said, still unable to look up.

Ronnie worked at the latch until he finally got it unlocked. He quietly lifted the windowpane. "Now what?"

"Climb through!"

"I...I don't know. Besides, there's a funny looking box thing outside the window full of dirt."

"Just do it, Ronnie, and stop making excuses!"

"I can't! It's too far down."

"Just put one leg through the opening and leave the other inside!"

"Huh?"

"Like you're riding a horse, for goodness' sake!" Drake said tersely. "Once you're up there, I'll go back and grab the rope so I can lower you down."

Ronnie gulped and lifted one foot cautiously. "Well...I'll try." He pushed himself up through the opening and did just as Drake had instructed him. He kept his body flat against the concrete with the windowpane above him, one leg inside the room and the other dangling on the outside. "Hurry, Drake!" he whined. "I'm scared!"

As much as Drake wanted to jump off the couch and grab the rope, he reminded himself to stay quiet and keep his movements slow and silent. He picked up one end of the rope and triple-knotted it around his waist. Then he stepped onto the armrest of the couch and tied the other end firmly around Ronnie. "Now, I'm gonna go right over there and get the rope taut between us before you go climbing out the window. Ever seen someone repel on one of those animal rescue shows you watch?"

Ronnie shook his head.

"OK, well, lowering you down is fine too." He pointed his finger at Ronnie and said, "That is, as long as you don't squirm around too much. If you go kicking the building on your way down—"

"I won't."

Drake walked over to the other end of the room and gathered the rope in his hands until there was almost no slack left. "All right. You can do this, Ronnie."

"Drake, I'm scared. What if I fall?"

"You won't fall. I've got you, and I'll lower you down slowly."

"What'll I do when I reach the bottom?"

"Lay flat on the ground so no one sees you and wait for me."

Ronnie nodded his head, though not yet entirely convinced. He peered once more out the window into the darkness below him before clutching the rope securely in his hands. *OK,* he told himself. *Don't be afraid. Just do it.* He pulled his other leg through the window and let his body slide off the edge.

The rope jerked Drake forward as it became taut, triggering him to wrap his already-white fingers around the rope even tighter to keep from losing his hold. He was afraid Ronnie would scream or let out a cry, but to his surprise, Ronnie had left his perch in the window with ease. He kept a firm hold on the rope as he lowered Ronnie down to the ground inches at a time.

Then came a muted noise—a footstep maybe or a door closing. Drake stopped, his heart picking up speed. Every part of his body froze as footsteps shuffled by the door, then back again. He heard the muffled sound of the television and allowed himself to relax. *Just do what you gotta do and do it fast*, he thought. *You may not have much longer.*

A little faster now, Drake began lowering Ronnie again. *C'mon, Ronnie, you gotta be close to the ground by now. I ain't got much rope left.*

The rope suddenly went limp. A second later, Ronnie gave the rope two quick tugs.

He had made it down safely.

Leaving the rest of the rope on the ground, Drake climbed up on the armrest of the couch and stared up at the small window above him. *I have to fit. I'll make myself fit. I can't stay here and risk being killed.* He stretched his arms up, but the window was too far away to get his fingers through the opening. He stepped down on the floor, eyes still locked on the window. *Who am I kidding? There's no way I'll reach it. I'm stuck.* He leaned close to the window and whispered loudly, "Psst. Ronnie!"

"What?"

"Is there a tree or something sturdy nearby?" he said, a little louder now. With all the guys watching television in another room and raving loudly from too much beer, Drake was certain he wouldn't be heard.

"Uh...yeah, a big one right here."

"Good. Take your end of the rope and tie it around the trunk. Make sure to make at least three or four good knots in it."

"Gotcha!" Ronnie said, scurrying off.

I just hope the kid knows how to tie knots better than I do, Drake thought. Moments later, two more tugs came at the rope, along with the words, "I got it, Drake!"

Drake wasted no time and began scaling the wall—if he could even call it that. His feet kept slipping on the smooth concrete walls, and his hands burned as the course strands of rope grazed against his flesh. Nevertheless, he continued to strenuously use his arms to pull himself up higher with each faltering step he took, regardless of the pain. He was so worried that at any second, Ronnie's knots would come undone and he would smack the floor with a loud thud, bringing a crowd of half-drunken gang members in the room all at once. He was shocked that Ivan hadn't killed him already for betraying him. *Quit thinking about it. You're alive, aren't you? Make it count.*

When Drake came close enough, he threw one leg up and pushed it through the open window. Now he had a secure hold. The rest from there was easy, and he simply used both leg and arm muscles to lift him up to the window. *Now for the hard part,* he thought, examining the window doubtfully.

It seemed a little bigger when he was sitting next to it, but he still had his doubts about being able to fit through. Sitting in the small hollow of the wall with his skin shaded by the bluish-orange tint from the blending of the moonlight and a flickering street lamp, he realized he had no choice but to go through. If it broke every bone in his body, he was going through that window.

Drake peered outside and was relieved to find that the ground wasn't as far down as he had imagined it to be. *I guess I'll be going feet first, then.* Outside the window was a rectangular-shaped brick flower box, only without the flowers. As small as it was, at least it would give his body some support so he wouldn't instantly plunge to the ground.

Drake slid his other leg through the opening and slowly leaned back, wriggling inch by inch through the small window. It was like doing the limbo, only this time he couldn't risk losing the game. He could only envision what Ivan and the rest of the gang would do to him if they happened to burst into the room and find him like this. Not exactly the best way to die. No, he was determined to get out this window with his entire body intact.

Drake sensed the window getting increasingly smaller once it framed his stomach. He held his breath and sucked his stomach in, forcefully pushing himself a little further through the window. He could feel the support of the flower box leaving him. *Just...a little...more.* He slipped his hands through the space beside his chest and gripped the outside of the building with both hands. As his fingers dug into the cracked brick wall, he sensed a thick, warm liquid oozing from his fingers and creeping down his hands like external veins. *Relief,* he thought, gasping. *It hurts. Too much...pressure.*

Draining what was left of his energy and closing his eyes in an attempt to ignore the pain, he dug his fingers deeper into the bricks and pulled aggressively.

Like a vacuum, air raced into his lungs as soon as his chest made it through to the outside. He ducked his head and brought it through the window, welcoming the crisp night air as it cooled his warm cheeks. Pushing himself up to a sitting position on top of the narrow flower box, he was finally able to look down and see Ronnie.

Ronnie was waving him down with both hands. "Hurry up, Drake!"

Drake felt the flower box begin to give way underneath his weight.

"C'mon, Drake!" Ronnie urged, waving his hands faster now. "We gotta go!"

Drake pushed his legs off the side and jumped to the ground. He landed in the thick grass below and rolled on his back, grateful that the weeds had broken his fall and muffled the sound of his crash. He hurriedly untied the knot around his waist and stood, searching the area for a place to run.

That's when he saw them. He hadn't been able to see them from the window earlier, but now there was no mistaking their presence.

Fences. Nothing but nine-foot chain link fences everywhere he looked. The only place there wasn't one was behind him, and that was blocked by the building itself. To his left was a window where he saw the light blue hue of the television casting itself onto the sidewalk not six feet away from where he stood. To his right, on the other side of the fence, was someone's backyard where an ugly pit bull lay sleeping with a twitching leg. That left only one place.

Right in front of him. The moonlight glistened off the towering chain link fence, enhancing all nine feet of its seemingly inescapable features. Drake glanced at Ronnie and discerned that his thoughts were the same as his.

"What are we gonna do, Drake?" Ronnie said, his voice sounding lonelier than ever.

"We're goin' over the fence, that's what. It's the only way."

"But I'm scared."

Drake wanted to shout at him and tell him to quit acting like such a baby. However, he exhaled slowly, knelt down on one knee, and looked up into Ronnie's teary eyes. "I'm scared too, Ronnie. But we can't let that stop us. Look how far we've come."

Ronnie's lower lip stuck out as he struggled to keep from crying.

Drake sighed and said, "Look, just pretend there's a hurt animal over this fence and you have to save it." It was a cheesy line, but he hoped it would be convincing.

Ronnie thought about it. "Or I could just pretend my life's in danger and I'm running away from the bad guys."

Drake stood up slowly and raised an eyebrow. "Yeah, that would probably work, too," he said awkwardly. "Come on. I'll help you." He put Ronnie on his shoulders and told him to grab the fence and hang on tight.

Ronnie clung to the fence like a cat does a carpet when it's bath time. Drake wanted to laugh, but now was definitely not the time for joking around. Now was the time for action. Neither of them would ever be laughing again if they didn't get a move on.

Drake could have climbed the fence ten times faster if he hadn't been so concerned about not making a sound. Because the chain link fence was along a strip of asphalt, it made an unpleasant scraping sound every time the fence rattled. That meant Drake had to be extra quiet and even slower in his movements. With a little more slow motion and the right sound effects, he'd be the spitting image of the six-million dollar man in action.

"All right, Ronnie," he said once he was at eye level with him. "I'll be right here when you climb, OK?"

"OK," Ronnie said, almost doubtfully.

"You go first, and I'll be right behind you. Just don't look down." Drake waited until Ronnie was a few feet above him before climbing again. "When you reach the top, you'll climb over the fence to the other side and—"

"Climb *over* the fence?"

Drake stared at Ronnie. *And at what age is common sense supposed to kick in?* "Yeah, what else? You expect a slide or somethin' to get you down?"

Ronnie bit his lip.

"Just do what I say, OK? There's a bunch of weeds on the other side, so it's not like you'd break any bones if your foot slips and you accidentally fall."

Ronnie's eyes grew large. "You mean I might actually *fall?*"

"Oh, just forget I said anything! Keep climbing!"

It wasn't long before Ronnie reached the top. Drake met up with him quickly to help him over the fence. "You can make this as easy or as hard as you want it!" he said, prying Ronnie's pallid fingers away from the fence. "C'mon, if they find us, they'll kill us!"

"But what if I fall?"

"At least you'll get to the ground sooner!" Drake said. "Get over it, Ronnie. You're stronger than you think. On the inside, I mean. Don't be afraid. Don't you see you've already made it this far? The rest is a breeze from here."

That seemed to calm Ronnie's nerves, or perhaps it was just Drake's wishful imagination. Ronnie glanced at Drake sheepishly and said, "Thanks. Sorry for acting like such a baby."

Drake allowed himself to smile. "You can thank me when we're both on the ground. Now go."

With a new sense of courage, Ronnie puffed up his chest, stiffly brushed the tears from his eyes, and went down the fence so fast that even Drake was amazed.

"Good. Now go over to that bush over there and wait for me." Drake swung one leg over the fence and got his footing.

Then he heard a door open inside the building.

Ivan swore.

Drake turned his head in the direction of the window and heard a gun click. Before he had a chance to react, a sharp pain entered his left leg.

Then next thing he knew was that his body smacked the ground hard as another shot took a chip out of the pavement only inches away from his head.

Ivan was trying to kill him. *Kill.* Drake tried to scramble to his feet, but his body wasn't working right. It was his leg. That's right. He had been shot.

Try crawling. He dropped to the ground and elbow-crawled toward a tree. He was losing blood; he could feel it sting as it left his body. He just hoped he didn't lose consciousness from the pain before the next bullet turned his world black.

The pain in his thigh made him want to throw up. It was all he could do to keep from passing out. Another bullet fired, barely missing him again as he crawled behind a thick-trunked white oak. He thought he heard Ronnie crying and screaming for him to get up, but all he could concentrate on was the pain. The throbbing, blinding, sickening pain. He tore his fingers into a mass of dirt and roots and heaved the rest of his body behind the enormous tree. There, behind two and a half feet of impenetrable wood, he crumpled to the ground without any strength to go further.

Still, he felt anything but safe. He sensed that in a matter of minutes he was going to die. He wanted to die. He couldn't imagine a pain worse than this. Lying face down with uncontrollable shaking hands covering his head, he tried to look down at his leg, but couldn't force himself to do it. He could feel the warm, sticky fluid seeping and intermittently spurting from his leg and was almost glad he couldn't see.

"Ronnie," he said hoarsely. Unknown to him, Ronnie had already been there beside him the whole time. "Ronnie..." He sucked in a deep breath of frigid air and found it difficult to continue speaking. "Go, Ronnie. Go hide. Don't...don't let them find you." Ronnie tried to argue, but Drake just shook his head weakly. "Go."

Tears streaming down his red cheeks, Ronnie turned and fled.

Drake was too tired to watch him run off, so he let his head fall to the damp earth, content to die there. He didn't want to live anymore. He hated his life, and this kind of death was exactly what he deserved. *I just hope I die before Ivan comes out here and finishes me off.*

He stared impassively across the street and watched as the street-lights began to swirl and form a huge, orange blur. Then other colors were added—bright blues, purples, greens, and pinks. The sickeningly intense brightness of the colors made him close his eyes. But they were there too, tormenting him, playing cynical games with his mind as the reality of death settled in. *Then let me die. I want peace.*

Drake opened one eyelid and drew in another labored breath. He thought he saw the flashing lights of a police car in the distance just before he lost consciousness.

Chapter 16

HEALING PROCESS

The first thing Drake Pearson saw when he opened his eyes was a large bouquet of mixed, colorful flowers. *Am I dead?* he wondered, struggling to keep his eyelids from falling closed again. The room was an off-white color, and he had a migraine. That was about all he grasped before his world went dark again.

For the next twenty minutes, his eyes kept fluttering open on and off. If he could only lift his head to look around, he would, but even moving an inch seemed impossible. So he was content to simply gaze around with complete oblivion. The light in the room—added to the intense glow from the broad window to his right—was too bright, and he couldn't hold his eyes open for more than a few seconds at a time. *Oh, man, it hurts. I wish someone would close the blinds.*

He wanted to reach down and touch his leg, but he felt so drugged that he wasn't sure he had arms anymore. What time was it anyhow? What day was it? And what was going on in his body that was making him feel this way? Motionless and utterly worn out from who knew what, he decided not to fight his fatigue any longer. He let his eyes stay shut and merely listened to the sounds around him.

People walking. A recurring beeping. Moaning in another room. Someone crying. Everything was so loud that the conflicting noises hurt his ears. *What is this place?*

He opened his eyes again—bad idea. A wave of nausea punched him in the gut. He sealed his eyes shut, wondering where this pain was coming from and why he was experiencing it in absolute confusion. He tried not to think about it; thinking only seemed to intensify the nausea.

Slowly, the sour taste of vomit filled his mouth. He swallowed a thick gob of saliva and pushed the bitter flavor back down to his stomach. His bottom lip quivered. His entire body began to shake. He tried moving his arm again. His brain told him he was wiggling his fingers, but his other senses gave no evidence of it. Either his whole body was numb, or he had no body at all. *If I am dead...No, this is stupid. I have to wake up. This has to be a dream.*

If only he had feeling, he would pinch himself. *Wake up, wake up! C'mon, you stupid body, work!* How frustrating not to have any control over his own body. It was as if he were paralyzed from his head to his toes. The only part of his body that seemed to have retained any of its normal qualities was his brain. He still felt the same, thought the same, but everything else was completely wrong. His irritation soon progressed into rage, but realizing he could do nothing but lie in this position, he stopped fighting.

Drake opened his mouth to release a lengthy yawn and sensed tears rising to his closed eyes. *Gotta get outta here,* he kept repeating to himself. *Gotta...* He felt sleep coming and welcomed it gratefully. Maybe things would be different when he woke up next time.

As long as Drake had slept, he still felt as tired as he had been when he first drifted off to sleep. Hesitantly, he opened one eye, hanging in suspense that just maybe he would wake up in a different place.

But, no. Same room, same white walls, and same old migraine pal. Only this time, he wasn't seeing things through double vision. Whatever drug that had been in his body earlier seemed to have wore off while he had been asleep, and that at least made him feel a little less dead.

He shifted his body slightly and for the first time became conscious of the pillow under his head. *At least I can feel that. What a relief. For a while there, I swore I was going crazy.* He peeked again and saw that the flowers were still there. More colorful perhaps, or had his brain simply not been up to par then and remembered them differently?

The light didn't bother him so much anymore, so he took the time to study every detail of the room more closely. The parted blinds were long and thick, the wallpaper was end-of-the-spectrum white, and the chair in the corner seemed as isolated and confused about its presence here as he was.

He heaved a sigh and straightened his legs. What a relief to know they were still part of his body. He sensed his strength coming back, though that strength seemed so insignificant now.

He flinched. *Ouch! What was that?* Another surging pain ran down his leg, then faded as quickly as it had come. *The gunshot. Wasn't that yesterday, or has it been longer?* He gasped. *Ronnie! Oh, man, what happened between then and now?*

He tried to push himself up, but he was brought down again as another throbbing pain coursed through the nerves in his left leg.

Something stirred beside him. He froze, waiting for nothing in particular but dreading it nonetheless. Then, a familiar voice said, "Drake, are you awake?"

It was Andrew. "Yeah," Drake answered groggily, sounding nothing like himself. "Where am I?"

Seeing Drake was too weak to turn his head, Andrew picked up his chair and moved it on the other side of Drake's bed. "The hospital."

Drake sighed and closed his eyes. "Guess a lot happened last night I never knew about. Or was that even last night I got shot?"

"It was last night. I called the police after you left and gave them everything you told me. It took them awhile, but they tracked down Miller's Diner and located from there where those men were holding Ronnie. The gunshots also gave them a big clue."

"Did they have to put up a fight?"

"I wouldn't call it a fight. They had those thugs surrounded and in handcuffs in no time." He coughed up a laugh and said, "You don't mess with the Springfield police. Those guys were behind bars so fast they didn't know what hit 'em."

Drake wasn't smiling.

Andrew subdued his pasted-on smile and said in a lower voice, "I'm sorry you got shot."

"Huh, isn't that ironic? I don't feel sorry one bit."

Andrew avoided that impending argument by saying, "Good news is the doctor said you were shot in the muscle of your upper leg, barely missing your femoral artery and femur. No fractures, no life-threatening bleeding. It'll take time to heal, of course, but after that you'll be able to—"

"Leave."

Andrew paused and focused on the swirled marble tiles on the floor. "I wasn't going to say that."

"Why would it be any other way? If you'd only seen the look on Ronnie's face when he...wait a minute, where is Ronnie anyway? Is he OK?"

"He's fine. He came running out of the bushes as soon as he saw me step out of one of the police cars. The first thing out of his mouth was that you were asleep under a tree. I knew that didn't sound right, and when I came to investigate, I found you lying there bleeding. I rushed you here immediately."

"Why are you still here? Don't you have more important things to do than watch me lay here helplessly?"

"Ronnie and I spent the night. He's still here, actually, sleeping in a pull-out cot beside you."

Drake folded his arms close to his chest. This room was cold enough to hang meat. He heard deep breathing beside him and thought about all Ronnie had gone through in the last twenty-four hours. "He must hate me after all I've done," he said quietly.

"Hate you?" Andrew shook his head and said, "Just the opposite. He's talked non-stop about you and how brave you were. He even bought you something with his own money." Andrew reached across Drake's bed and grabbed a teddy bear decorated with a halo and wings. He set it next to Drake's hand. "He got it because he called you his guardian angel. As soon as we walked into the gift shop, he knew that's what he wanted to get you. It took all his money to buy it too. All of twelve dollars and forty-eight cents. But he wanted to buy it. Said you were worth it."

Drake looked down at his crisp sheets. *Go ahead and rake me over the coals.* He touched the bear's soft fur and withdrew his hand. "I don't feel worth it. Why can't he see I was the reason he was kidnapped in the first place? Why didn't you tell him that first day that it was me who made the phone call and set you up? It would have solved a lot of problems that way."

Andrew leaned forward and clasped his hands together. "It wouldn't have really mattered, would it? He wouldn't have believed me. In his eyes, you're a hero. Don't you see? He wants to be your friend so badly if you'll only give him a chance."

"I said I was leaving before, and this time I mean it before I go screwing up something else."

Andrew looked hard at Drake. "You'd do that to Ronnie?"

"If he had enough sense, he'd realize it was for his own good that I leave."

"No, if you had enough sense, you'd realize what a great friend you've been ignoring for so long. He looks up to you."

"I know. You've told me that a billion times now, but you aren't putting that guilt trip on me. It's not gonna work."

Drake was bullheaded enough to argue with a pole. Andrew had let him rant long enough, and he wasn't going to let him win this time. "If you feel any guilt, it's your own conscience trying to wake you to reality. In that bed over there is a seven-year-old who loves you to death, but you're treating him as if he means *nothing* to you."

"He does mean—"

"How do you think that makes him feel, Drake? Yes, granted, it was your fault he was kidnapped. I'm not going to try to hide that, and yes, it made me very angry. But what are you gonna do? Go walking out of his life as if he never existed? For the past few weeks, you've been part of our family, whether you see it that way or not. And families have a really hard time letting each other go."

Drake let his mouth fall open in unbelief. "Well, try to look at it from my perspective! I feel like such a failure. Everything I've done since I first came here has been wrong. I lied to you, I lied to Ronnie by not telling him the truth about me in the first place, and I even managed to pull off lying to myself. I thought I could change, and wanna know something else that's hard to believe? I thought *you* could change me. It took me this long to find out *I* was the problem. No one else. It's *me*. I can't be part of your lives because I know I'll just fail at that too."

"How do you ever expect to get better if you're always beating yourself up? You don't think you're good at playing the piano, you've complained about the yard even though I told you that you did a great job, and you're always putting yourself down."

Drake looked at him blankly. "My life stinks, OK? I'm living proof of what my old man said I would be. Nothing. If he could see me now, he'd tell me that a thousand times over."

"Then who are you gonna listen to? Him or yourself? You're not bound by what other people say about you. You're only bound by what you confess over yourself," Andrew said.

"You can't wipe away eighteen years that easy. You don't know who I had to live with. Dad berated me all the time, and it was a battlefield almost every night just to see who would win the shouting match. You don't realize what I had to go through every single day of my life. I could say the sky was blue, and my dad would swear up and down that it was a different color. No matter what I said, it was wrong. I could buy him a pack of cigarettes for his birthday, and he'd complain that it was the wrong kind. You don't know what it feels like to have someone you live with hate you like that. He told me once I couldn't change. He said I could never climb the ladder and have nice food and clothes like everybody else because I was born trash and would always stay that way." Drake bit his lip and said, "You know what? He was right."

Andrew stretched out his hand and gently smoothed down a wrinkle in the hospital sheet. If he had thought Drake seemed distant before, he seemed even further away now. Andrew had the feeling he was no longer part of Drake's world. Just a memory, a person who would soon be forgotten in time.

But God had bigger plans, better plans. Plans to fulfill and revive. Andrew wasn't ready to give them up. "I know you've been through a lot, Drake, but you can't use that as a crutch for the rest of your life. You *can* rise above."

"No, I can't," Drake said sharply. "I tried, and look where it got me."

"Well, then is it me who's stopping you? Do you have this idea in your head that I have some sort of resentment toward you? I've forgiven you, Drake. It's over, so let it go," said Andrew sincerely.

"You just don't know when to quit, do ya? I've already made up my mind. I'm not goin' back. As soon as I get this stupid leg back to walking again, I'm gone."

Andrew wondered how long his patience would hold out. The needle felt like it was teetering on the edge of empty. "Do you know why I took Ronnie in, Drake?"

"Look, I don't need—"

"No, hear me out. I took Ronnie in because I saw a need and I met it. If you're telling me you don't have a need, then maybe I'm the one who's deceived. The motive for me helping you isn't so that it will in some way make me feel better, as if I've done my good deed for the month. I want to help you because I care. I want to see you happy like I see Ronnie happy, and you've done nothing but fight me the entire way."

Drake glared at him. "I'm leaving because I never wanna see that look on Ronnie's face again. I can't. When he looked at me last night...it hurt. He trusted me. Me, the one who had put him there." He shook his head. "But he doesn't see that. You obviously don't see that either."

"The only thing I see right now is hurt and anger in your eyes. Don't try to hold it in, Drake. It'll only hurt you."

"What's one more bruise?" Drake said caustically. "I'll get used to it."

"Drop the ego, Drake. If you don't want my company, fine. But don't go through life walking with your head high acting as if nothing ever bothers you. Everyone hurts. I'm not trying to make light of what you've been through in the past. All I'm trying to do is point you in the direction of your future and support you with positive words instead of negative ones."

"Future? Like..."

"Like playing the piano. Don't roll your eyes; you know it's the truth. Drake, your playing is excellent. You know me well enough to know I wouldn't lie to you. You are so full of talent, and the sad thing is, you don't even know it. Sometimes I don't even think you care."

"You don't think I care?" Drake flared back, wanting to yank every IV out of him and find his strength again. "You don't think there've been nights when I've soaked my pillow with tears because the pain inside hurts that bad? You don't think I wanna change? I'd trade my life with you in a heartbeat, but life doesn't work that way, does it? You deal with what you got stuck with and go on."

"It doesn't have to—"

"No, I'm through fighting it. I'm empty. I've wasted my life doing my own thing my own way, and it's done nothing but hurt me and those around me. There is no turning back. I'm sorry I used you, because that's the reality of it. I used you because it was good for me, but even the selfish person deep inside knows that using you for even one more day is wrong. I'm not going back. I'll only hurt you again."

Andrew stood. "Well, even if you're calling it quits, I'm not giving up on you. I know I may be nothing more than an old-timer to you, and I also know that Ronnie can sometimes rub you the wrong way, but we love you. Ronnie may not be your definition of a friend, but I assure you that that seven-year-old over there would do anything in the world for you. If not for me, stay for him. He really needs a friend right now."

Drake found himself speechless. He was unsure whether he should feel angry or humiliated. He had never expected the conversation to end like this, and though he usually had a sharp comment to fire back as the last word, he was left feeling empty. Ashamed. And yet strangely, he felt incredibly thankful.

No one had ever talked to him that way before. His dad had yelled at him plenty of times, but Andrew was oddly straightforward and caring at the same time. Was it possible that it was all true? Why couldn't Andrew have just called him the foulest name in the book and left with a thunderous door slam? That's what he deserved. But this? Andrew going as far as telling him that he loved him? When was the last time someone had told him that? The thing that really bothered him was that Andrew actually sounded like he meant it.

Andrew gently nudged Ronnie, waking him from his sleep. "Ronnie, get up, buddy. Time to go."

Ronnie rubbed his eyes and sat up straight. "I want to talk to Drake first."

Drake forced his eyes closed. *No, just go away, Ronnie. I wouldn't know what to say if I talked to you.*

Andrew shot a quick glimpse at Drake. Better luck next time. Right now, he was gone. "Not now, Ronnie," he whispered. "Drake needs his rest."

Drake heard paper crumpling as Ronnie said, "Can I put this up first? I want Drake to have something to look at when he wakes up."

Andrew examined it. Sometimes the simplest words of a child were enough to shake someone to the truth. "It's beautiful, Ronnie. Of course, you can." He grabbed a role of tape he saw one of the nurses leave earlier and tore off a piece. "Here, show me where you want it and I'll hang it up."

Ronnie put a finger to his lips as he inspected the wall. "How about right there in front of his bed?"

"Sounds perfect." Andrew adjusted the picture and taped it to the wall. He patted Ronnie on the back and discreetly tried to press down the rooster tail that had shaped in his hair while he had slept. "Maybe we can come back and see him tonight."

"All right," Ronnie said dolefully, lowering his head.

Andrew grabbed something and moved next to Drake, noticing he was still pressing his eyes closed. "I'll leave this with him, just in case he wakes up and needs something to do."

Drake felt something weigh down on the bed near his hand, but he refused to look until Andrew left the room.

"Goodbye, Drake," Ronnie said, lightly touching Drake's hospital gown. "Make your leg get better soon so you can come home with us. But even if it still hurts when you wake up, I hope the bear I got you will help. I know you can't hear me 'cause you're sleeping, but I'll go ahead and say I love you anyway. Thanks again for saving me."

Tears burned in Drake's eyes. *Just go. Please, go.*

"Come on, Ronnie," Andrew said, slipping an arm around Ronnie's shoulders. He led him from the room, but couldn't help but glance once more at the person he wanted so desperately to find peace. *I leave the rest in Your hands, God.* He gently pulled the door closed behind him.

Drake opened his eyes, a sea of tears distorting both corners of his vision. Beside his bed, almost touching his fingers, lay a Bible.

Chapter
17

ONE SHEPHERD

Like a never-ending cycle, nurses came in and out of Drake Pearson's room every half hour to check on him. The lunch they brought him of chicken noodle soup and tasteless crackers was so disgusting that he didn't even try to make himself eat it. The only thing that tasted normal to him was the Mountain Dew. He swirled the liquid around with his straw, watching the fizzing iceberg of crushed ice drown in his foam cup. Welcome to the pits. When a bobbing chunk of ice becomes fascinating, life has officially reached rock bottom.

The nurses encouraged him to drink the broth, going off on a long spiel about how his body needed fluids, how his recovery was determined by the health of his body, blah, blah, blah. Did he ask for a lecture on medical science? Drake told them he wasn't hungry and pushed the tray away, hoping they wouldn't bother him about it anymore.

"Is there anything else I can do for you?" each nurse would ask before leaving the room.

Drake's answer was always the same. "No, but thanks anyway." He was ready to get out of here. He was jumpy on the inside and wanted above anything else to have a change of scenery. However, the nurses had already forewarned him that he had to stay until late in the afternoon for further observation, making sure he didn't have a reaction to the medicine they had given him or develop an infection.

"But that's crazy," he had protested.

"That's protocol," the doctor had replied with a smile.

"I feel almost completely normal now. Just help me out of this bed and I'll show you."

"Sorry. I know you're eager, but I doubt you'll be walking on that leg without the help of crutches."

"Crutches? How long will I have to use those?"

"A week to ten days maybe, but don't worry. You'll be back on your feet again soon enough."

Drake doubted it. He had tried arguing, insisting that he felt perfectly fine, but nothing worked on these bloodhounds. He learned from the doctor that he had been shot in the upper thigh, just as Andrew had said. The bullet had torn through muscle and soft tissue, barely missing his bone, and exited the other side. They had cleaned the wounds thoroughly, put him on some oral antibiotics, and had given him large doses of pain medication—which he soon discovered he needed more than he had realized. He looked forward to tonight when he could finally be up on his feet again, even if he did have to use crutches.

Once Drake regained most of his strength, he—slowly and extremely carefully—used the buttons beside him to elevate the back of his bed. He cringed as another flash of pain struck his leg, stopping him from daring to go any higher.

Wait, what was that on the wall in front of him? He straightened and leaned his head forward.

Ronnie's picture. Andrew had taped it on the wall before he left. Drake felt ashamed for almost forgetting about it. He studied the picture and smiled at the three stick men with arrows under them pointing to the words "my family." They were all smiling as they stood beneath a colorful rainbow. Drake's eyes glanced up at the large words written in the clouds, then quickly looked away.

Jesus loves you. Or so it said.

Drake looked back up and stared at the words. *Jesus loves me? Then tell me where He's been all my life.* He appreciated the thought, but how could he accept something he knew was a lie?

A nurse cracked his door open and peeked inside. "Just making sure you weren't asleep before I come barging in on you," she said, smiling.

Drake put a hand behind his head. "No problem. Hard to sleep when you got IVs in anyway."

"Well, I just thought I'd ask if there was anything—"

"No, thanks," Drake said, stopping her before she had the chance to continue.

She reached for an odd-looking device connected to the bed. "Now that you're feeling back to normal, you may want to watch some television. This controls the volume and that button allows you to scroll through the channels."

"Thanks," Drake said, taking the device in his hand. "What's that button for?"

"It's in case you need to alert us of anything or have a question."

"Oh, OK. Probably won't need that then, unless I can persuade the doctor into letting me out sooner."

The nurse laughed. "Don't think that'll work, but we'll try to get you out of here as soon as possible."

Drake flipped through the channels until he finally stopped on a movie that was already an hour into the plot. He fiddled with the device the nurse had given him, trying to find out which button turned off the closed captioning at the bottom of the screen. After trying every button, he gave up and turned off the television. *Who cares? I've seen it before anyway, and the acting is lame.*

His eyes drifted around the room until they landed again on Ronnie's picture—specifically on the words in bold. *Just leave me alone,* he thought. He tore his eyes away from the picture and concentrated on the ceiling. *What do I care? Why should it bother me? I know what the truth is.*

He reached over to the tray beside his bed to take another sip of his drink. When he did, however, he noticed Andrew's Bible still lying beside him where he had left it. *Is there nowhere I can go to get away from this harassment?* He huffed and weighed the Bible in his hands. Maybe he could just take a peek. After all, it wasn't like he'd read it and find himself page-turning until the end. His motives were solely because he was bored and had nothing better to do.

Drake indifferently opened the Bible. John chapter 1 fell open because of a bookmark Andrew had placed there. He looked at the page and wrinkled his forehead. It looked like any other ordinary writing to him. What made this book so special that it stood above every other? *Hmm. Guess I'll just have to find that out for myself, but it's only because I'm bored and tired of staring at the wall. Maybe if nothing else, it'll be so boring that I'll finally be able to go back to sleep.*

Drake haphazardly leafed through the delicate pages of the Bible. After reading several chapters, the stories were just what he had expected them to be—exaggerated, questionable, and completely far-fetched. *Demons fell down before Jesus, water was turned into wine, people rose from the dead, an insignificant meal was stretched to somehow feed a crowd of five thousand people, water was walked on, and those who were blind saw clearly? Please.*

Even in the short amount of time he had been acquainted with Andrew, Drake had always figured him to be a practical man with a good head on his shoulders. But this? He seriously bought into all this? Maybe there had been a man named Jesus on the earth at one point in time, but what was the meaning of it all? To say that He healed people who couldn't walk and cast out demons sounded like the definition of a cult to Drake.

OK, so maybe Jesus might have been a good person who showed compassion for others, but people shouldn't run with the idea and create a fantastical story based on what He did in life.

As good of a deal as that sounded—everlasting life and the whole package that came along with it—Drake was still holding back. He found nothing in it for him. Sure, it was good for the people who had received the healings and miracles, but that was then. What good was the Bible for people today? What good was it for *him?*

Drake could clearly see that Ronnie was right—Jesus did have love. Of all the reading he had done, he admitted that much. But Jesus also must have had His favorites. Drake had never seen God work on his behalf, and why? Because he was a sinner, and sinners didn't go to Heaven. They went to hell. That seemed fair enough, but somehow it bothered him when he saw Ronnie's picture. Jesus may have loved him at one time, but not anymore. He loved people like Andrew and Ronnie. Good people. People who made Him proud. Drake had failed miserably at that a long time ago.

Every time nurses came into Drake's room, they gazed at him curiously as they found his eyes still focused on the open Bible resting on his stomach. "Is your television working OK?" one of them finally asked.

"Oh, yeah."

"Well...would you like some magazines? We have sports and hunting—"

"No, this is fine," Drake answered, offering a smile. He knew they must have thought him strange and possibly even delusional to be reading something for nearly two and a half hours now without putting it down once. Difference is they could walk. He was confined, on the other hand, to his bed with an ancient manuscript that might as well have been written in Hebrew. What else did they expect him to do with his time?

The nurse just nodded her head politely and left the room, still wearing a confused look on her face as she closed the door behind her.

Drake turned his attention to the end of the Book of John in the eighteenth chapter. Judas, one of Jesus' friends, had just betrayed Jesus, and Peter had disowned him three times. What kind of friends were they? Jesus was popular enough; why so many enemies and not enough support?

For so many years, he had pictured Jesus differently—weak, frail, and without any human feelings whatsoever. But after reading about how He had been questioned unfairly and brought before this guy named Pilate, Drake was beginning to have second thoughts. Just earlier in chapter 17, Drake had read the prayer Jesus had prayed just prior to being arrested. He had said, "Father, I want those You have given Me to be with Me where I am, and to see My glory, the glory You have given Me because You loved Me before the creation of the world. Righteous Father, though the world does not know You, I know you, and they know that You have sent Me. I have made You known to them, and will continue to make You known in order that the love You have for Me may be in them and that I myself may be in them," (NIV).

Be in them. What does that mean? What was Jesus saying when He said, "Father, I want those You have given Me to be with Me where I am"? What an odd prayer. Drake didn't know Jesus had ever prayed. Never thought He had reason to. Why would the God of the universe take time to pray for those who were about to betray and disown Him? He could have struck them all dead, yet He didn't. He did the unthinkable and actually prayed for them. *Strange. I would have gotten ticked and told them all what I thought of them. Why didn't He?*

Drake sighed and turned the page to chapter 19. He read to himself just above a whisper, "Then Pilate took Jesus and had Him flogged," (NIV). He stopped reading and stared at that statement. Flogged? He flipped the page back, speed-reading through what he had already read. *Am I missing something? Jesus was innocent, right? I mean, it's not like I'm actually interested in this...it just doesn't seem fair. No one could bring anything against Him, at least from what I can make out of all this.*

Unable to find what he was looking for, Drake turned back and continued reading. "The soldiers twisted together a crown of thorns and put it on His head. They clothed Him in a purple robe and went up to Him again and again, saying, 'Hail, king of the Jews!' And they struck Him in the face," (NIV).

As Drake continued reading, a sick feeling arose in his stomach, and he was unable to continue. He had heard the stories and seen the pictures, but no one had ever told him it was this bad. *Even if Jesus was supposedly God-slash-man at this point, He still would've had feelings, wouldn't He?* It almost made him mad just reading it. They had whipped Him, they had mocked Him openly, and they had beaten Him without cause. How could anyone ever treat a human being that way, especially someone who was blameless?

Drake knew what was coming next—the crucifixion. He had always known what a cross was and knew what it stood for, but never before had he known the one who had been on that cross. Now, after almost three hours of reading about Him, he knew who it was who was about to be killed on that universal symbol of shame.

Drake had seen his share of gruesome scenes in movies and video games, but nothing compared to this. The Bible didn't go into detail about the crucifixion, but even the sound of the word denoted that it must have been a horrible way to die. Jesus was stripped of His clothing, nailed to a wooden, splintered cross, and then left there for the entire world to laugh at and humiliate. Even after crying out with thirst, the only thing the soldiers gave Him was wine vinegar fed to Him from a sponge. How inhumane. How inconsiderate. Drake honestly didn't think he could treat his worst enemy this way.

Then, after all the torture, Jesus died. The great Hero of the world gave up His Spirit, as the Bible put it, for those who could care less about Him. Even though it was an expected ending, it enraged Drake. He would have rather read that Jesus called down fire from Heaven and vaporized them all where they stood. That was what he would have done if he had been in Jesus' position. But an ending like this was simply unfathomable. Why would anyone do that?

Drake fingered the bookmark he was holding and noticed a beautiful picture of sheep in a field printed on it. Beneath the picture were the words, *"I am the good shepherd. The good shepherd lays down His life for the sheep"* (John 10:11 NIV).

Drake's eyes gazed back up at the picture. He had just read that verse somewhere earlier, and now here it was again. He turned back to John chapter 10 and read it again for himself. *Those were Jesus' words. So that's what He meant when He said...He knew He would die soon.* He glanced down at the verse and read to himself, *"I am the good shepherd; I know My sheep and My sheep know Me—just as the Father knows Me and I know the Father—and I lay down My life for the sheep. I have other sheep that are not of this sheep pen. I must bring them also. They too will listen to My voice, and there shall be one flock and one shepherd,"* (NIV).

Drake held his breath and thought, *Could it be that when Jesus said He had other sheep that were not of His pen, He was referring to people who didn't love Him?...People like me?* He looked down at the bookmark again and found that the reference to John 3:16 was in parenthesis. With a new interest aroused in him, Drake quickly found the verse and read it aloud with a trembling voice, "For God so loved the world that He gave His one and only Son, that whoever believes in Him shall not perish but have eternal life."

That wasn't a misprint he had read; it clearly stated that *whoever* believed would be saved. Could that possibly include him?

Drake's mind spun with questions he had never entertained. Honestly, he didn't know if he was ready to think about such things. Life would be a whole lot simpler staying the way it was. Still, there would always be the nagging question...

A light tap on the door ruptured Drake's thoughts. *Not another one.*

Surprisingly, it was a new face. "Not sleeping, are you, Mr. Pearson?" An elderly man in doctor garb decorated with credentials encased in glossy, plastic cases strode toward his bed with an outstretched hand. "Hello. My name is Dr. Paul Eerdman. Just wanted to check in and see how your recovery is coming along."

"Are you the one who did surgery on my leg?"

"That's me."

"Thanks." *I think.*

"I'm grateful the bullet did no life-threatening damage, though I imagine those words don't help when your leg's throbbing."

"Not much. How does the inside of a leg look anyway?" The nausea was over now, so Drake figured he might as well ask.

The doctor chuckled. "A mass of muscle, tendons, and stringy veins...I just finished a cheeseburger and curly fries, so I'll stop there with the details."

"No cafeteria food for doctors, huh?"

Dr. Eerdman gave him a knowing look.

"I don't blame you. They tried to make me eat some of their soup, but the noodles were decomposing in my bowl."

The doctor laughed. "I'm glad to see you're in high spirits."

Drake tried to smile. *I'm glad you think so.*

Dr. Eerdman rose and shook Drake's hand again. "Well, I'll let you get back to resting. If you have any questions about your recovery, don't hesitate to ask. That's why I'm here."

"Thanks. I've appreciated the company."

The doctor stopped when he caught a glance of the Bible lying next to Drake. "Good reading choice."

Drake looked at the Bible. "A friend left it." It felt like a blow to the gut to downplay his true emotions. If there was ever anyone to answer his questions, it was this man. *Ask him. That's why he's here.*

"Talk to you later, Mr. Pearson."

Drake wasn't sure what he was searching for or if he would find it, but he had so many questions he needed answered that to pass up this chance would be mental suicide. On the flip side, finding out could prove even worse. Without giving it another thought, he dared to take the step. "Wait."

Dr. Eerdman turned.

Drake stared down at the Bible and had to coerce the words from his mouth. "There is *one* more question."

Chapter
18

APPALLING REALITY

Dr. Eerdman rolled a padded stool next to Drake's bed. "I'm listening."

"I don't really know if you can answer my question or not. See, it's not about me. It's about someone else."

"Well, I can certainly try," Dr. Eerdman said. "What's your question?"

Drake lightly touched Andrew's leather-bound Bible. "I wanna know what a crucifixion is. What it means. I mean, I know what the definition is and all, but I want to know what really happened." Those words sounded so strange coming from his mouth. For now, he could pass it off as the medicine in his body. He felt anything but himself; fatigue had visibly taken its toll, added to the string of events that seemed to last more like a lifetime than a week. God was just a fleeting form of escape for him right now. Soon, this temporary phase of insanity would pass and he would go on with life as he always had.

The doctor adjusted his glasses and said, "You're a Christian too, huh?" Before Drake had the chance to protest, he continued. "As a doctor and a Christian, years ago I decided to do some extensive research about crucifixions and found them to be rather...how should I say this? Horribly inhuman? You can choose your own description of it if you're sure you want to know what it entails." A grave expression darkened his countenance. The unsteady flickering from the fluorescent light above accentuated the shadows of wrinkles etched across his forehead.

"I remember the first time I studied it," he said softly. "It was hard. I cried for days."

Drake raised an eyebrow.

"No, seriously," the doctor said. "I had always known what Christ did for me, but at the same time, I really didn't know. And because I didn't know, I couldn't truly appreciate it. The cross represented everything horrible and sickening that man could devise, and when I learned that my Lord had to go through that, it was..." He swallowed and rubbed the back of his neck. "...it was difficult to accept." He paused, allowing that weight to settle. What was coming next was the hardest climb. "Crucifixion was a common type of punishment in the heathen nations, so the details are pretty graphic. That is, if you still want me to tell you."

Drake forced himself to nod. The urge to hear the truth felt like gravity. He couldn't make himself understand why he should care about any of this; it was like something deeper was reaching out, begging him to listen. "Just tell me. I wanna know every detail. I know this may sound like a strange request, but I need to know."

"If you're sure..."

"I'm sure."

Dr. Eerdman sucked in a breath of air as if he were testing his lungs on a spirometer. "OK, then." He wrinkled his brow as if trying to remember—and possibly because it was a disturbing topic for him to discuss. "Crucifixion was regarded as the most horrible form of death, usually reserved for only the worst criminals. The punishment began by scourging—another word for whipping, only this was much worse. The Roman whip was a heavy mass of strips of cord, each piece dangling with toothed fragments of metal or bone. Anything to create the maximum amount of agony. The back was the part most bloodied by the whip, but some Romans went beyond cruelty and beat their prisoners in the hands, face, and belly, until almost no piece of flesh remained untouched by their whip."

Drake absorbed the words, almost guiltily. It pained him to hear something so gruesome, even if he did choose not to believe it. But it seemed so real and alive the way Dr. Eerdman presented it. He was so focused on his statements that even wasting time to blink was out of the question. All of his descriptions were built detail upon detail, as if he had gone through this single event a million times in his head. Maybe he had. He was devoted to what he believed—Drake credited him with that much—even if that belief did happen to be a scarred, torn fragment of the life of a man who gave so much for seemingly so little.

"Because of this treatment," Dr. Eerdman continued, "the victim usually died tied to the whipping post before ever making it to the crucifixion site. But if the victim was able to survive, he was then forced to carry his own cross to the place where he would be executed. It was normally just outside the city, but even a short walk was enough to make the victim collapse. After being stripped of all his clothing, the victim was sometimes given a drink of vinegar before he was nailed to the cross."

"Why vinegar?" Drake said.

"Because it contained other ingredients that helped deaden the pain."

"Oh," Drake said, knowing that even if Jesus had been given the strongest pain medicine, it would have been insignificant compared to the agony He must have endured.

"You sure you want me to continue?" Dr. Eerdman asked concernedly, seeing how pale Drake's cheeks were getting.

Everything the doctor had already told him was enough information to make Drake want to throw up for a week, but what he had heard was only part of what had happened. "Yes," he answered, almost gagging. "I want to know."

"If you insist. Upon arriving at the place of execution, the person's arms were then stretched along wooden crossbeams, and either at the center of the palms or clean through the wrist, a thick, blunt nail was driven through each hand and into the cross with a mallet. After that—"

"After that?" Drake gasped. "What could be any worse than that?"

Dr. Eerdman pursed his lips. He could get into serious trouble for sending a recovery patient back into shock. "There's still a lot more left."

Drake let his head sink into his pillow and closed his eyes, not wanting the doctor to see that tears were already beginning to form in his eyes. "Go ahead," he mumbled. "I'm listening."

"Then, through either each foot separately or both feet at once, a thick, blunt nail was hammered to tear its way through muscle and veins until it was driven deep enough to penetrate the cross on the other side. From there, the cross was raised and allowed to fall in place into a narrow hole in the ground. As the cross plunged into the hole and came to a sudden halt, the already lacerated tendons were further torn as the weight of the man's body jerked downward, causing the nerves to throb with incessant agony. This position made every slight movement extremely painful and caused the victim to push up every few seconds just to do the once simple task of exhaling.

"The victim was in constant torment as he waited for death—if only death would come. Because of the numerous lacerations on the body, inflammation by exposure to the sun's heat made the slashed flesh burn. The arteries, particularly in the head and stomach, became swollen with an over-abundance of blood. There was also dizziness, a high fever, and horrific cramps. He experienced all this in front of the crowds that formed to watch the most revolting death imaginable.

"Often several hours passed before the victim finally died. Death was sometimes rushed by breaking the victim's legs or delivering a solid blow under the armpit. But they didn't break Jesus. He died at the power of His own words."

Drake didn't know what to say. He lifted his eyes to meet the doctor's and said in a quivering voice, "Thank you. You've answered all my questions."

The doctor stood up brusquely, teary-eyed himself, and left the room.

Drake sat there in horror, trying to imagine how Jesus must have felt. One leg surgery was pushing his pain threshold; he couldn't comprehend seeing his flesh lying on the ground after a brutal lashing and feeling his blood draining from multiple wounds. The doctor had certainly left out no details, just as he had asked him not to.

But how could words describe that kind of death? Words were just words, and even words had limited meanings. Was there a word stronger than pain? Could a word really describe how it feels when a rusty nail is pounded through the tendons of a person's hands and feet? Can a word ever convey how it feels when pieces of serrated metal slashes the skin from a person's back, legs, face? He had never heard about that part. Even in the churches he had been in, Jesus' death had always been portrayed as something less than what it really was. No one would have wanted to see the true picture of Jesus. The naked, humiliated, bruised, swollen, beaten, and bloody part of Jesus.

Drake put a hand to his head and felt sweat seeping through his pores. No one had ever before taken the time to explain to him what Jesus' death really meant. It wasn't just a few whip marks on His back.

It wasn't just a handful of nails in a cross. It was the most horrible way a person could die, and yet Jesus *chose* to die that way.

Maybe Christians could find comfort in knowing that Jesus died for them and that they would gain entrance to Heaven one day, but to Drake, it did nothing but cut him deeper.

Drake gazed out the glowing window beside his bed and repeated to himself that something that happened thousands of years ago didn't have anything to do with him today. History was like that—its memory may last, but it's dead just the same.

I don't want to think about it. He should be focusing on resting, not this. The nurses would have a fit if they knew this was going through his mind on top of the empty stomach they had already lectured. He needed to clear his mind and focus on himself. *That's right. Pull everything back into focus and realize you're recovering from a bullet wound.* There was no guilt in that. He owed it to himself to save this for another day. His recovery was number one...*and the person who died for you ranks where?* The more he thought about it, the sicker he felt.

Drake turned away from the window, away from the world, away from the sky that seemed to penetrate his being like searing eyes. He had to get out of here. This room was contaminated with something. He knew because he was certainly not himself. Maybe he could find a button to push somewhere that would give him enough medicine to knock him out for five or six hours.

Discolored, flashy images of whips and spikes toppled back into memory. An innocent face streaked by matted blood and spit contorted as another cluster of serrated bones and metal removed a chunk of flesh from His shoulder. Drake turned back to the window and breathed like he was going through trauma. *Suck it up and be strong. You're better than this.*

The image flickered, then left his mind.

Drake squeezed Andrew's Bible in an attempt to calm his shaking hands. If only someone had told him this sooner, maybe he could have gotten his life straight and accepted what Jesus had done for him. But it was too late now. His life was a wreck. Why would God ever want to take him like this? He had gone his own way and ruined his life. Who was he to think that Jesus, after all He had already done for him, should ever take him back? It simply wasn't right. To ask such a thing would almost make him feel as if he were only putting Jesus through more pain.

Slowly, Drake lifted his eyes to Ronnie's picture on the wall, past the people and the rainbow and...

Jesus loves you. Drake stared at the words—resolute to keep his eyes fixed there until the full depth of those words sank in. *Why did You have to do that, Jesus? Can't You see that I'm not worth it?* he thought, almost angrily. *Make it say something else!* His body heaved forward, and tears fell freely from his eyes now. He thought about the doctor's words and all the sickening images of Jesus' crucifixion.

Drake grabbed the pink tray beside his bed and threw up on it.

When supper was brought to him, Drake refused it.

"Are you sure you're feeling OK?" one of the nurses said after cleaning the vomit tray. "I could bring you a popsicle. Grape or cherry?"

Drake set down his empty cup of Mountain Dew and said almost pleadingly, "Please, when can I get outta here?"

"A nurse will be on the way with your crutches shortly." A knock came at the door. The nurse turned and smiled. "There she is now."

Drake relaxed. Finally.

The nurse moved toward the door and opened it. "Oh, hello. I thought you were the nurse. Well, come right on in. I'm sure Mr. Pearson'll enjoy the company."

Drake craned his neck and saw Andrew and Ronnie standing in the hallway. "Don't worry," he said, letting his weary head fall back down on his firm, cool pillow. "I'm not asleep or anything. You can come in."

Andrew walked in slowly behind Ronnie, who was already eyeing the tray of untouched food.

Drake took a carton of vanilla pudding from the tray and held it out. "Want it?" he said.

Ronnie moved toward it, then quickly drew back. "No, I shouldn't. Go ahead."

"I hate pudding and I hate vanilla even more. You might as well eat it." He handed the pudding to Ronnie, along with a plastic spoon.

"How have you been?" Andrew said tentatively.

"'Bout the same," Drake answered, carefully avoiding his IVs as he scratched a patch of dry skin on his hand. "Don't know what the doctors are makin' a big fuss of. It's not like I can't walk."

"From what I hear, you'll be getting your crutches soon."

Drake grimaced. "How long will I have to use those again?"

"Probably a week. Maybe a little longer. All depends on when the tissue in your leg heals."

Drake looked at Ronnie and tried not to laugh at the creamy pudding mustache coated above his upper lip. "Thanks for the picture and bear, Ronnie. You didn't have to do that."

"I wanted to," Ronnie said, scraping his cup to get out the last spoonful of pudding. He glanced up and smiled at Drake. "We made a pretty good team out there, huh?"

"Oh, uh...yeah, guess we did, didn't we?" He took a fleeting glimpse at Andrew before turning his eyes to the floor.

Andrew took a step closer and touched the tray near Drake's bed. "Did you get any reading done?"

Drake looked at the Bible and shrugged. "A little. Television wouldn't turn on, so I picked it up for a while. Slept most of the time, though." He pursed his lips and said no more. Why was he doing this to himself? Was it because the Bible had bothered him more than he had expected it to? Was it because the more he tried not to believe it, the more it made him ache on the inside? Try as he might, he couldn't explain the way he had acted. It had tormented his mind to the point he had to vomit to discharge the sickness he felt.

And now? Now to lie about it? To act as if it meant nothing? Drake knew he was only hurting himself, but it was better than facing the holy God he had read about with a fog of sins clouding his life. If he disgusted even himself, how much more did he disgust God?

Andrew sat on the chair next to the bed and cupped his hands around his knees as a faint frown covered his face. A little reading was better than none, he guessed. He had hoped for more, even a slight interest. But perceiving Drake's tone of voice, there had been no such reaction. "Do me one last favor, Drake. Stay with us until you're able to walk without your crutches. That way, I'll know you'll be OK when you leave."

"Let's not argue about this again."

"No one's arguing."

"Then here's a head's up."

"You're not even listening," Andrew mumbled.

"I'm trying to be reasonable."

"Reasonable? All I'm asking for is a week!"

"Weeks are the same as years to me. I shoulda been gone yesterday."

"So I got in your way?" Ronnie said, his turn to join in now. "You wanted to leave and I ruined your plans?"

"Whoa, hang on, buddy. You're way off base. I never said—"

"Last night, we were a team," Ronnie said, his face now striped with tears. "Least, I thought we were. You showed me I was braver than I thought I was. You taught me to find something good in even the really bad...what's the word?"

"Situations," Andrew quietly offered.

"Yeah, that. For the first time, I felt what it was like to have a friend. I don't care if it was just one or two or...oh, I don't know how many hours it was, but I was kinda glad we were tied up 'cause I had someone to talk to. And you did talk. You made me feel better inside, even about the scary things I was too afraid to think about by myself. I knew everything was going to be OK when you came."

Drake fumbled for words. "I'm...I'm glad we both came through safe." Pitiful. Was that all he could say? No genuine feeling, no sympathy? Ronnie spits out phrases like a psychoanalyst, and all he could come up with were a few hollow words barely glued together. Pitiful.

"That's why I don't want you to go," Ronnie sniffled, wrapping one hand around the cold metal bar beside Drake's bed. "Andrew doesn't want you to go either. I think he really wants to tell you that, but sometimes he just doesn't know how to say it."

Andrew peeked at Drake.

Oh, he knows, Drake thought. *Probably took lessons from you.*

"Drake, look at me," Ronnie said.

Drake looked at him. How he had changed so much from that timid little kid half falling out the window last night to the bold person standing before him now giving him the lecture of his life. He may have been seven years old, but he deserved to be heard.

268

"Drake, you have to stay. We're a team. A team can't split up."

"Ronnie, don't make this hard. You know I have to go."

Ronnie stared at him incredulously. "No, I don't know *why* you have to go! I thought we were a family. I thought we were friends."

"I already went through this, pal," Drake said, rubbing his weary head.

"You don't care about us," Ronnie sobbed, moving away. "Why did you even come if you were just gonna leave? Didn't you know we'd like you? I thought you were gonna stay with us forever."

Drake put an arm around Ronnie and pulled him close. "Don't cry, kiddo. You know I care about you."

"If you cared, you'd stay. I'm sorry if I made you mad or somethin'. Is that why you're leaving? Mommy and Daddy always left when I made them mad. I'm sorry if I did anything wrong, Drake. I didn't mean to."

Drake wrapped both arms around Ronnie and hugged him tightly. "Ronnie, you have never done anything to make me mad at you. If I've gotten mad, it was because I was mad at myself, not you. I could never be mad at you. Don't ever think that. I love you, Ronnie, more than you'll ever know. And it means the world to me for you to say I'm your friend." He pulled away and wiped the tears from Ronnie's cheeks. "If you really want me to stay..."

"I do, Drake! I do!" Ronnie cried, hugging him again.

Andrew sat in the corner alone, afraid that if he tried to join in, this moment would fragment like delicate glass. He was still the outsider; the one Drake consistently pulled away from. But Ronnie had gotten through to him successfully—no small accomplishment. He wanted Drake to be true to his word for Ronnie's sake, because that fighter had earned it. And as long as there was a glint of hope, he was still pushing, still praying, that Drake would find a friend in him too.

Drake closed his eyes and let Ronnie squeeze the life out of him. Andrew was right. He had been surrounded by love all this time.

All he had to do was open his eyes and see it.

Drake was a little shaky climbing out of bed, even with a nurse holding one arm and Andrew bracing the other. This feeling of hopeless incompetence was what babies must experience when learning to take their first steps. Now all he needed to complete the picture was someone on the other end of the room with outstretched arms telling him in a baby voice, "Come on! You can do it! That's it! That's it!" No, wait. Ronnie was already doing that.

Drake felt lightheaded as he gradually shifted his weight to his good foot. His body felt strangely off balance with the floor, as if the ground were sitting at a thirty-degree angle. "I'm OK. I can do it," he kept saying, trying to stand on his own. Andrew and the nurse must have known better, because they didn't leave his side.

Drake couldn't believe how weak he felt, especially in the leg where he had been shot. The area was extremely tender, and when he bent over to reach for his shoes, he quickly realized he wouldn't be putting them on his feet by himself for a while. Even a diminutive amount of pressure on his wound restrained him from doing the simplest of tasks.

"Set me back down," Drake said quickly, reaching for the bed. "I'm feeling sick." Andrew and the nurse lowered him to the mattress.

"Is it nausea?" the nurse said.

"No, just gravity. Give me a sec and I'll get over it." What was taking place inside his intestines sure felt like nausea. But Drake wanted to get up, get going. This room and its Antarctica air made him hope he never had to visit a hospital again.

The nurse held one of the crutches up to him and adjusted it according to his height. "There," she said, snapping it into place. "When you're up to it, see how this feels."

Drake wrapped his fingers around the gray padding and moved the crutches under his arms. He slowly lifted himself off the bed and onto the ground. "Much better," he said, fumbling to keep his balance. Truth was, standing up was more painful than lying down, but right now, he would tell the nurse about anything she wanted to hear if it meant staying out of that stiff bed.

Shifting his entire weight onto his good leg, Drake moved the crutches ahead of him a few inches and gently rocked his body forward. "Hey, this ain't bad at all. I'll be cruisin' in no time."

Andrew smiled, relieved. "Glad to see you up on your feet again. You don't feel nauseous or anything, do you?"

"Not at all," Drake lied, already having located the pink tray in case he needed to get to it fast. "I'm just ready to get outta here and see some color again." Drake gave a nod to Ronnie and said, "What do you say, little man? Ready to go?"

Ronnie walked over to his picture and peeled the tape off the wall. "Don't forget your picture."

No, can't forget that. Drake tucked the picture under his arm and swung his legs forward as he took another step with his crutches. He wouldn't admit it in a million years, but he was glad he had a home to go to tonight instead of the streets. A bed, good food, and especially the support of Andrew and Ronnie was what he needed most to make his recovery a speedy one.

Chapter
19

TEARSTAINED PAGES

After being helped out of the car, Drake Pearson shuffled slowly up to the front door, only to watch Andrew struggle to beat him to it first and open the door for him. Drake wasn't about to get used to the idea of being treated like a patient again, but at least Andrew seemed sincere in his motives. A little too obliging perhaps, but nonetheless helpful.

"I'll pull the covers back on your bed," Ronnie volunteered.

"Thanks, but I don't want to go near a bed again for a while," Drake said kindly. He examined the flight of stairs. "As a matter of fact, I don't figure I'll be seeing a bed for a long time. Not the one upstairs, anyway."

"Then I'll make you a bed on the couch tonight," Andrew said.

"Thanks," Drake said.

Ronnie tugged the coffee table toward the wall so Drake wouldn't bump into it as he walked toward the couch to sit down. "I want to sleep down here with Drake! I can make room."

Andrew helped Ronnie lift the table over a bump in the rug. The house would feel so different in a week, if Drake still decided to go. The guest room would go back to being empty, one less chair would be filled at the kitchen table, the back door rug would be less muddy, and the sounds from the piano would sleep for a few more years. He hadn't missed God, Andrew kept telling himself. People were responsible for their own choices. But understanding those choices was the toughest part. And saying goodbye.

"He needs someone to look after him and get him water and stuff if he needs it," Ronnie continued. "Please, Uncle Andy? Pleeease?"

Andrew looked at Drake and shrugged his shoulders. "Looks like the decision's already made. You know as well as I do that getting into an argument with Ronnie is useless. He always wins."

"So that's a yes?" Ronnie said, waiting for a response with wide eyes.

"That's definitely a yes," Drake said. "You can keep me company if I can't sleep, because the way I feel now, I'll probably be awake for days."

"Yes!" Ronnie pumped his fist up and down before racing up the stairs. "I'll get a piece of paper and write down all the things we can do tonight!"

"Oh...you really don't have to do that!" Drake called up to him.

"Don't worry!" Ronnie hollered back. "I'll have a list ready!"

"No, seriously, Ronnie. I was just exaggerating about..."

Ronnie's door slammed shut.

That works too, Drake thought. He turned and faced Andrew. Why did Ronnie always have to bolt from the room and leave him and Andrew alone in such an awkward atmosphere? Drake grabbed his imaginary shield and prepared for "one of those" conversations.

Andrew shed his jacket and draped it over a chair. If he put this off now, he may never get another chance. "So, uh, you said you got some reading done?" he tried to say casually.

"Yeah." This conversation was going to be as short as Drake could make it.

Andrew set his Bible down on the coffee table. "I noticed you read the crucifixion of Jesus."

That made Drake look up. "How'd you know I read it?"

Andrew pursed his lips.

"Oh, I get it. The bookmark was there. Well...it was there because it fell out and I didn't know where to put it, so I just stuck it in somewhere. Sorry." Whew.

The pain on Andrew's face was clear. "Drake, don't lie. I know you read it. You don't have to hide it."

"What are you talking about?"

Andrew looked at him, hoping an all-out war wasn't pending. "There were tearstains on the page, Drake."

Drake looked away and scowled. "I don't know what you're talking about."

"I'm not condemning you for it. I was just wondering if you wanted to talk about—"

"There's nothing to talk about, OK? Why do you have to dissect everything? What if those were your own tears on that page? What if the pain in my leg was so bad that I happened to leak a few tears while the pages were open?"

"On the page of the crucifixion, Drake?" Andrew sighed and ran his tongue over his bottom lip. He wasn't about to let this subject slip away. Not after running ten miles to reach it. "I'm not trying to single you out; I just wanted to know."

"Know *what*? Know that I bawled like a baby for over half an hour just because I couldn't make Jesus' crucifixion make sense in my mind? All right, so I cried. And I cried more after that when I realized I couldn't have any of it because I was so messed up on the inside."

"Drake, you've got it all wrong—"

"Boy, you can say that again," Drake said, forcing a laugh. "I read the stories, the chapters, the parables, and I believe it. Surprised? I guess I've known all along there was a God. There has to be. But when I read about Jesus...when I understood His pain, I saw myself for the first time and I despised it. I knew what sin was because I felt it eating me up the more I read about Him. And it hurt." He stomped his crutch on the floor and clenched his teeth, hating that the feeling was returning. "As bad as the pain in my leg hurt, knowing this hurts worse."

"But that's why Jesus came, Drake," Andrew said, unable to subdue a smile. "To bridge the way back to God again. You don't have to be afraid."

Drake clawed his fingers into the padding beneath his hands. "How can I not be? It's easy for you. What have you ever done in life that's bad?"

"I've lied. I even stole something before."

"There, you see? Stuff like that's insignificant. I'm talking about big things, like taking a kind man for granted, causing an innocent kid to get kidnapped, even something as big as committing a murder."

"Murder?"

Drake shook his head. "Just throwing that out there. You get my point."

"Show me."

"Show you what?"

"That even something as terrible as kidnapping or killing someone is unforgivable by God."

"Well...maybe not in those exact words, but my own common sense tells me that. Look, I didn't mean to get into this with you. I shoulda just kept my mouth shut, but as always, it ends up like this."

"Drake, don't clam up again and refuse to talk to me. I'm trying to work things out, but it seems like every time we speak, there's an argument."

"Like my dad," Drake said, a lump rising in his throat. "If we can't get along, then maybe it's better if we don't talk to each other."

"Don't do this. I'm not against you. I want us to get along. I really do."

"Well, obviously that's just not gonna work out, is it? Look, you've been kind to me and I'm grateful that you're letting me stay here until my leg heals, but you and me are complete opposites. Things just don't work out between us."

"Why do you say that? I'm not the one trying to push away. Don't you understand that I *want* us to get along? Why do you want me to stay out of your life so badly?"

Drake moved toward the fireplace, remembering how his dad had looked in the dark shadows of his old house. His face had looked so evil, even with his eyes closed and unmoving; Drake's knuckles had bled slightly after the hit, never slackening from the rock-solid fist he had used as his only weapon. Drake looked up at Andrew, suddenly feeling like a stranger here. "Because if you only knew the real me, you would have never opened your door to me in the first place. You may think you know who I am, but you really don't. I'm not the kind of person you would get along with."

"I've tolerated you so far. Doesn't that mean something to you?"

Drake wished he could offer a different response, but he honestly had to shake his head. "No, it doesn't. I don't see the value of it. Why are you trying to invest in my life when it's done nothing but blow up in your face? I'm not a profit, Mr. Andrew; I'm a loss. If taking in a homeless person for the month was a little scheme your church devised, then sorry, but it's failed. I'd like to think that you taking me in has changed me in some unimaginable way and my life will never be the same because of it, but I can't.

"I showed up at your doorstep a miserable, homeless teenager, and in a week or so, I'll be leaving out that door the very same way I came in." He rubbed his face and longed for rest. "I really do thank you for taking me in. Thanks for feeding me and giving me a bed. I've never had it this good before. But I can't accept this, just like I can't accept what it says in that Book of yours."

Andrew gazed at him with sad, yet compassionate eyes as he listened. "Then you're robbing yourself of something very special," he said softly. "I wish I could make you see that. If Jesus didn't come for the sinners, who'd He come for? The good people, as you call them? Look around, Drake. Is there anyone in this world who's good? Is there anyone deserving of Heaven?"

Drake lowered his eyes to the floor. Déjà vu. Hadn't he had this same conversation with Ronnie at Ivan's hideout? Scary how those two worked together without realizing it.

"No, not one," Andrew said through the silence. "Jesus isn't keeping you out of Heaven. You are. You see the sin in your life, and that's good, but your problem is you're struggling to hold on to something that's killing you. Yes, you've sinned, Drake, and so have I. We both recognize the sin in our lives, but the difference between you and me is that I gave it to God.

"That doesn't mean I'm free to do whatever I want to do. Thankfully, when Jesus came into my heart, I was ashamed of my sin and truly wanted to change. I still mess up, though, but I refuse to let my sin keep me from God. That's why every day I ask Jesus for forgiveness. You can have forgiveness too, if you'll just ask for it and accept what Jesus has already done for you."

Impossible. Nothing Andrew could say or do would make him see differently. Forgiveness was just another crutch of Christianity. Drake could barely manage walking with two crutches, so a third would only make him trip. "I can't," he said plainly. "After all He already went through, why should He do anything else for me? I had my chance, and I blew it. It'd be wrong to ask Jesus into a heart that's filled with nothing but obscene thoughts and ugly desires. Why should Jesus carry my burden? It's not His to carry."

Andrew took a deep breath. "But that's why He died. Don't let His death for you be in vain. You're already so close. You've read the Bible, you recognize your sin, but you're pushing salvation away when it's the only thing that can save you." Andrew moved over to the couch where Drake sat and chose the cushion on the end, purposefully leaving a space between them. Despite his obvious effort, he noticed Drake stiffen when he sat. Andrew was beginning to feel as if he couldn't breathe in his own home without being accused of spreading the plague. *God, I'm trying. And I still believe in miracles...hint, hint. You know I'd greatly appreciate the support right now.*

The ceiling fan rocked above them, cooling the room but not doing much for their heated argument. "I love you, Drake." Had he said that out loud? It was meant to be a thought, not spoken audibly. He looked at Drake. Drake was staring back at him, just as startled to hear those words as he was.

"Drake..." Andrew began. He had to say something now after those words. But what? *Just speak from your heart. Honesty may be painful, but its motive is always love.* He cleared his throat and listened for the Holy Spirit to help him begin. "It hurts me to hear us fight, but I love you enough to tell you the truth. If you die without Jesus, you *will* go to hell. I know you don't feel worthy of Heaven, but neither do I. That's the whole point. If we could somehow make it to Heaven on our own, what would be the purpose of Jesus' death? Salvation is just as much for you as it is for me or Ronnie, but until you grasp that for yourself, you'll always be living life the same way."

Drake gazed toward the other end of the room. "I'm tired of this merry-go-round conversation of ours. I told you, I have nothing more to say."

"Then I won't make you." Andrew picked up Ronnie's picture from the table and smiled. The stick man that was supposed to be him had hips cocked sideways, as if frozen in a disco. That must have been caused when the car hit a pothole, since Ronnie had scolded him while they were driving to the hospital.

Drake heard Andrew chuckling to himself and turned his head. "What's so funny?"

"This," Andrew said, pointing to the disjointed figure on the picture.

Drake suppressed a laugh. "Looks like a bad case of arthritis."

Andrew set the picture down and gazed up at him. "Hey, it did my heart good to hear all those things you said to Ronnie in the hospital room earlier."

So the conversation was changing again. Crank up the merry-go-round. "I wasn't doing it for you."

"I know. That's what made it special."

Drake thought about that. "I don't know. What he said made me feel different. Made me really feel sorry for all I put him through when he hugged me like that."

"Ronnie really does love you, Drake." Andrew chuckled and said, "I just hope you're prepared to stay up late with him tonight, 'cause he'll be talking your ears off."

A smile crept across Drake's lips. "Yeah, well, I'm kinda looking forward to it."

"Knock, knock!" Ronnie said for the quadrillionth time.

Drake forced himself to keep from sighing. His eyelids were falling lower over his eyes with every lame joke, and he wasn't sure how much longer he could hold out. The clock said one thirty. His body told him it was much later, especially when he heard Andrew's snoring move into its second stage. Lucky him.

"Drake!" Ronnie complained, slapping the side of the couch with the back of his hand. "I said, 'knock, knock!'"

"Yeah, yeah, I remember. Who's there?"

"Yul."

"Yul who?"

"Yul never know!" Ronnie exclaimed, bursting out in laughter.

"Ha, ha," Drake said, trying his hardest to sound like he was having fun. Even if the jokes were incredibly corny, at least this was better than watching Ronnie play with his crutches—his legs kicking wildly in the air every time he took a running jump. He tucked his pillow under his head and said wearily, "Hey, I've got a joke, Ronnie."

"Really?"

"Yeah. Knock, knock."

"Who's there?"

"Justin."

"Justin who?"

"Justin time to go to sleep."

Ronnie didn't laugh. "Aw, c'mon, Drake. You don't really mean it, do ya?"

Drake covered a yawn. "I'm tired, buddy. Maybe we can finish this tomorrow, huh?"

Ronnie heaved a sigh and squirmed into his makeshift sleeping bag. "There's still a lot left on the list..."

"We can tackle the Amazon jungle some other time."

Ronnie folded his arms. "Funny."

"You mean that's not on your list?"

"Now I'm gonna dream about lizards and tigers tonight. Thanks."

"Are tigers in the Amazon?"

"How should I know? I'll tell you what I find after I get done dreaming about 'em," Ronnie said, flopping over on one side.

Drake stretched his arm across the small end table beside him and flicked the lamp off. Then he turned over on his side and threw the covers over his shoulder. The couch wasn't too bad to sleep on, except for the barely noticeable way the cushions curved toward the back of the couch. Drake buried his cold feet underneath the mound of covers and peeked at the clock one last time. All was quiet in the house except for the low hum of the AC running along with the refrigerator. He couldn't remember the last time he had felt this tired.

Except for the night he had murdered his dad. With all that had happened to him lately, he had somehow managed to push that thought out of his mind. Or so he thought. Now it all came back to him in one long, crashing wave of remembrance. Every little detail, every word spoken, every action taken, every gut-wrenching feeling on the inside of him after he realized what he had done.

And on top of all that, he hadn't allowed himself to grieve yet over the death of his mom. His whole world seemed to be spiraling faster and faster down a path of destruction, and crying almost didn't seem worth the effort anymore because he knew it couldn't change reality. Too bad there wasn't an eraser for the past. Andrew had mentioned something called forgiveness, but Drake was beyond reach. Beyond hope.

Drake lay on his back and stared at the ceiling. Jesus was probably up there somewhere looking down on him and shaking His head at the accident He had created. That's how Drake viewed himself. An accident. He had crashed and burned, fallen for the world's lies hook, line, and sinker. Now Andrew was trying to give him the false hope that there was still a chance for him. *I wish he'd just leave me alone. It hurts enough to know what kind of a person I've turned out to be, but for someone to tell me that God still loves me only makes me more angry. I know he's just trying to be nice, but it's not helping.*

"Drake?" Ronnie said, pushing his covers down so he could see Drake's face.

"I told you, buddy, no more jokes," Drake said, burying his face in his pillow.

"This isn't a joke. I wanted to tell you about a dream I had last night after we took you to the hospital."

"Was it a long dream, 'cause I ain't—"

"No, not too long. Maybe I dreamed it 'cause I cried all the way back home and it made my stomach hurt. I dunno."

"What were you crying for?"

"I thought the doctors might not be able to fix you and you could die. Uncle Andy told me they shot you, and I thought you might die while I was sleeping."

"Ah, Ronnie, don't worry about me. You know I'm fine."

"I know you are now, but I was scared then. Anyway, after I got home, I went straight to bed—after praying for you, of course."

Of course.

"And then I dreamed a dream. I dunno, but it kinda felt different. Like I was really there. Know what I mean?"

"Yeah, I know what you mean," Drake said, watching Ronnie tiredly through one drooping eyelid. "Just get to the dream."

"The dream. Right. Well...I sorta dreamed about Heaven."

"Heaven? Well, I guess that's always a nice thing to dream about, right?"

Ronnie was strangely silent before saying, "Drake...you wasn't there."

Now it was Drake's turn to be quiet. "What do you mean I wasn't there?" he said slowly.

Ronnie's eyes were squinted as he said, "Uncle Andy and me was there, but I didn't see you anywhere. I asked some people around, but they didn't know either. So I started looking for you. I looked everywhere, and I kept looking for you, but you wasn't there. Then I felt scared. Drake, if you wasn't in Heaven, that meant you was in hell."

Drake couldn't explain the sudden shakiness that had come over him. "Ronnie, that was just a dream," he assured him. "A bad dream. You don't have to be afraid for me."

"But I *am* afraid, Drake." Ronnie's voice had never sounded as grave as it did now. "I have to ask you this, or else I might have that dream again." Nothing could have prepared Drake for what he heard next. "Drake, are you going to Heaven?"

Drake looked away and drew in his blanket closer to his body. "I dunno, Ronnie. How would I know?"

"I know that I am. And I know Uncle Andy's gonna be there too, 'cause he believes in Jesus like I do. I just want to make sure you are gonna be there with us. I don't wanna be up there one day looking for you forever. And I don't want you to go to hell. I want us to be together in Heaven, not away from each other. If we aren't, that means we'll never see each other again. So are you going to Heaven, Drake? Are you?"

"That isn't up for me to decide."

"Yes it is. All you have to do is—"

"No, it isn't!" Drake snapped. "It's not that easy."

"So...you don't know if you're going to Heaven or not?"

"No, Ronnie, I don't. I guess I'll just have to find out when I'm dead, won't I?" Drake turned and covered his face with his blanket. Gah, he wished religion would leave him alone.

Chapter
20

PIERCED

Drake Pearson was running. Faster. Faster. His heartbeat pounded like an echoing explosion. It was beating too quickly; he should be dead. His body was on the verge of collapse, and yet he kept running...

A shadow overlapped his. Something was chasing him. Something big. Drake took a left and quickly peered behind him into the thick smoke.

It disappeared.

Drake panted as he pushed his legs to run harder. Sweat clung to his face like icy fingers. It wanted him; its breath on his neck felt like fire. What had happened to the world as he knew it? Everything was colorless—the sky was pitch-black and the world a murky gray. Suddenly, every building, street sign, person, and even the asphalt underneath his feet began to gradually melt and sink into the ground.

And he was sinking.

Drake tried running faster to escape.

Thunder sound waves rippled through the sky. In a flash, the earth ruptured and swallowed him where he stood. Drake fell for only an instant before he smacked the ground. Bones shattered, and yet only a vague perception of pain told him he was dying.

He lifted his dazed head and found he was in a small, empty room. The temperature was cold. Too cold for any human to survive. The goose bumps on his body felt like needles to his flesh. He had to get out of there but was no longer able to move his legs.

Panting deeply, he lay there in terror, studying the room. It too was colorless, except for the words JUDGMENT DAY written on the floor in smeared red.

Blood red.

Drake looked down and studied his body as more cold chills ran up his arms and legs. His body was deteriorating in front of his eyes—flesh taking on the form of liquid and blood concreting to stone. He was dying. Fast.

Without warning, two doors on both sides of him split open. One powerful hand reached through one door and another hand reached for him through the other.

Both hands seized him at once and began pulling him in opposite directions. Drake could feel the blood rising to his head as he tried to fight back, but whatever strength he once had was worthless now.

"Choose this day whom you will serve!" a voice boomed from above.

"Guilty!" another voice shrieked from below. "Guilty! There is no other punishment but death!"

Drake was being pulled harder. He knew that if he held out much longer, his entire body would be torn in two. He had to let go of one hand, but which one?

Tears welled in his eyes at the excruciating pain. His body weakened as he felt himself going unconscious. With no strength left in him to fight back, he gave up and let his head fall to his chest.

"Guilty!" the voice cried again. "He's mine!"

Drake's head lolled to the right. The horrible noises and sights seemed to fade away as the beating of his heart came to an abrupt halt. His eyes fell on the hand that refused to let go.

Pierced. With a nail.

Jesus Christ.

Drake sat up immediately, gasping for air. Beads of sweat clung to his wet hair and face. He pressed both hands against his chest and tried to control his breathing. *Just a dream. Just a dream.*

He touched his face to make sure he was still alive. His hands were normal, feet were normal. Ronnie was still sleeping soundly beside him on the floor. *Oh, thank God.*

His voice stopped short at those words. The running, the room, the doors, the voices...all seemed too real to be a dream.

And the pierced hand. Even with his eyes open, Drake could still see it as he had in the dream. He held his trembling hand in front of his face. *It was there. I saw it, holding onto mine. Jesus was holding my hand, pulling me toward Him.* He forced his eyes shut, desperately trying to visualize the scene again. *I felt it. It wasn't a dream. It was real. I was there... at Judgment Day.*

It was all too much to take in. *So it's really real then. Judgment Day is the place you go when you die.* Drake sat back and closed his eyes. He wasn't ready for eternity, and he knew it. He wasn't ready to be pulled into a place he knew nothing about. The thought of an endless afterlife petrified him.

Drake stared at the door across the room. He could still faintly hear the railing words, "Guilty! Guilty!" stabbing at his soul, as if some sick creature were begging to take his life. He had wanted to scream, to tell the voice he wasn't guilty, but how could he? He *was* guilty. Guilty of practically everything there was to be guilty of.

So that raised the question: why had Jesus pulled him in His direction? Why hadn't He just given him up to the place where he belonged? Why hadn't He *let go?*

"Forgiveness," Drake said, just above a whisper. It was something Andrew had mentioned, saying that all he had to do was ask for it. Impossible. He had nothing to offer in return, so trying to reach God was pointless. Still, the dream tormented him. The more he tried to reason against it, the more it burdened his heart.

Ever since the day of the murder, he had wanted to tell someone—anyone—if only it meant being relieved a fraction from the corroding guilt that was steadily melting his life away. He had almost blurted out the truth to Andrew several times, but every time he had stopped himself just before opening his mouth. And every time he had hated himself all the more for keeping his dark secret locked inside.

Drake quietly picked up his crutches and lifted himself up off the couch, careful not to wake Ronnie. It took him five minutes to maneuver around the bulky furniture—only to leave him half-tripping across the rest of the room after catching his foot on the hump in the rug. He caught his fingers around the television and regained his balance.

Ronnie stirred, then rolled over on his stomach. Thank goodness, he was a deep sleeper.

Drake gripped his crutches and headed toward the back door. His mind was on nothing but getting outside where he could be alone.

The night air chilled Drake as he closed the screen door gently behind him. Two dogs were barking in the distance while an upset owl seemed to question their identities with a recurrent, "Who? Who?" He stopped to listen, wondering why he had decided to come out here.

Chill bumps covered his exposed arms, and he considered going back inside and catching up on his sleep. *Who am I kidding? I can't go back to sleep. I don't even wanna go back to sleep. How do I know I wouldn't just have that dream again?*

Because there were only two steps down leading to the yard, Drake had no problem getting off the porch. The grass tickled his bare feet as he lowered his good foot to the soft ground below. The enchanting feeling of being almost invisible in the darkness took him back years to those rare nights of sneaking out his bedroom window as a child. He never went anywhere; he just wanted to climb a tree and listen to the crickets sing.

To him, the night was filled with not only sights and sounds, but also with smells. No one ever believed him when he told them that, but he knew it to be true. The distinct aroma of a dew-saturated fog, accompanied by the faint perfume of honeysuckle, and the rare scent the earth gives off when the ground releases its heat were all as alive and real to Drake as the layers of stars above.

Life had changed since then. The little boy climbing trees was now a self-convicted felon with a second-rate escape plan. Time was a good painkiller.

Drake hobbled toward a nearby maple and went around to the other side to make sure he wouldn't be seen if Andrew happened to go to his window. He rested his back against the wide trunk and laid his crutches on the ground beside him. With all the darkness enclosing him, he almost felt as if he were in his dream again. But this time his senses were fully alert, and he felt a heaviness in his spirit that no dream could possibly convey.

Drake placed the palms of his hands against the cool dirt and breathed. If he were to die right now, what would the next seconds be like? Wasn't it already too late for him?

Drake stared at the stars with moist eyes, so confused. *I didn't ask for the dream. I didn't ask for any of this...I'm not ready.*

His lip quivered as he continued to stare up at patches of the night sky through the lacework of leaves and branches rustling above him. Someone had to be up there. Someone who loved him enough to keep holding on. "Jesus," he started, not sure what he should say or how he should say it. "Jesus, my life is a wreck."

That wasn't the right way to talk to God, was it? It was time to get to the point of why he had come out here. "If You're even listening... You shouldn't waste Your time with me. The voice...what I heard in the dream...I really am guilty, so You can let go now."

Drake sat still, not knowing if he was waiting for a response or going to add something else. Was that what he really wanted, for God to let him go? It was what he deserved. Sin had to be paid for. But it still wasn't what he wanted deep down.

"I don't really want You to let me go," he added, feeling the need to talk again. "It's just that I don't think there's a way out of it now. If I could come to You as a better person, I'd feel OK about it. But the fact is, I never wanted You in my life before now." He bit his lip and ran a hand through his hair. It was a struggle just to get the words out.

"Jesus, I've wasted everything I have. I killed my father, I hurt Andrew and Ronnie in ways I never thought possible, and I'm afraid that I'll hurt You too if You come into my life. I really want Your love and Your forgiveness, but I'd just be using You like I've used so many other people in the past for my own gain."

Like a torrent, tears began streaming down his cheeks. "I don't want You in my life because I'm so ashamed of it. My heart isn't pure. It's ugly. I have nothing to offer You in return."

Drake broke down and cried, pounding his fist in the dirt softened by last night's rain. "Say something!" he said loudly. "Anything! Just let me know You're at least listening and I'm not talking to myself again!" He covered his face with his hands and sobbed. "God, show me You're here. I want to believe."

He reached out a hand and held the tree beside him to steady himself. He felt a deep indention where his fingers were, and wiped away the warm tears from his eyes to look. Carved into the bark were three greenish-brown words: *Andrew, Ronnie, Drak.* Drake's name was spelled without an e. *Ronnie*, he thought. Carved to the left of Andrew and Ronnie's names were tiny crosses.

Beside Drake's name, however, there was nothing but bark.

Oh, Ronnie. I had no idea. He turned and rested his back against the solid trunk. Instantly, he heard the sound of glass breaking beneath him. Drake pushed himself to the side, noticing for the first time that he had been sitting on a mound of recently removed dirt. He shoveled the dirt away with his hands and found a buried broken jar. Inside was a note. Drake carefully removed the large pieces of glass before pulling the note out. *Wonder what it says.* He unfolded the paper and recognized Ronnie's handwriting.

Jesus, plees let my momy and dady be nise to me agin. I want to see them, but I'm still a litle skared.

Jesus, plees also help Drak. I love him alot. He needs to no you love him to, cuz I want him to go to heven with me one day.

Drake pressed the note to his heart and clenched his teeth. If someone was trying to get his attention, it was working. He had asked God to speak, and here was his answer.

Every feeling of worthlessness faded away as Drake fell to his knees despite the pain in his leg and lowered his face to the ground. "Jesus, I want You," he cried, not caring anymore if the whole world heard him. "Forgive me of my sins. I need You tonight and for the rest of my life. Please, if You can somehow take this life and make something beautiful out of it, then I give it to You."

The next thing Drake heard was the faint sound of someone calling his name. He lifted his head and saw Andrew running toward him in a wrinkled white tee and plaid pajama pants.

"Drake, Drake!" Andrew called, rushing to his side. "What happened? Did you fall? I heard you saying something out here and I—"

Drake hurriedly lifted himself off the ground and embraced Andrew. This man had given him so much and showed him incredible love at times when he least deserved it. "Thank you, Mr. Andrew," he said, his tears soaking through the man's thin shirt. "Thank you for everything."

Andrew was caught off guard by this unexpected gesture. Slowly, he wrapped his arms around Drake's shaking back. An indescribable emotion flooded his heart and the two held each other for a long time. *God, I don't know what You did, but I thank You for doing it.* Andrew wasn't concerned about asking questions or trying to get an explanation for the embrace. The only thing that mattered was that something had finally clicked in Drake's head, and now it was all coming out at once. He was just glad he was there to receive it.

Drake gently pulled away and looked Andrew in the eyes. "I was wrong," he said, steadying his voice. "I thought I was right, but I was so wrong."

"Wrong about what, Drake?" Andrew quietly prodded.

"About God. Jesus. I never knew He really cared until now. I had a dream tonight...it was so real. It felt like I was dying, and then there He was, holding my hand, like He was trying to pull me back."

"Jesus?"

"Yeah, now I finally know what it feels like to really hold His hand." He inhaled a deep breath of chilled air and said, "I gave Him my life tonight. All of it. I know it may not seem like much, but it's all I got."

Andrew embraced Drake again as tears streamed from his eyes. "That's all God ever asks for, Drake. I'm so happy for you. You don't know how much I've prayed—even pleaded with God—for this day to come." He let go of Drake and smiled. "And now it's finally here."

Drake tried to smile back, but a new fear swept over him, and he looked down. "Uh, there's something else," he said, darting his eyes away.

"Something else?"

Drake balled his hands in a fist and tried to keep from shaking again. He wasn't ready for this. "That first day when you asked me why I came here..." He blinked twice and bit the inside of his cheek. "I lied to you."

This was unexpected, but Andrew wasn't surprised. "Go on."

"I told you I hitchhiked up here. I told you I was gonna hole up in a shelter until I found a job. Those were just lies I made up to cover up the truth."

"I don't care why you came here. That was never an issue."

"But—"

"You don't have to explain anything to me. If you were out of money or got kicked out of your house, that's none of my business."

"I made it your business when I stepped foot in your house. This is something you need to know." Drake took another long breath before saying, "You know how that phone call you got from the police made me so upset?"

Andrew nodded his head. "I remember."

"I was afraid of being caught."

"Being caught? Why would you—" Andrew stopped and closed his mouth. "Drake," he said gravely, "what did you do?"

Drake closed his eyes before he spoke, not wanting to have to face the shock on Andrew's face when he told him the truth. His pulse quickened as he said almost silently, "I killed my dad."

The color in Andrew's face blanched. For a long time, he said nothing. Shock wasn't a realistic enough word to describe how he felt. Staggered was more like it. Every feeling of joy he had felt only moments ago seemed to fade away into a mixture of horror and astonishment. Even Drake's tears on the back of his shirt were disappearing in the breeze, almost convincing him they had never been there to begin with. He wanted to say something, but every time he tried, he couldn't seem to get past the first word.

"That's why I insisted on leaving," Drake said, shifting his weight uneasily as he watched Andrew sit down on the porch step with his mouth half open. "I never wanted to hurt you or Ronnie, but after killing someone, I could never trust myself again. You deserve to know the truth. I couldn't keep it inside any longer."

"Why, Drake?" Andrew said eventually, his voice breaking. "Why did you do it?"

"Because I found out my dad had murdered my mom!" Drake blurted, unable to keep it inside. "Why is that so bad? The law kills murderers all the time, so why am I being tracked down like a rabid animal? It's not fair I have to live the rest of my life this way!"

"Shhh," Andrew cautioned, searching the surrounding houses for any lights being turned on.

"I was angry," Drake whispered, "but I never planned it to go that far. It was an accident. I hit him, I expected him to fall, but not hit his head on the fireplace and stop breathing. The whole thing was a stupid mistake, but how can I explain that to the cops?"

Andrew shook his head, out of answers this time.

"It took me a long time just to convince myself that I never really intended to kill him. I wanted revenge, but it turned my life into a living nightmare. Now I see things at night. I have dreams. I hear us fighting."

"Oh, Drake," Andrew said, lowering his head to his hand.

"Now I can't go back. I can't change things. I accepted Jesus into my heart, and believe me, it was the real thing, but that doesn't mean I won't live with my dad's murder for the rest of my life." Drake sighed as he lowered himself onto the porch step beside Andrew. He looked up at the sky. Even the moon had been scared off. "I'm just talking to myself again. Why should you even care what I have to say? Now you know the whole, rotten truth about me."

"I'm listening, Drake, just as I've always been. It's just...hard to hear all this at once. I never knew—"

"That I am a murderer?" Drake said, his jawbone rigid. "I know. I wanted to tell you so badly, but I couldn't make myself face you. You're the only person who's ever believed in me. I didn't wanna lose that."

Andrew crossed his arms tightly against his chest to conserve his body heat. "What are you going to do now?"

Drake lowered his head. That was one question he wasn't prepared to answer. "I'm scared," he admitted. He was tired of thinking about the future. It only left him hurting more when it was over.

"I realize that, but if you expect me to still believe in you, you have to give me something to believe in. That involves taking responsibility for your actions. I know that's a tough word, but it's something we all face."

"You don't hate me?"

"I'm certainly not condoning what you did, but I could never hate you, Drake. What's done is done. There is no changing the past, so what I'm concerned about now is what you're going to do about it. Are you going to keep running away from something that will chase you to your grave, or are you going to make it right once and for all?"

"I know what the right answer is," Drake said miserably. "I just don't know if I'm ready yet. I'm afraid of getting the death sentence, and even more afraid of dying."

"It's up to you. I can't make you decide."

"Can I think about it tonight? I'd like to get some sleep before I make my decision."

Andrew nodded slowly. "As long as you stick to your word and don't run out on me before morning."

"I will. I'll let you know tomorrow." Drake grabbed his crutches as Andrew helped him off the porch step. "Should I tell Ronnie?" he said, leaving them both in still silence again.

Andrew thought for a moment and finally said, "That too is up to you."

Chapter 21

HARD CHOICE

The rest of the night, Drake Pearson fought the idea of going back to Missouri and turning himself in, even after he had vowed to himself only days earlier that he would never resort to that—ever. But everything was different now. He had asked Jesus to come into his heart, and that had changed his whole perspective about how he would now live his life.

God, get me out of this, he prayed. *I'm so afraid.* Even with his blanket and shirt off, his entire body glistened with sweat. *I don't have to go back, do I? I mean, I asked for forgiveness. That's enough, right? Haven't I already suffered enough as it is without having to face that too?* He stared up at the ceiling fan, water rushing to his eyes as the stiff breeze blew down on him. *Jesus, give me the strength to do what's right. I don't wanna live the rest of my life feeling this way.*

Drake closed his tired eyes and wondered if he should tell Ronnie. The kid was so young; could he even bear news like that? Telling Andrew was one thing, but explaining something like that to Ronnie would be like scaling Mount Everest with one hand. Ronnie's mind was so pure and innocent, so what would he think when Drake told him he had murdered his own father? That would forever kill his trust in Drake, only leave him confused and hurt.

Drake massaged his forehead and thought, *But won't I be hurting Ronnie just as much by not telling him?* Ouch. He didn't want to look at that side of it. In fact, he didn't want to think about anything except what was good for him and what would keep him safe. *Still the same, selfish old self, aren't ya, Drake? C'mon, God. You're supposed to make this easy, right? Supposed to make everything magically work out to a happy ending.*

Drake rolled his head to the side and watched Ronnie's covers rise and fall as he breathed. *No, I shouldn't expect You to do that. No matter how I look at it, whether I wanted it to happen or not, this is still my fault and I have to pay for it. I just thank You that You'll be with me when I go through it.*

Maybe it was because Drake was up most of the night and he felt about as alive as a rock, but it seemed to him that Andrew came downstairs earlier than usual. Drake sat up and thrust his pillow underneath his back. "What's up?"

Andrew pushed Drake's blanket aside and sat down beside him on the couch. "Just thought I'd check to see how you were doing. I heard you moving around a lot last night."

"You were up too, huh?" Drake said, wiping a sticky film away from his eyes.

"Spent most of the night thinking about you."

Drake glanced up at him, then quickly darted his eyes away. "Yeah, me too."

"Have you made up your mind?"

Drake interlaced his fingers and nodded slowly. "I can't run from it anymore." He breathed deeply and said, "Just promise me one thing first."

"If I can."

"Promise me you'll come visit me. I don't know all the procedures and stuff they have to go through or how often they'll let you visit, but it'll kill me if I never see you guys again."

"Of course we will. But you know what that means, don't you?"

Drake looked down. "It's better if Ronnie knows."

"When do you want me to take you back to Missouri?"

"As soon as possible, if that's OK. I know it seems too early, but you don't understand. I can't live like this one more day knowing what I've done."

Andrew rose from the couch and walked into the kitchen. "Then I'll make you a big breakfast before we go. I know you'll...Drake, I'm sorry. I didn't mean for it to sound that way."

"It's OK. If it's all the same to you, I'd rather not eat. I don't have an appetite right now."

"Where you goin'?" Ronnie said as Drake emerged from the bathroom with a new set of clothes on.

Drake spun around. "When'd you get up?"

Ronnie shrugged. "Just now."

"Oh, well...go eat breakfast or something."

"Already did. Want to hear my dream about the Amazon?"

"Some other time."

"There weren't any tigers, but I did see a giraffe. Weird. I don't think they're supposed to live there either."

"I said some other time."

Ronnie walked closer to Drake to see his face more clearly. "Hey, what's wrong? You look sad."

Drake hobbled into the living room and glanced up at the stairs. He heard water running. *Fine time to take a shower,* he thought. *I don't wanna tell him by myself.*

"So where are you goin'?"

Drake wanted to tell Ronnie to leave him alone and go watch Animal Planet, but he had already rehearsed a thousand times in his head how he would tell Ronnie the news. "Ronnie, sit down," he said hesitantly.

Ronnie sat, eyebrows wrinkled.

Drake forced a smile despite the fact that he was squeezing the life out of his crutches. "Last night I found the note you put under the tree."

"You did?"

"Yeah, and I read it. Ronnie, your words made me realize what I've been ignoring—you, Andrew, and especially Jesus."

"Jesus?" Ronnie said, excitement in his eyes.

Drake nodded. "I asked Him into my heart last night." He tapped his chest with his finger and said, "He's in here now, just like you said He'd be."

Ronnie leaped from his chair and hugged Drake. "Drake, I'm so happy for you!" He let go, as if suddenly remembering something, and backed away slowly. "But if Jesus came in your heart, why do you look so sad?"

Drake gulped and tried to figure out exactly how he would explain this. "That's what I wanna talk to you about. Because I have Jesus in my heart, that means I have to get rid of the old stuff. Y'know, throw away all the junk to make room for Him."

Ronnie just sat there, listening intently to his every word.

If only Ronnie had been running around the room and half-listening, this would have been so much easier for Drake to get through. But when he looked at him like this, it gave him a churning feeling in the pit of his stomach.

"So that's what I have to do," he said, wondering how long he could avoid reaching the main point. "Get rid of the bad stuff." He scooted next to Ronnie and rested his hand on his knee. "Ronnie, you don't know how hard this is for me to tell you."

"You can tell me, Drake," Ronnie said. "I'm listening."

I know. That's why it's so hard. Drake fingered the tassel on the embroidered pillow beside him and said, "Ronnie, you know how your dad made you mad sometimes?"

Ronnie stared down at his floppy socks and nodded.

"It really hurt, didn't it?"

"A lot."

Drake wrapped his arm around Ronnie's narrow shoulders, fighting everything inside him that screamed against telling Ronnie the truth. "Well, Ronnie, that's how my dad was, only I was a lot bigger than you, so things usually got ugly."

Ronnie stared up at him in horror. "Did he hurt you?"

"Never hit me, but I found out something about him one day that made me *really* mad at him." There was movement at the top of the stairs, and Drake glanced up.

Andrew was standing at the top with his hands on the rail, listening to him as tears moistened his eyes.

Drake nearly broke down right there. "So I came home after finding out what he did," he choked up. "I had enough of him, so I..."

"You what, Drake?"

Drake clenched his teeth. "I hit him. And he fell. I didn't know it would happen." A tear leaked from his eye, and he briskly wiped it away. "I said something to him after that—I don't remember what it was now—but he never moved. Never got up."

Ronnie observed the dark shadow line on the side of Drake's face. "You mean..."

"I killed him, Ronnie," Drake said, somehow maintaining eye contact when all he felt like doing was hiding his face.

"No," Ronnie mumbled, standing up. "No, I don't believe you."

"It's true, Ronnie," Drake said, his lips tight as he spoke. "You asked me where I was going, so here's your answer. I'm going back home so I can turn myself in to the police."

"No!" Ronnie screamed, running upstairs and smearing his cheeks with his tears. Andrew rushed to his room, but Ronnie slammed the door and shouted, "Leave me alone!"

Drake had never felt so depressed in all his life sitting in the front seat of Andrew's car, staring out the windshield as a gray world passed him by. It had been practically a re-creation of the Battle of Bunker Hill just to get Ronnie out of his room and into the car. Ever since they had left the house, Ronnie had sat with his arms crossed, refusing to talk to anyone. Andrew was just as quiet, only he at least moved slightly when he had to turn the steering wheel. Ronnie looked like a statue ready to shatter into a million pieces any second.

"You don't have to try to be so macho and hold it all together, Ronnie," Drake told him after watching him for five minutes in the rearview mirror. "It's OK to cry. I had to."

Ronnie began tearing up, so he turned his head and moved out of Drake's sight.

Drake sighed and rested his head against the window. "I shouldn't have told you. Either of you. I should've just waited till my stupid leg healed up and did all this by myself."

"No, it was better you told us," Andrew said, trying to hide the waver in his voice. It was the first thing he had said since they had backed out of the driveway. "Besides, I'm glad I'll be there to support you."

Drake waited for Ronnie to say something. When nothing came, Drake realized his lips would obviously be sealed for the entire trip. He couldn't stand this kind of pain.

Two hours later, Andrew spotted a fast food joint and pulled into the drive-through. "All right, everybody tell me what you want to eat. There's chicken, fries, burgers—"

"I'm not hungry," Ronnie interrupted.

"May I take your order?" a voice said cheerily through the tiny machine.

Andrew turned and faced Ronnie. "But, Ronnie—"

"Me either," Drake said.

Andrew looked at Drake and said slowly, "Me either *what?*"

Drake shrugged and said, "I'm not hungry either. But you go ahead."

"I don't believe this," Andrew said, shaking his head. "Drake, you didn't eat breakfast. You have to be starving."

"Sorry, but I don't even wanna look at food right now," Drake said.

"Nope," Ronnie said.

"Sir?" the voice asked. "Are you ready to order?"

Andrew glanced at them both and waited for a response. Finally, he stuck his tongue in his cheek and leaned his head out the window. "No thanks. We all suddenly lost our appetites."

"You didn't have to tell her that," Drake said after Andrew pulled back onto the main road. "Now she probably thinks we thought the food on their menu looked disgusting."

"I don't know why everyone has to be so stubborn," Andrew replied.

Drake threw his hands in the air. "No one's being stubborn! I'm just not hungry. Sorry, but you can't really blame me, can you? I mean, it won't be much longer until I'm—"

"I know, all right? I don't care about the food!" Andrew said sharply. "I know it won't be much longer until we get there and they take you away. Don't you think I know that? Don't you know that's all I've been thinking about this entire trip?"

"OK, then, so why are you so mad at me all of a sudden?" Drake said heatedly. "I just said I wasn't hungry. Gah, you'd think the sky was falling or something by the way you're acting. Just turn around then and order me some fries if it'll make you feel better."

"For the billionth time, it's not about the food!" Andrew shouted.

"Then what?!"

"I just don't want to let you go yet, OK?! I was just trying to kill a little time," Andrew said, his voice trembling now. "I'm sorry. It's not you. It's not you either, Ronnie. I just...wanted us to be together a little longer. I don't want to have to let you go yet, Drake. Not yet."

Drake felt his face flush. "I didn't realize," he said gently.

"Just ask if they'll let you come outside and see us one last time before we leave, all right?" Andrew said, rolling down his window to allow the air to cool his face.

Drake nodded his head and mumbled, "Yeah."

Two more hours passed, until suddenly the roads turned familiar and the town hiding so many bad memories climbed into view. The engine rumbled as Andrew put the car in park and sat there with his seat belt still buckled. "I guess this is really it, huh?"

Drake's leg bounced nervously as he stared down at the tiny, black spokes in the floor mat. "That's what it looks like," he said, welling up.

Ronnie sniffled in the backseat.

Drake gazed outside his window and listened to the rain hiss as it cascaded on the warm pavement. "I'm sorry I drug you both into this. I never wanted it to be this way."

"We'll write and visit as often as we can," Andrew said, forcing himself to smile and sound positive. "Isn't that right, Ronnie?"

"I guess so," Ronnie answered halfheartedly.

Andrew pulled the keys from the ignition and shoved them deep in his pocket, leaving them all in an awkward silence as a stiff wind rocked the car.

Drake finally unbuckled. "I know you're just trying to waste time, but please don't make this any harder than it is. I have to go."

Andrew leaned over and hugged Drake one last time. "I'm gonna miss you, you know. You've meant so much to me. I'm just glad I can let you go knowing you have Christ going with you."

"I'll miss you both too," Drake said sadly. "Gonna hate leaving that beautiful piano behind."

"I'm gonna hate not hearing you play it," Andrew said, trying to keep the conversation going. "Just take care of yourself, all right?"

"I will." Drake turned and looked around his headrest to see Ronnie. "C'mon, Ronnie. Can't I even get a goodbye from my best friend?"

Ronnie looked up and rubbed his red eyes before throwing his arms around Drake's neck. "Don't go, Drake," he cried. "I'm not mad at you anymore. I couldn't be mad at you." He glanced at Andrew and said, "Make him stay, Uncle Andy. He doesn't have to go."

"I'm afraid I can't do that, Ronnie," Drake said, dabbing Ronnie's tears with his sleeve. "It wouldn't be right." He looked up and caught himself staring into Andrew's eyes.

"Goodbye," Andrew said, his voice unsteady.

"Bye," Ronnie said. He let go of Drake.

Drake brushed away his tears, grabbed his crutches from the back-seat, and stepped out of the car. The large drops of rain pelted down on his head, but he hardly noticed. The only thing that registered in his brain as he walked up the path to the sheriff's office was that he was leaving behind the best part of his life. He fought the urge not to look back, but as he reached the doors, his eyes darted toward the car one last time.

They were still watching him, tears lingering in their eyes.

Drake looked away and gently wrapped his wet fingers around the tarnished brass handle in front of him. *God, help me. I know I'm doing the right thing, but it feels so wrong.*

He stopped for only a few seconds to stare silently at the town. Linhurst Peak looked different in so many ways; then again, maybe it was only his perspective that had changed. As he stood in front of the county sheriff's office, he felt a calming peace knowing that he was not the same person who had left here running from a murder. A thousand bad decisions couldn't stand up to the one good decision he was now making.

Slowly, he pulled the door open and walked inside. The atmosphere was a few degrees colder, and the sounds of staplers clicking and men and women pecking vehemently at keyboards seemed to match the rhythm of the white ticking clock on the center wall. Wood paneling covered the walls, revealing its undisturbed history while darkening the overall appearance of the room.

Drake cleared his throat and approached a man in a crisp, chocolate brown and gold uniform cradling a phone to his ear from behind his cluttered desk. The man held up a finger and switched the phone to his other ear as he scribbled something down.

Drake studied the pictures on the man's desk as he waited. He assumed that the picture of a young woman with three children gathered around her was his family. *They all look so happy. Lucky guy.* He remembered Andrew had called him family once. Drake had rolled his eyes at it. But then again, he really couldn't blame himself. The only definition to the word "family" he knew meant a broken home. *He was so kind to me, and I was such a jerk.* He looked at the clock on the wall. *Maybe I have time to say goodbye to them one last time. They said they'd wait for me.*

The man said goodbye and set the phone down on its receiver. "Can I help you?"

Drake tore his gaze away from the clock and looked up. "Huh?"

"Can I help you with something?"

"Oh, uh, yeah. Sorry." Drake's heart trembled against his rib cage. He had to force the words out of his mouth. "I have information regarding a murder," he said slowly, expecting the officer to slap handcuffs on his wrist and lead him down a long, dark hall where he would never see the light of day again.

"A murder?" the man said, almost skeptically. "In that case, I'll have to refer you to homicide."

Drake nearly jumped at those words. "Oh, am I in the wrong place?"

The man stood up and pointed down the hall with his finger. "Nah, homicide unit's three doors down to the right. I'll buzz Frank and let him know you're coming."

"Thanks," Drake said, not honestly meaning it. He walked down the hallway and found HOMICIDE UNIT in bold, black letters on the door, just as the police officer had told him. He lightly touched the doorknob and noticed his hand was shaking. He pressed his fingers against his closed eyelids and prayed a quick prayer. A sudden stillness entered his soul, stopping his trembling, as a soft warmth passed over his heart. *You're doing the right thing, Drake. It's hard, but don't back down. Not after coming this far.* He slowly opened the door.

The man inside stood and reached across his desk to shake Drake's hand. "Name's Frank."

Drake hesitantly offered his hand. "Mine's Drake."

"Nice to meet you, Drake."

Yeah, you won't be sayin' that in a few minutes.

"Have a seat," Frank said, gesturing to a folded chair leaning against the wall.

Drake rubbed the palms of his hands together. "I'd rather stand, if that's OK."

Frank shrugged and returned to his seat behind his desk. "James tells me you have information on a murder. Is that correct?"

"That's right," Drake said nervously.

Frank stood up and moved to a nearby filing cabinet. "Name please?"

"Ben Pearson."

Frank fingered through the worn folders and pulled out one near the front. "One of our recent cases," he remarked as he checked the date. His eyes scanned down the page until he found the report. "Found dead of a gunshot wound to the head Tuesday night—"

"W-wait...what?" Drake said, walking around the desk to read the file himself. "Gunshot wound? But he wasn't shot."

"I'm sorry if this is coming as a shock to you. Because you came in here with information, I assumed you already knew the cause of death."

"No," Drake said, shaking his head in disbelief. "No, I didn't." That chair would come in handy right now.

"I can't imagine how you wouldn't have known. It was all over the local news for days."

"Do you know who shot him?" Drake said, his mind still reeling.

Frank pursed his lips and set the folder on his desk. "Clive Roland. Based on interviews from friends, he was supposedly one of Ben Pearson's drinking buddies. He and Ben were both very drunk when they got into an argument in the bar. Those standing around didn't think anything of it since nothing usually came of their arguments, but then Clive pulled a gun from his pocket..."

"I understand," Drake said, turning away.

"Roland shot Ben in the head before turning the gun on himself. There was also an old gash mark on the back of Pearson's head, but we weren't able to find the cause of that." Frank shuddered. "Horrible scene. Nothing could have prepared our men for what they saw that night."

Drake's chest burned like fire at the thought of what had happened to his father. He didn't know why he should feel so surprised, though. He had always expected something like that to happen. *Dad must've known it too. He just didn't care, that's all. But I did. As hard as it was for me to do, I still remember caring for him a little. Now that it's actually happened, I'm not sure how to feel.*

Frank gave Drake a moment to take in the news before saying, "The case was decided by the judge two days ago, but if you have other information that would—"

"No," Drake said, already heading toward the door to leave. "I must've just made a mistake." A horrible mistake that almost took his life too. "Thank you, sir," he mumbled. He opened the door and never looked back. When he opened his mouth to exhale, he tasted the salty tears falling from his eyes. *Shot. All this time, I was really innocent. I didn't kill him. I didn't kill nobody. I'm not a murderer.* The tears stung his eyes as he pushed open the sheriff's office doors and hobbled as fast as he could toward Andrew's car.

Andrew opened the door for him. "What is it? What'd they say?"

Drake put his hand to his head and looked at him, wondering if Andrew would even believe what he was about to say. "I didn't kill Dad," he choked up.

A puzzled look came over Andrew's face. "Say again?"

"I know it sounds crazy," Drake said, rubbing his tears away as fast as they fell. "I mean, I thought I did it. I had been so sure..." He closed his mouth as his eyes fell to the floor. "He was shot. Somebody shot him. But I didn't know. I would have blamed myself for his murder all my life if I hadn't come down here."

"You mean—"

"I left him unconscious. After he fell and I saw the blood...I didn't stay long enough to see if he was still alive. He wasn't moving. He looked dead, but..." Drake stared down at his hands—the hands he had thought were responsible for murder—and an indescribable surge of relief covered him. "He woke up," he said quietly. "He went to a bar...got in another fight and someone shot him."

Andrew put a hand on Drake's shoulder and held it there. "And all the way up here, you were prepared to do the right thing. I'm proud of you, Drake."

"It's strange. It's like a weight lifted off of me when I heard what happened to Dad. But at the same time, reliving that moment all over again was still painful. I never wanted him to die, as angry as I was. Now I know I was never part of his death."

"The Bible says the truth will set you free."

Drake smiled slightly—something he thought he would never do again. "The truth sure set me free today."

"So...you're not going to jail anymore?" Ronnie said uncertainly from the backseat.

That beautiful reality set in. As Drake's tears dried, he felt life permeate into his body and his heart embrace that part of him he thought he had lost. "No, buddy. Not anymore."

Ronnie grinned. "Then that means you can come home."

Home. That really was the word, wasn't it? And a family. Now life could be worth living again. Drake instantly looked to Andrew, who, by this time, was smiling too. "Can I?"

"Is that what you want?"

Drake's voice trembled as he said, "I can't imagine anything I've ever wanted more."

Andrew put the car in reverse and stole a glimpse at the sky. "Me either."

"Oh, wait," Drake said, taking off his shoe. He lifted the flap of his heel and pulled out the six one-hundred dollars bills hidden beneath. "Just one more thing I gotta take care of first."

Andrew looked at the money curiously. "What are you going to do with that?"

Drake nodded his head toward Ronnie. "Saw a pound about two miles back. Think maybe they have a spare box we can take a beagle home in?"

"A beagle!" Ronnie squealed. "Thank you, thank you, thank you!"

"I never knew you wanted a beagle, Ronnie," Andrew said. "I don't mind buying you one."

Drake put his hand on Andrew's arm. "Please. Let me do this."

Andrew smiled and pulled out of the parking lot without another word. Ronnie, on the other hand, couldn't stop talking.

And for once, neither could Drake.

Epilogue

So that's my story, and even if you had told me the ending ahead of time, I probably wouldn't have believed you. Life seemed to drift back to the way it was when I first came here, only now I have to occasionally brush puppy hair off my pillow. But I don't care. It's just great to have a real home.

Exactly one month after I came back, Andrew got a brilliant idea and took us all to a picture studio to have our "family" picture taken. He had always called me family. Now, for the first time, I actually believe it.

To this day, I've kept that old angel bear Ronnie gave me on my dresser, and the picture he drew is still on the wall. It serves as a constant reminder that God can still do whatever God wants to do. My leg healed just as the doctor said it would, and now I can finally walk without a limp. I never forgot that car salesman either. He couldn't stop grinning when I told him about how I had asked Jesus into my heart. I even offered to repay the money he had lost on the truck, but he waved off my statement with, "Be blessed." Amazing guy. I never thought I'd see the day when I felt so complete in all my life. It's great.

Still more surprises came my way when the church asked me if I would join the praise team and play the piano. Apparently, Andrew had spilled to them behind my back that I played, but I don't mind. It makes me glad to know I'm able to take something I love and do it for the glory of my Savior. I've written two worship songs already—not bragging, but they're pretty good. Oh yeah, I decided to start giving Ronnie lessons after he came incredibly close to dropping to his knees and begging me to teach him every day. He's learning fast. In a month, I'll bet he passes me up.

"Hey, everybody!" Andrew hollered from downstairs. "Come look!"

I caught Ronnie staring back at me as I ran out into the hallway. It was a race to see who could get down the stairs the fastest.

"Well, what do you think?" Andrew said, taking a seat on the couch as he stared up at something.

I looked up above the fireplace and saw our picture mounted. "You finally found a frame that fit," I said, sitting down beside him.

"Yeah, and the perfect spot too!" Ronnie said.

I smiled as I looked at the picture. "Now that's a picture."

Andrew put one arm around me and the other around Ronnie. "No, Drake. That right there..." He paused and admired the picture before saying, "That's family."

ABOUT ASHLEY WILLIAMS

Ashley Williams, always a devoted reader to a fast-paced novel, began her path toward becoming a Christian novelist at age fifteen. More than just wanting to create characters that lived on in her reader's minds, Ashley desired to write fiction that unashamedly glorified the name of Jesus and brought readers to a deeper understanding of who God is. She then enrolled in Jerry Jenkins' Christian Writers' Guild, determined to deliver a solid, well-crafted message to her readers. In 2009, she published her first Christian book titled *A Father's Betrayal: Condemned to Die*—a story about persecuted Christians in Pakistan.

Born in Texas, Ashley now lives in Tennessee with her parents, two brothers, and little sister who are a constant encouragement to her dreams. Ashley had been homeschooled since the first grade and is now in college continuing to pursue her love of writing. She stays very involved in her parents' ministry alongside of her siblings, and finds happiness in reading God's Word, spending time with her family, and writing.

If you enjoyed this book, let Ashley know at ashleyfiction@hotmail.com or check out her Website at www.ashleywilliamsbooks.com.

DESTINY IMAGE PUBLISHERS, INC.

*"Speaking to the Purposes of God for This Generation
and for the Generations to Come."*

VISIT OUR NEW SITE HOME AT
WWW.DESTINYIMAGE.COM

FREE SUBSCRIPTION TO DI NEWSLETTER

Receive free unpublished articles by top DI authors, exclusive
discounts, and free downloads from our best and newest books.
Visit www.destinyimage.com to subscribe.

Write to: Destiny Image
              P.O. Box 310
              Shippensburg, PA 17257-0310

Call: 1-800-722-6774

Email: orders@destinyimage.com

For a complete list of our titles or to place an order
online, visit www.destinyimage.com.